Praise for

STEALING THE

DRAGON

"Dashiell Hammett by way of Jerry Bruckheimer—with some Jackie Chan thrown in for good measure. If you like your private-eye adventures fast, funny, and action-packed, you're going to love this book!"

– Steve Hockensmith, author of
Holmes on the Range and *On the Wrong Track*

"Take one smart, funny detective. Add one beautiful, deadly Chinese assassin. Mix in an ancient secret ingredient that people will kill for, then stir violently. I gobbled up the chapters, and an hour later I was hungry for more. Tim Maleeny delivers."

– Marshall Karp, author of
The Rabbit Factory and *Bloodthirsty*

"*Stealing the Dragon* is a raucous, sizzling, no-holds-barred delight from the get-go. Tim Maleeny propels readers down the darkest alleyways of Hong Kong, Tokyo, San Francisco, and the human condition with scathing wit and style. Keep an eye on your socks—this is a debut sure to knock them right the hell off with an auspicious bang."

– Cornelia Read, author of
A Field of Darkness

"A crime noir tour of San Francisco's Chinatown, conducted by an occasionally abrasive but nonetheless likable detective and a haunting, unforgettable assassin who lead the reader down alleys that are worlds away from the usual tourist haunts."

— Joe Hartlaub, *bookreporter.com*

"Crisp. Sharp. Great characters. A page-turner with appeal to both men and women. Tim Maleeny's first is just the beginning for this talented new writer."

— Rita Lakin, author of
Getting Old Is the Best Revenge

STEALING THE

DRAGON

FORTHCOMING BY TIM MALEENY

Beating the Babushka

Fall 2007

A CAPE WEATHERS INVESTIGATION

STEALING THE
DRAGON

TIM MALEENY

MIDNIGHT INK
WOODBURY, MINNESOTA

FIRST EDITION
First Printing, 2007

Book design by Donna Burch and Joanna Willis
Cover design by Gavin Dayton Duffy
Cover photograph © Eryk Fitkau / The Image Bank / Getty Images

Midnight Ink, an imprint of Llewellyn Publications

Library of Congress Cataloging-in-Publication Data
Maleeny, Tim, 1962–
    Stealing the Dragon / Tim Maleeny—1st ed.
        p. cm.—(A Cape Weathers investigation)
    ISBN-13: 978-0-7387-0997-0 (alk. paper)
    ISBN-10: 0-7387-0997-2 (alk. paper)
    1. Private investigators—Fiction. 2. Smuggling—Fiction. 3. Triads
(Gangs)—Fiction. 4. Murder—Investigation—Fiction. 5. San Francisco
(Calif.)—Fiction. I. Title.

PS3613.A4353S74 2007
813'.6—dc22

                                                                2006046899

Midnight Ink
2143 Wooddale Drive, Dept. 0-7387-0997-2
Woodbury, MN 55125-2989, U.S.A.
www.midnightinkbooks.com

Printed in the United States of America

To my parents,
Robert T. Maleeny and Ruth S. Maleeny.
For everything.

1

Cape Weathers just wanted to know what time it was before he died. It wasn't much of a prayer, but it was all he could manage on short notice.

Cape was on his back, looking up at the clock tower as the Russian tried to strangle him. He could feel his larynx start to collapse as the gangster shifted his weight and tightened his grip, all three hundred pounds of him crushing the air from Cape's lungs.

Broken ribs stabbed as he tried to breathe. His vision started to fade and Cape knew he'd black out any minute. Then he'd be dead. But he could still see the clock tower jutting upward into the fog, and he couldn't help himself. He wanted to hear the bells ring one last time.

He also wanted to kill the son of a bitch that was strangling him, but Cape had learned to set realistic goals.

Cape managed to free his right arm and swung frantically, trying to get an angle on the giant's head. The Russian spat in his face and squeezed harder. Cape heard a wet cracking sound and figured he'd lost another rib. He fought the pain and kept punching, telling himself this would be over soon, one way or another.

An audible crunch and sudden pain in his throat, his attacker relaxing his grip as if Cape had just died.

Maybe he had.

Cape snapped his head back, away from the hands, banging the back of his skull against the pavement. White spots flashed as he watched the Russian's head flop to the side, eyes rolling back, the thick tongue drooling blood across Cape's chest.

The barbed tip of an arrow protruded through the Russian's neck, the wooden shaft slick with blood. It had struck the back of the neck and penetrated far enough for the tip to pierce Cape's throat a fraction of an inch. He held his breath and got his arms under the Russian, heaving the lifeless body across his own until he could sit up.

Cape felt his ribs and found most of them intact. The cracking noises had been arrows hitting their mark. Two more were just below the shoulder blades, their feathered ends pointing back toward the tower. Cape followed their line of sight and saw a lone figure standing on the balustrade above the clock, dressed in ninja black with bow in hand. Even though he couldn't see a face, Cape knew who it was.

Then the fog swallowed the tower and the figure vanished just as the bells started to chime.

———————

Cape smacked the alarm clock with his right hand and twisted himself awake. The sheets were soaked, his left arm pinned beneath his body, the cold air coming through his bedroom window making him shiver. Forcing himself to sit up, he swung his legs over the side of the bed, stood up, and walked naked to the bathroom.

He didn't turn on the light, but the morning gray was enough to show his reflection in the mirror. He noticed his sandy hair was damp as he leaned across the sink. Two blue-gray eyes stared back, the lines around them multiplying as he forced a smile. *Yeah, still here and in one piece.* He gingerly touched the narrow scar on his throat.

When a dream is really a memory, when does it fade away? The scar was almost a year old, but the dream still haunted his sleep.

Cape didn't mind the scar; it was better than the alternative. But he was really getting sick of that damn dream.

2

It was time to abandon ship.

The eternal twilight of the ship's hold gave no sense of time, but she guessed it was almost dawn. Almost twelve hours since the last meal, and the crew usually stuck to their schedule.

Almost two hundred men, women, and children were huddled together in the cargo hold of the decrepit freighter, their collective fear palpable. Twenty had died during the eight-week voyage from Hong Kong, their bodies thrown overboard by the crew. The lingering stench of sweat and fear hung like a fog in the stale air.

She sat perfectly still in one corner of the huge hold, close to her fellow passengers but not crowded. A couple of older Chinese men had recognized her—if not by name, then for what she was, and gave her a wide berth since the voyage began. The whispered rumors traveled fast that first day, and for the rest of the trip she kept to the shadows.

She looked at her fellow refugees, most sleeping fitfully, clutching the person next to them whether related or not. An old woman rolled over, causing a rat to scurry for another place to keep warm. A young boy retched against the steel hull only a few feet away. She looked away, not wanting her eyes to bring him more shame, wondering if he'd survive, sick with the knowledge there was nothing she could do for him.

An adolescent girl cried quietly in her mother's arms, the older woman's face an expressionless mask. The girl had been taken by the crew on a regular basis, then returned to her mother bruised and sobbing. She had probably been raped, as had many others. Sometimes they didn't return at all.

She put her right hand to her breast, feeling the weight of the package concealed under her ragged clothes. It seemed to have become heavier with each leg of the journey, but she knew that was exhaustion taking hold of her imagination. At least that's what she wanted to believe.

Shafts of sunlight thin as a spider's web broke through the cracks in the deck above. It was almost time. She closed her eyes, took a deep breath, and focused her energy, as she had been trained to do since she was a little girl.

Rusted steel beams roughly four feet apart ran along the walls of the hull, exposed ribs in the belly of the ship. Laying sideways, she pressed her open palms against the nearest beam, then set her feet firmly on the one below. She pushed and arched her body to match the curve of the hull.

Carefully, she moved her left arm two feet, followed by her left leg, all the while maintaining pressure to keep her off the deck. In agonizing increments, she scuttled across the beams, a massive black spider working her way to the center of the web. Fifteen minutes later, she was directly below the hatch, looking down at the huddled refugees. A few were awake and watching with a blend of fear and hope, but none were willing to meet her gaze. She tried to control her breathing. Pressing hard against the facing beams, she swung her left arm around, pivoting in the cramped space.

Staccato footsteps on the deck, followed by the rattle of chains as she heard the padlock on the hatch. She braced herself, arching to keep as much of her body in shadow as possible.

The hatch swung open with a harsh creak of hinges, pale sunlight blocked by the silhouette of a man. He blinked, squinting at the black square below his feet until his eyes adjusted.

The shadows moved. He felt something grab his right leg behind the knee, yanking him down to the steel deck and knocking the wind out of him. He sat up, dazed and angry.

The deck was empty.

Maybe he'd tripped. He'd felt like shit all morning, drank too much last night. Just like every other night and every morning on this floating prison.

Clutching the edge of the hatch, he leaned forward cautiously, peering obliquely into the hold. The weak sunlight showed only refugees huddled together, sunken eyes staring at him anxiously from thirty feet below. Cursing and spitting, the crewman shook his head and began to stand up.

He never saw the hand that grabbed his collar, but he felt the force of the foot against his spine as it shoved him through the hatch. It happened so fast he didn't have time to yell. He plummeted through space, the refugees parting like the Red Sea, clearing the floor before he hit the deck with a sickening thud.

Long seconds ticked by as he lay there unmoving, then he groaned and raised his head. He tried to sit up and almost fainted, realizing too late that both his arms were broken. Twisting his head around, he looked at the men and women huddled nearby, an imploring look on his battered face.

The faces that looked back were no longer filled with fear—bright fires of hatred were lighting their eyes. As quickly as they had moved away, the ragged mob converged on the lone crewman. The hatch slammed shut just as he started to scream.

She heard a muffled cry and whirled around as a lone seagull cut across the bow of the ship. Her eyes narrowed as she looked at the hatch, wondering if she'd heard the gull or a cry for help from the lone crewman.

I hope he isn't dead yet. Some deserve to see it coming.

She hoped her calculations were correct. They were due to arrive in San Francisco that morning, maybe even within the hour. The crew would be awake soon and start moving refugees into the empty containers on deck. A heavy fog wrapped around the ship like a blanket, but she could just discern the ghostly outline of land.

The Golden Gate Bridge should be visible anytime now.

She stepped carefully across the deck to the starboard side. Glancing at the black water, she estimated the distance, wondering if the nylon rope around her waist was long enough. Stealing a lifeboat would make too much noise, so she had to stay hidden until they were almost at port. They would unload the containers filled with cargo like every other ship, leaving the refugees onboard until nightfall. Then they would turn the operation over to their Chinatown contacts while they got drunk in a local bar.

She thought of all the people trapped in the belly of the ship. Entire families who sacrificed everything just to escape their homeland, parents who sold themselves into slavery so they could give their children a chance they never had.

Her original plan was to leave no trace, hoping the crew would come to the conclusion that the guard had fallen to his death, knowing none of the refugees would expose her. She thought of the girl crying and the look in the mother's eyes, the woman's expression not recriminating or even angry. Simply determined, devoid of fear. There was something in those eyes that neither the crew nor a daughter's suffering could take away.

She touched the package beneath her clothes and reminded herself why she was there, then cursed under her breath and shook her head at her own foolishness.

We cannot choose what fate will bring us, or when it will arrive.

Words from her childhood invaded her thoughts.

Death is an ally. Use him wisely.

She closed her eyes and sighed, then crept across the deck until she was directly below the wheelhouse. At this hour there would only be two men in the forward cabin, if that. The others should still be belowdecks. Reaching around with her right hand, she pulled a black anodized knife from behind her back, the tip of the blade angled sharply in the style of the Japanese *tanto*. Its weight against her spine had been a cold comfort during the long journey.

She heard voices a few feet away and realized there could be more than two men inside the cabin. She knew the number didn't really matter. If she had learned only one thing, it was that nothing was certain in this life, except death.

She tightened her grip on the knife and stepped through the cabin door.

3

"It's big, ain't it?"

Howard McClosky had been asking his wife Betty the same question for the past five minutes. It was a question he usually asked in the bedroom, a thought that almost made her smile, but she kept her mouth shut and gritted her teeth. She knew Howard got a little touchy about their private life and besides, she was trying her damnedest not to puke.

"And it's getting bigger," was all she said, glancing at the huge container ship and trying not to turn green. She turned away after a second and locked her eyes on the deck between her feet.

They were squeezed alongside the starboard rail of the *Alcatraz II*, a twin engine powerboat that ferried people from Pier 39 to the infamous island prison. They'd come all the way from Lubbock, Texas, and stood in line for three hours with thirty other people who were now crammed aboard right next to them, holding on to the rails for dear life. The tour guide had warned them San Francisco Bay got pretty choppy this time of year, but Betty thought he could have been a little more specific with the folks from out of town, which was pretty much everybody. Either that or hand out Dramamine on the dock. The sky that day might have been blue through the breaks in the fog, but the currents were hellacious. As far as Betty was concerned, it was *The Perfect Storm* out here. She expected to see George Clooney float by any second.

"It's funny how your whole perspective changes once you're on the boat," mused Howard, totally oblivious to the rolling of the deck. Last time Betty checked, he was the only one onboard not staring at his shoes. She figured it must be all that spicy food he ate—the jalapeños fucked up his stomach so bad he couldn't feel a thing. Probably why he farted so much, now that she thought of it. She started humming to herself to keep her mind off the waves. *Howard, my husband, the flatulent sailor.*

But to Howard, she just nodded dumbly as he continued his monologue.

"Like that big one there," he said, jutting his chin at the massive container ship cutting across the bay. "A few minutes ago, it looked like we were a couple of miles away from Alcatraz and that ship was just coming under the Golden Gate. Now you'd swear we're gonna hit the island any second and that ship is gonna meet us there, even though you gotta figure the captains would keep us at least a couple hundred yards apart. It's gotta be a code or regulation, don't you think?"

Betty looked up at the big ship, sensing Howard needed some kind of response. Even at home he needed at least an "uh-huh" or "I see what you mean" to egg him on, not satisfied asking a purely rhetorical question. Hard enough being married to such a talker, but to provide constant feedback, well, being a woman was never easy. Not wanting Howard to get pouty, Betty tore her eyes away from the undulating deck to verify Howard's insightful observation about optical illusions.

Howard was right. The freighter looked as tall as a skyscraper, blotting out the sun, looming so close she thought she could touch it. She looked past Howard and saw the captain's face as he shouted against the wind at one of the crew standing near the bow. Whipping her big hair back toward the freighter, Betty saw the rivets in the hull, the dull scratches in the paint, even smelled the sour tang of oil from somewhere in the boiler room. Her eyes glued to the black ship, Betty reached out, grabbed Howard's hand, and started screaming.

A second later, the impact knocked the smaller boat right out of the water. The sound of metal hulls colliding drowned out the passengers, the wind, and the churning water below. The powerboat bent nearly in half, shooting twenty feet into the air before landing against the rocks at the base of Alcatraz. The passengers and crew flew off the deck like Ping-Pong balls shot from a cannon, splashing into the water a good thirty yards from the island.

Betty and Howard, still hand in hand, hit the water hard and sank a good fifteen feet before their natural buoyancy brought them to the surface. Betty's hair broke the water first, followed by Howard in the midst of a sentence he'd started just before Betty got her scream out, something to do with relative distances at sea.

Betty gasped. The water was ice cold, the current yanking them and twisting them around. She tilted her head back and tried to keep her mouth above the waves, her eyes glued to the mammoth black hull just fifty feet away. The container ship had run aground on the banks of Alcatraz, the sharp metal prow digging into the coarse sand, the giant vessel listing sharply sideways.

Betty thought she heard a Klaxon somewhere in the distance, but she couldn't be sure. As the waves lapped against her ears, it sounded like a large group of people were singing, or maybe screaming, a muffled chorus somewhere nearby. She saw spots and figured she was losing consciousness, but she still clung to Howard and figured she'd be all right. All that hot air should keep them bobbing on the surf till the Coast Guard arrived.

I knew there was a reason I married you, she thought happily, squeezing his hand beneath the waves.

4

San Francisco Bay looked like the freeway at rush hour.

The container ship listed drunkenly on its keel, the bow stuck in the loose shoal around Alcatraz, the stern braced by two tugboats commandeered by the Coast Guard. Two cutters idled on either side of the huge vessel while a harbor patrol boat circled Alcatraz Island to maintain a secure perimeter.

Just beyond this tenuous ring of authority, chaos reigned. Sailboats, powerboats, and even a few rowboats jockeyed for position as tourists, locals, and reporters tried to get a closer look at the spectacle.

Overhead, a Coast Guard helicopter hovered noisily, its rotors blowing foam off the already choppy water. Within an hour of the accident there had been almost eight helicopters in the sky, most of them from television news bureaus. The choppers from Channel 5 and Channel 7, two stations in a fierce ratings war for the right to call themselves "The Bay Area's Favorite News Source," almost collided directly over the ship. That prompted the Coast Guard to establish a no-fly zone enforced the rest of the day.

Onboard, the scene was no less frenetic, the deck crowded with the Coast Guard, INS, Customs Service, Harbor Patrol, FBI, and the San Francisco Police. It got so jammed that uniformed cops were sent to keep order after an FBI agent took a swing at a guy from Customs when the two men bumped into each other.

The almost two hundred refugees and what remained of the crew were taken ashore and held in a makeshift command center on Treasure Island, the former naval base. Interpreters were already there, trying to figure out what happened.

Back on the ship, it was obvious something had gone terribly wrong.

The area immediately outside the main cabin was cordoned off with yellow tape, which caused an eddy in the foot traffic across the deck. Two homicide cops stood just inside the tape watching the forensics teams go to work.

"I think I'm gonna be sick," Vincent Mango announced, bracing an arm to compensate for the slant of the deck. He was dressed immaculately, an Italian sport coat offset by pleated slacks cuffed over Ferragamo shoes. His tie was a subtle shade of green, which, at that precise moment, seemed to match his complexion.

"It's all in your head, Vinnie," said the man next to him, voice booming like the surf. Almost six-eight and built like a defensive lineman, Beauregard Jones looked enormous even against the backdrop of the ship. He wore jeans, a black T-shirt, and a leather shoulder rig holding a Beretta stretched taut across his chest. He wore no jacket, smiling broadly at his partner as if he were immune to the cold, his ebony skin shining from the spray off the water. He said, "You can't be seasick if you're not at sea."

Vinnie tried to focus on a spot between his feet, the only part of the deck that didn't seem to be moving. "I hate boats."

"It's a ship, Vinnie," replied Beau, "not a boat."

"Whatever."

"Nah, this shit's important," Beau insisted. "You tell those guys with the Coast Guard you on a boat, just see if they keep takin' you seriously. Next thing you know, we won't get a ride off this thing."

The prospect of staying onboard got Vinnie's full attention. "OK, it's a ship."

"That ran aground," said Beau. "It's like standing on a pier."

"Don't tell me how I feel," snapped Vinnie, who risked raising his head to glare at his partner. "The deck is rolling."

"Aye-aye," said Beau amicably. "But I'm tellin' you—we ain't movin'. The boat's stuck."

"I thought you said it was a ship."

"Whatever."

Vinnie leaned over and spat between his feet. "Let's change the subject."

"Fine."

"So what do you think?" Vinnie jerked his chin toward the cabin.

Beau squinted against the wind and frowned.

"This is a freak show, Vinnie."

Vinnie nodded slowly. "That's what I think. You sure this is gonna be ours?"

Beau shook his head. "Hell, no. At best, we're gonna have to share."

"You must've dealt with the feds before, when you were in Narcotics."

"Lots of times," replied Beau. "Mostly DEA, but the boys from the bureau showed up once or twice."

"How was it?"

"A cluster fuck, usually," replied Beau. "They didn't share information, got in the way during the investigation, then took credit after the bust went down."

"Swell," said Vinnie. "I can hardly wait."

Beau smiled at his partner. "This one's gonna be worse."

"How you figure?"

"Remember all those news choppers were here earlier?"

Vinnie nodded but didn't say anything, his gaze returning to the spot between his shoes.

"We're gonna have reporters up our asses till this is over. And since the nice Chinese folks down in the ship's hold probably didn't have green cards, visas, or even a *get-outta-jail-free card*, you just know the fuckin' State Department is gonna stick their noses in. That makes it political, which means the mayor'll get involved."

Vinnie moaned. Beau couldn't tell if it was because of the jostling of the ship or the mention of the mayor.

"Guess we don't get a lot of choice in the matter," muttered Vinnie.

"*To serve and protect*," intoned Beau solemnly. "Or is that just the motto of the L.A. police?"

"I think it's 'protect and serve' in San Francisco," said Vinnie. "We serve later than they do."

"That sounds about right," agreed Beau. "But either way, we're stuck out here till the next chopper arrives to take us back to dry land."

"When are they gonna fly the stiffs out?" asked Vinnie.

"Guy from forensics says it'll be at least another hour," replied Beau. "I just hope we're not in the same chopper."

Vinnie risked standing upright and took a deep breath. "What was the count?"

Beau took a small black notebook from his back pocket and gave it a cursory glance. "Four."

"That include the guy in the hold?" asked Vinnie, grimacing. "The one who fell?"

Beau frowned. "We both know he wasn't killed by no fall."

"Yeah," Vinnie shrugged. "So that makes five?"

Beau glanced again at the notebook. "Just eyeballing it, I'd say we've got a broken neck, at least one crushed larynx, one 'no visible causes,' and one extremely fatal stab wound."

Now it was Vinnie's turn to flinch. "Want another look?"

"Not really," replied Beau, shaking his head. "But we probably should, before it gets cleaned up."

The two men walked around the side of the cabin to a heavy steel door set between the round glass of the windows overlooking the deck from the bridge. Slumped against the bottom of the door was a Chinese man in his early thirties, a scraggly growth of beard at the very base of his chin. The rest of his face was long and narrow, his almond-shaped eyes staring vacantly at the two cops.

Embedded in his chest was a knife approximately eight inches long, the blade an anodized black material that seemed to absorb all surrounding light. A rusty trail of dried blood ran from the center of the door to the back of the man's head, tracing the path of his collapse. Still clutched in his right hand was a gun, a small-frame automatic. Less than a foot away, a brass shell casing gleamed dully in the afternoon light.

Written just above his head on the left side of the door was the number "49." It had been scrawled using the same dark paint that once flowed freely through the dead man's veins.

"Jesus," Beau muttered under his breath.

"This wasn't the refugees," said Vinnie.

Beau nodded. "Most didn't look strong enough to walk without help, let alone kill someone holding a gun," he said, adding, "But they did a number on that guy who fell."

Vinnie grimaced again. "Don't remind me."

Beau turned to look along the length of the deck. "The others were clean, Vinnie," he said into the wind. "Really clean."

Vinnie followed his gaze, then looked at the windows of the cabin. They were streaked with grime but otherwise unremarkable. He knew there were three more bodies inside, but you couldn't tell from where they were standing. There had been no signs of a struggle and almost no blood.

"After this guy out here, it happened fast," mused Beau. "Not a lot of people know how to kill like that."

"That could narrow the field."

"That's what I'm thinking." Beau's eyes drifted out of focus as he stood facing the Golden Gate Bridge in the near distance. The wind picked up and Beau hunched his shoulders, seeming to feel the cold for the first time that day.

Vinnie noticed the expression on his partner's face. "You're not thinking of someone in particular?" he asked incredulously.

Beau shook his head, his eyes shifting their focus to Vinnie. He forced a smile before answering.

"No, not necessarily."

5

"THE SNAKES ARE POISONOUS, you know."

The man behind the desk seemed calm as he spoke the words in Cantonese with practiced ease, his voice deep and resonant. His black hair shone dully in the subdued lighting of the office, slicked back from a high forehead that was smooth and unlined. The corners of his mouth curled into a smile as he talked. It was only his eyes that betrayed anger. They were utterly black, each pupil indistinct from the iris, two bottomless wells that threatened to swallow anyone who met his gaze. That was one of the reasons Chan did not look him in the eye.

The other reason was that Chan was hanging upside down, a heavy, braided cord wrapped around his right ankle. Directly beneath him a trap door had opened in the hardwood floor, revealing a hole roughly four feet square. In the dim light it was difficult for Chan to see the bottom of the shaft, but every few seconds *something* stirred in the darkness, the reflected light betraying sudden animal movement.

And if Chan ever doubted what lay beneath him, the sound made it all too clear. When the hatch opened, a reptilian susurrus flooded the room. To Chan it sounded like the rasp of silk sheets being dragged over a corpse, and in his mind's eye he saw his own face revealed.

A heavyset man of around forty, he swung awkwardly above the opening. His hands opened and closed reflexively as he tried to stop turning in circles.

"You're positive it's missing?" The man's voice was calm but insistent. The same question had been asked several times already this evening.

"The case was empty, *lung tau*," Chan cried, his voice unnaturally high.

The man behind the desk did not acknowledge the title, *lung tau*. Dragon Head.

He'd carried the appellation for so long, at times he forgot his real name.

"I see, the cabinet was empty," he said pleasantly. "And who was guarding the room?"

Chan jerked frantically, trying to face his captor. "I was on guard, *shan chu*," he said, trying to sound respectful. "But I swear—" He gasped abruptly as the rope lurched downward three feet.

Chan's inquisitor took his finger off a button set into the wide teak desk. As he did, a figure standing in the shadows behind him leaned forward and spoke quickly in his ear. The second man faded into the shadows almost as quickly as he appeared, but not before Chan caught a glimpse of the ragged scar running the length of the man's face. Even from his inverted position, Chan recognized his accuser and knew, at that moment, there would be no escape.

"I will find it!" cried Chan. "I will bring it back—*it is my responsibility.*"

The man behind the desk pursed his lips as he placed his index finger on the button. When he spoke again, his voice was almost friendly.

"Not any more."

As he pushed the button, the rope slipped through the pulley and released. He watched impassively as Chan disappeared from view, and the slithering became a dull roar, the movement of the snakes like a crashing wave.

The trap door snapped shut, cutting short Chan's scream and chasing the liquid sound of vipers from the room.

The Dragon Head leaned forward, his hands steepled in front of him. Without turning, he spoke to the man in the shadows, his voice sounding loud in the sudden quiet of the room.

"A bit melodramatic."

"But there is something to be said for tradition." The man with the scar stepped from the shadows. His black hair was cropped close to his skull, the scar starting just below the hairline on the right side and zigzagging past his eye until it ended at the corner of his mouth. As he smiled, it twitched like a lurid bolt of lightning trapped in his skin, the scar tissue catching the light at odd angles. "He talked quickly, wouldn't you agree?"

The man behind the desk nodded. "Too bad he had nothing to say." He sighed deeply. "You will find it and bring it back."

The lightning bolt danced in the shadows. "Of course, *lung tau.*"

"And you will find the one who took it from us."

"And bring them back, also?"

"Only the heart," came the reply. "I only want the heart."

6

"Are you trying to take advantage of me?"

Cape Weathers sat behind his desk and tried to think of a suitable answer. The man asking the question was supposed to be his client, after all, so he should take the question seriously. On the other hand, the man in question was a pretentious prick, a sub-species found crawling around the upper echelons of San Francisco society. They were known to consort with unctuous assholes and pseudo-intellectuals, two other life forms common but not unique to the Bay Area.

"Actually, I was trying to decide whether or not to shoot you," replied Cape pleasantly. He leaned forward in his chair and began rummaging through his desk drawer.

"I beg your pardon?" Richard Choffer was clearly used to being in control. He pursed his lips menacingly as he tried to force Cape to make eye contact with him. The scion of a famous publishing magnate from New York, Richard had moved to San Francisco fifteen years ago to start his own publishing empire with dad's money. Now he had a successful line of titles that the critics liked to call picture books for adults—a series of heavily art-directed books on photography, music, and pop culture. *Batman, Pez Dispensers, Diners Across America.* Every photo was given its own page and two lines of copy, then bound into a handsome volume suitable for gift-giving when you ran out of ideas for gifts.

Cape had no problem with the way Richard made his living. It was arguably more respectable than the way Cape made his. And the books were undeniably successful—he'd even bought one or two himself over the years. He could even look past Richard's insistence on being called Richard Choffer, *Esquire,* or the fact that his business card said "Literary Director," even though most of his books had barely fifty words from cover to cover. It must have been hard growing up in dad's shadow, which obviously stretched all the way from New York to San Francisco.

But Cape couldn't abide being lied to, especially by a client.

"Ah, here it is," announced Cape cheerfully. In his right hand was a matte black revolver, a Ruger .357 Magnum that held six cartridges. It had a size and heft that made it intimidating, especially if you weren't used to guns.

"Wh-what are you doing?" demanded Richard, his thin lips drained of color. Cape casually dropped the gun onto the desk, causing Richard to jump in his seat.

Cape looked up from the desk as if he'd forgotten Richard was sitting across from him. "What?"

"Explain yourself, sir," said Richard. The words came out in a rush, but he was secretly pleased he'd been able to keep his voice under control.

Cape leaned forward and looked at Richard for a long minute before answering. Without realizing it, Richard leaned back in his chair and drew his knees together.

"I agreed to take you on as a favor to Bob Grecken," said Cape. Mentioning the name of a well-known San Francisco lawyer would matter to someone like Richard. "And you hired me to determine if your chief financial officer was embezzling from your company."

"I know why I hired—," began Richard, but Cape raised a hand to cut him off.

"But what you really wanted to know was whether or not your wife, who also works at your company, was having an affair with your chief financial officer."

"I said it was a possibility," said Richard. "I didn't mean—"

Cape's hand rose up again.

"Bullshit."

Richard blinked but didn't say anything.

"You didn't want to come out and say it, or maybe Bob told you that I don't take divorce cases anymore," said Cape. "But you probably figured in the course of another investigation I might notice a few indiscretions along the way, and then you'd have what you wanted in the first place."

Richard's eyes narrowed. "What are you implying?"

"I'm not implying anything," said Cape, his voice taking on gravel. "I'm telling you that you're a moron."

Richard's eyes doubled in size.

"Here's how it breaks down," said Cape. "You're boffing your secretary, a seemingly nice but hopelessly naïve twenty-three-year-old with literary aspirations. And your wife—who is not nearly as naïve as your secretary—is on to you."

25

Richard's mouth dropped open.

"And you signed a prenuptial agreement that would make Bill Gates fear for bankruptcy," continued Cape, "since there was an infidelity clause in the document. I guess your wife knew enough about your past indiscretions to protect herself, or at least guarantee that she could tear your balls off if you ever fucked her over."

Richard's mouth started working but nothing came out. With his eyes bugging out, Cape thought Richard looked like one of those bobble-head dolls.

"But the best part," said Cape, his tone softening as he smiled, "is that *you're* embezzling from your own company."

Richard's right eye started to twitch.

"Apparently those cocktail parties the local news is always mentioning cost more than you thought they would," said Cape. "Or maybe you've got a gambling problem—you've been to Reno three times in the last two months, and Vegas five times. It's probably the gambling."

"H-how…?" stammered Richard.

Cape ignored the question. "Then you cooked the books to frame your CFO, who, as far as I can tell, is a perfectly nice guy. He is a bit friendly with your wife, but not nearly as friendly as you are with your secretary."

"We… we're a privately held company," Richard protested. "I showed you only portions of our financial reports. What you're talking about is… is…," he trailed off lamely, realizing too late that protest was the quickest path to confession.

Cape shrugged. "I had someone hack into your network," he said matter-of-factly. "And the rest was straightforward detective stuff."

Cape briefly wondered how that would look on his business card:

CAPE WEATHERS

THE STRAIGHTFORWARD DETECTIVE

But then decided against it. Too many words.

"Bob...the lawyer...he said I could trust you," said Richard. His voice had dropped to barely more than a whisper.

"I talked to him myself," said Cape. "He said I was honest—there's a difference."

Richard didn't know what to say to that. Either that or he didn't understand the distinction.

Cape shrugged. "Just goes to show, you can't trust lawyers."

As he waited for his future ex-client to say something, Cape absently took note of footsteps in the hallway outside his office. A heavy tread—either someone big or a Clydesdale, he couldn't be sure. Finally Richard broke the silence.

"What are you going to do?"

"I told you already," replied Cape. "I'm going to shoot you. Given the litigation you'll be up against, I'm practically doing you a favor."

Richard smiled tentatively, one last attempt at charm. The lower classes were like animals—you had to demonstrate command of the situation at all times. Smile at the lunatic behind the desk and maybe this nightmare would end.

Cape picked up the gun. "You're an arrogant asshole who thinks he's smarter than everyone else, Richard," he said evenly. "And you lied to me." He pointed the gun squarely at Richard's chest and thumbed back the hammer.

Richard stopped smiling. He started to raise his hands in protest just as Cape pulled the trigger.

Click.

"Shit," Cape muttered. "Forgot to load it—gimme just a second."

Setting the gun down, Cape started rummaging through the desk drawer. A moment later he produced a box of cartridges and set them next to the gun. "Be just a minute." He didn't look up as he cracked open the cylinder and started inserting one bullet at a time.

The screech of wood against wood was followed by the crash of a chair as Richard bolted toward the door. He let out a yelp as he collided with Beauregard Jones, whose massive frame almost blocked the exit entirely. Richard bounced off Beau like a pinball and ran, his footsteps echoing down the hallway.

Beau leaned into the office and smiled. "Another satisfied customer?"

Cape shrugged. "Wait till I send him a bill."

"Got a minute?" asked Beau, taking a giant step into the office.

Cape stood and shook hands, then gestured toward the toppled client chair.

"As of that meeting you just witnessed, I'm currently unemployed."

"Glad to hear it."

"Thanks," replied Cape, trying to put some hurt into his voice. "And here I thought we were friends."

"That we are," said Beau. "It's why I'm here."

"What's the subject?" asked Cape. "With you it's usually women or murder."

Beau smiled briefly before answering.

"How about both?"

7

"You happen to look out your window yesterday?"

Beau's size 14 shoes rested comfortably on Cape's desk.

The office faced the bay, but any view of Alcatraz was blocked by the looming edifice of Aquarium of the Bay, which sat directly across the street at the entrance to Pier 39. A long walk down that pier led to a daily congregation of sea lions that had made the area a major tourist attraction, a bit of natural history you couldn't see back home. Unfortunately, every square inch of the pier itself was crowded with stores and booths designed to empty tourists' wallets long before they ever made it to the sea lions. With the addition of the GAP, the Hard Rock Cafe, and the Disney Store, the pier looked more like a strip mall than anything remotely related to nature or history.

But if you looked past the pier to the right, you could see the water and signs of mayhem from the day before. The police and federal agencies had cleared out, but the ship remained lodged at the base of Alcatraz. The tourist boat rammed by the ship was stuck bow-first in the sand on the far side of the island, the hull split open like an egg. All the crew and tourists had been topside, hurled into the water before the boat struck land.

The bizarre wreck had attracted a small fleet of sailboats and dinghies overloaded with passengers, most without life preservers but all wearing cameras around their necks. The Coast Guard and Harbor Patrol had a long week ahead of them until the two ships could be towed to the docks in Oakland.

"I was home yesterday," said Cape. "But I saw it on the news. Channel 7 said there was 'evidence of foul play' and Channel 5 said it was 'slaughter on the high seas.' Channel 2 put the whole thing in perspective with a segment called 'Ships of Death.'"

Beau shook his head sadly. "I wish their choppers had crashed."

"I take it you're involved."

Beau shook his head. "Not for long."

"You don't sound too happy about it."

"It's political," replied Beau, "and it's gonna get worse. You know District Supervisor Harold Yan?"

"Heard of him," replied Cape. "But never met him. He's the one running for mayor?"

"That's the one," said Beau. "Represented Chinatown for almost a decade, now wants to be the first Asian-American mayor of San Francisco."

"So?"

"So the current mayor was kinda hoping to get re-elected."

"I get it," said Cape. "And the mayor had a string of bad press lately. That accounting screw-up in the comptroller's office last month, and—"

Beau finished the thought. "And now allegations of police corruption. You see the story in Monday's paper?"

Cape nodded. "Any truth to the rumors?"

Beau hesitated before answering. "It started with a report that a few beat cops in Chinatown were taking bribes to look the other way on gang activity. Basic extortion scam, protection rackets. Now, do I think there's cops that would grease their palms to let something go?" Beau shrugged. "Maybe, especially in a tight-knit neighborhood like Chinatown. Same thing happened a couple years back with a few Latino cops in the Mission, but it blew over. A few bad apples."

Cape nodded but didn't say anything. He wasn't a cop and didn't pretend to be one.

Beau took his feet off the desk and leaned forward. "It's never more than a few cops, and it usually straightens itself out—the other cops see that it does, you understand what I'm saying? But for some of these young guys, it's not so black and white when they first hit the streets. All depends on where they grew up."

"So why all the press?"

"'Cause this time the press brought enough heat to trigger an Internal Affairs investigation," Beau replied. "And they're taking a hard look up the ladder, all the way to the assistant chief of police."

Cape recalled the article he'd seen in the *Examiner*. "The assistant chief … isn't he Chinese, too?"

Beau nodded. "Matter of fact, he is."

"So like you said, it's political."

"Very." Beau blew out his cheeks and sighed. "I got a boatload of Chinese people smuggled into the country and a crew that's mostly dead. I got District Supervisor Yan running for office, already putting heat on the mayor before any of this went down. Yan was on the morning news, calling this a 'humanitarian crisis affecting Chinese everywhere.' Asking what the mayor's gonna do about it."

"Oh boy," said Cape.

"So the mayor calls the chief," continued Beau, "who's already on the mayor's shit list because of the scandal in Chinatown. Chief calls the division commander, who calls me and Vinnie and says '*Men, we need a win on this one.*'"

"A win?"

"A win." Beau rolled his eyes. "But then the feds call the chief and tell him to back off."

"You've dealt with the feds before."

"Not like this," replied Beau. "This is really their turf. Murder took place on the boat, not in the city. I'm just a homicide cop ... I walk the streets, and every now and then trip over a dead body."

"But the mayor wants to be the guy who solves this case, huh?"

"Ain't gonna happen, though he needs the press," said Beau. "And he needs the votes. You know thirty percent of the voters in this city are Asian?"

"No kidding."

"How about that," said Beau. "But the mayor don't give a rat's ass about the case, or the people on the boat." Beau frowned. "I used to like that asshole mayor, too, him being a brother and all."

"See what you get for being racially biased in your voting?" asked Cape.

"There is no justice for the black man," muttered Beau. "Even *from* a black man."

"You want a hug?"

"Fuck you."

Cape laughed. "What do you want from me?"

Beau described the crime scene on the ship, including details that the newspapers didn't have yet. He described the corpses in detail and the apparent causes of death, watching Cape's expression carefully as he talked.

When Beau had finished, Cape pushed back in his chair and whistled soundlessly.

"So that's why I'm here," said Beau.

Cape raised one eyebrow but didn't say anything.

Beau said, "I think you should talk to your partner."

"My partner?" Cape said, frowning. "You mean Sally?"

Beau nodded. "Figured she might have ideas about this kind of thing."

"She's not my partner, Beau," said Cape. "She's a martial arts instructor. You know that ... she runs a school in Chinatown. We're just ...," Cape trailed off, realizing he didn't know how to describe their relationship.

"She helps you out on cases," said Beau. A statement, not a question. He shifted into cop-speak as he laid out the facts.

Cape shrugged. "Sometimes."

"She watches your back."

"Yeah," Cape replied tentatively.

"You trust her."

"Absolutely," said Cape. No hesitation.

"Then she's your partner," said Beau. Case closed.

"Fine," said Cape, holding up his hands. "So why don't you go see her yourself?"

"I might," said Beau. "But thought I should start with you, since we go back a ways. Besides, after six tonight, this ain't my case."

"You sure you're not looking for an excuse to see her?"

Beau looked indignant. "What's that supposed to mean?"

"You had a crush on her last year," said Cape. "You even tried taking one of her classes, didn't you?"

Beau smiled. "I came to my senses. A woman that could hurt me like that..." He trailed off, shaking his head. "It's bad enough I gotta worry about getting hurt when I'm on the job. The crush ended after that first class."

"The fact that she's gay was never a deterrent?"

"Considered it a challenge, you want to know the truth," replied Beau. "Never dated a lesbian before."

"That's because lesbians don't date guys like you," said Cape. "Or me... because they don't date guys, period. That's how it works."

"You learn that on Doctor Phil?"

"You're hopeless."

"Just messing with you."

"I know," replied Cape, "but you're still hopeless."

"Tell me something I don't know."

"How about you tell me what made you think of Sally."

Beau looked at the ceiling for a long moment before answering. "You didn't see the ship... the bodies. That wasn't the work of no refugees. What I saw... not a lot of people know how to do that." He lowered his eyes and studied Cape.

Cape met his friend's gaze.

"I bet Sally could do that," added Beau, his tone matter-of-fact.

Cape didn't know what to say, but he didn't like where this was going. He and Beau had been friends before he'd become an inves-

34

tigator, and Cape had never lied to him. He might have left things out from time to time, but he never lied. And though he'd known Sally just as long, there were things about her that Cape couldn't explain, even to himself.

"Last year, you were working on that case with the movie producer," said Beau. "And that Russian guy tried to kill you."

Cape unconsciously raised his right hand to his neck. "So?"

"So, he was shot through the neck with an arrow, as I recall."

"Did you search Sherwood Forest?"

"No, smart-ass, but we checked sales records at the sporting goods stores and the gun shops, talked to anyone we knew that had a quiver in their garage."

"Including Sally."

"She had a solid alibi—she was teaching a class," said Beau. "A couple of her students backed her up."

"And you didn't press it."

"Forensics said to look for a crossbow or a compound bow, the kind with all the pulleys. Said the distance was too great, the shot too hard for anyone to make with a regular bow and arrow."

"I wasn't the only one that guy tried to kill," said Cape, realizing too late he was sounding defensive. He took a deep breath before continuing. "And he'd already killed someone right here in the city—*your* city."

Beau held up his hands, palms out. "I'm not saying he didn't deserve it," he said. "And I'm not saying me and Vinnie looked real hard for his killer. The fact of the matter is that once the Russian wound up dead, the case was closed as far as the city was concerned. All the bad guys accounted for."

"So what *are* you saying, Beau?"

"You've taken on some heavy cases over the years and have managed to not get yourself killed."

"Thanks to Sally watching my back," said Cape, finishing the thought. There was no denying it.

"Yeah," said Beau. "And as your friend, I'm grateful to her."

Cape nodded. "But as a cop…"

"I've always wondered."

"But Sally's never even had a ticket for jaywalking," said Cape, knowing that wasn't really the point but wanting to say it anyway.

"Neither have you," replied Beau. "Doesn't mean you didn't cross against the light when no one was looking."

"You think the ship's a different story."

Beau nodded. "I don't know jack shit about the crew, the refugees, or the dead Chinese. And I can't move around Chinatown like an Asian cop could."

"And there's a rumor of corruption among the Chinese cops on the force," said Cape, understanding now where this was going. "So the feds are cut off from that angle."

"Right."

"And you think I should ask Sally to help?"

"To start, I'd just ask her a few questions," replied Beau, sounding like a cop again. "Sally grew up in Hong Kong? Moved here maybe ten years ago?"

"Yeah, as far as I know."

"The ship came from Hong Kong."

Cape studied Beau carefully before responding.

"Sally's one of the good guys."

"Then I'm on her side," said Beau. "But I think like a cop. Everybody's a suspect till proven otherwise."

"I thought it was *innocent until proven guilty*."

Beau shook his head. "Nah, that's the courts. You know the system. It's like catch-and-release fishing—we catch them, and the courts let them go."

"There must be some leads," Cape insisted.

"After the feds and SFPD finish interviewing the crew, the refugees, the shipping company, and the port authority, they'll have enough leads to keep this investigation going for the next ten years."

"So?"

"This isn't a lead," said Beau. "It's a hunch."

Cape nodded. "Thanks for coming to me first."

Beau looked at his watch. "Like I said, after six it's not my problem. But if I go see Sally, then it's official—gotta fill out paperwork, her name goes in a file. You know the drill."

"Thanks just the same."

Beau smiled. "Besides, paying a surprise visit to Sally didn't seem like a big idea."

"For what it's worth," said Cape. "I trust her completely."

"I don't doubt it," replied Beau. "But how well do you *know* her?"

Cape started to respond but caught himself, realizing he didn't have an answer that would satisfy either one of them.

8

—

"Sally, your parents are dead."

Just like that. No preamble. Nothing to soften the delivery. Li Mei's face was a mass of wrinkles that seemed to crack open as she delivered the news. The old woman looked at the five-year-old with an expression that begged no questions.

When Sally just stood there, Li Mei spoke again, this time in Cantonese.

"They've gone from this place, Sally." Li Mei's dark brown eyes were kind but unblinking. "And now we must leave." She turned the small girl around with a gentle shove. "Go and pack your things."

Your parents are dead.

Go and pack your things.

Everything happening at once. Even at five, Sally sensed her nanny was trying to distract her, keep her off balance before shock could set in. Push her away before reality could touch her.

It was an old trick. Don't look at the cut on your knee, look at me.

Sally dug her heel into the carpet and stared at Li Mei as if she didn't recognize her, the five-year-old looking in that instant as old and jaded as her ancient Chinese caretaker. Sally had her Japanese mother's jade green eyes and lustrous black hair, but her cheeks were painted with freckles, a genetic gift from her Irish-American father. These and other telltale traits she got from her parents, but her will was all her own.

"Tell me," she demanded, looking as if she would know if any details were omitted.

So the old woman sat down on the floor and took the little girl in her arms. Sally's father had left the Army base around four and drove to Shinjuku station in downtown Tokyo, where he picked up her mother every day after she finished work. Most Japanese did not drive if they could avoid it, preferring to take the trains and skip the traffic, but her father was so very American. He said he preferred doing things himself, he liked being in control. Likewise, many Japanese women didn't work, but the family's rent was expensive since they moved off the Army base. And like Sally's father, her mother was independent in spirit.

Traffic was heavy that time of day, and it was dark by the time they headed home. That meant they probably never saw the truck that killed them. The driver was drunk and had neglected to turn on his headlights. The police said the only warning might have been a brief flash of sparks from the undercarriage as the truck jumped the median and struck their car in a head-on collision. They were both killed instantly.

"They did not suffer," added Li Mei, tears flowing freely down her cheeks. She said something else but Sally couldn't hear it over the roar of blood rushing in her ears. She searched Li Mei's face for something *else, a happy ending the old woman had forgotten, a story within the story that only Sally could hear. But now there were spots before her eyes, and her heart convulsed as if it had stopped. As she gasped for breath, she saw Li Mei's face dissolve in a waterfall of tears, replaced by the smiling faces of her mother and father.*

That was the last thing Sally saw before she blacked out.

———————

The trip to Hong Kong was a blur, along with everything else about the next week. Li Mei explained that Sally had no surviving relatives, either in Japan or the United States, so the old woman was adopting Sally herself and taking her to Hong Kong. That was where Li Mei had grown up. She just knew Sally would feel at home there.

Even at five, Sally could sense a lie. Not a single official-looking person had come to the house to talk with her, bringing official-looking papers for Li Mei to sign. Li Mei and Sally had simply left Japan, boarding a ferry in Osaka that would take them to Hong Kong. Along the way, no one asked any questions that Li Mei couldn't answer. Sally didn't really care one way or the other, so she didn't say anything about it to Li Mei.

In fact, she had said very little over the past week, and Li Mei noticed that Sally was speaking less each day. She looked at her young charge and wondered what she must be thinking, now that her world had turned black.

Throughout her short life, Sally had generally been a happy child. A week ago, Li Mei would have called her precocious. But she was also strangely intense for a little girl, approaching every game or new activity as if it were a test. While the other girls giggled, Sally would frown in concentration. Only when she mastered the new skill would

Sally relax and laugh like the other children. To Li Mei it seemed that Sally was two little girls sharing the same body—one girl full of life and hope, and the other experienced beyond her years, earnestly preparing for some hardship yet to come.

Now that hardship had arrived, Li Mei could see the smiling, laughing side of Sally going into hiding. She hoped the two different girls that comprised Sally were friends, and she wondered if the hardened girl sitting next to her would ever share her happy playmate with anyone again. She suspected the smiling, hopeful side of Sally would be jealously guarded for many years, protected from the cruelty of the outside world. Li Mei prayed she was not lost forever.

It was an odd train of thought for the old caretaker, given their destination.

Li Mei had been anxious to return to Hong Kong for her own reasons, but she also had plans for Sally. Several times during the voyage she considered turning back but quickly derailed that line of thought by telling herself there was no better alternative. Sally did not belong in an orphanage—she had talents and potential that only Li Mei and a select few could recognize. And when the time came, when Sally was older, she would have a choice. That was what Li Mei kept saying to herself: I am not giving her away. I am giving her a choice.

If Li Mei wasn't completely convinced by her own argument, at least it kept her moving closer to their destination.

Hong Kong hadn't changed much since Li Mei had left, except to grow even bigger and louder, if such a thing were possible. There was no other city in the world that was so alive—not even Tokyo or New York. From the moment they disembarked at Kowloon, their senses were assaulted with the glare of neon, the smells of open cooking stalls, and the roar of traffic and the planes overhead. It was hot that time of year, steam rising off the street and choking the air with humidity. It didn't take long for Li Mei to get her bearings, and young Sally simply let the crowds buffet her along as she held Li Mei's hand and tried to keep up.

They spent their first night in a cheap hotel in the Kowloon district, the glare from a neon sign outside their window painting the room a lurid blue. That and the constant buzz of traffic five stories below kept Sally awake well into the night. It was after midnight when she spoke into the darkness, her small voice echoing around the room.

"Is he still alive?" she asked the ceiling. She could tell from the sound of Li Mei's breathing that she was also awake.

"Who, Sally?" asked Li Mei, though she already knew the answer.

"The man who killed my parents," said Sally, her voice very flat now. "The man who was drunk."

Li Mei hesitated, but only briefly.

"Yes, he survived."

"Will he go to jail?"

Li Mei sighed. "Yes, child, for a little while."

"But not forever?"

Another sigh as Li Mei struggled to find the words. "The police said he was the nephew of the man who owned the trucking company. His uncle was … is … a very important man. He plays golf with the Finance Minister."

"What does that mean?" asked Sally, not understanding what golf had to do with losing her parents.

"I'm saying …," Li Mei began, then faltered before finding an answer. "I'm saying that in this world, sometimes it is hard to find justice, Sally."

Sally thought she knew what justice was, but she wasn't sure. But if finding it meant the man who killed her parents would suffer, then she would look.

"I will find it," she said to the shadows and the neon.

Li Mei thought again of their destination and the weight of the little girl's words, then nodded to herself in the darkness.

"I know you will, child," she said softly. "I know you will."

9

DARKNESS HAD TAKEN THE city by the time Cape left his office.

The paperwork from Richard Choffer's case took him longer than anticipated, but he expected an angry call from Richard's lawyer in the morning and wanted everything to be in order. He called Sally earlier but no one answered. Just as well—he wanted to talk with her face to face.

He walked up Stockton toward North Beach, an uphill climb every step of the way. By the time he crossed Chestnut he could feel the burn in his calves. Walking even a few blocks in San Francisco was a workout, one of the reasons women in this city had such great legs. It was one of the reasons Cape liked living there.

At Lombard he passed Saints Peter & Paul Church where Joe DiMaggio wed Marilyn Monroe, the celebrity marriage of its time. The marriage didn't last long, and most folks had forgotten it ever took place, if they knew in the first place, and they certainly couldn't tell you *where* it happened. But forty years later the church had retained all its beauty, if not its fame. The Gothic spires pierced the night sky, twin monuments of remembrance and hope in a city with an increasingly short attention span.

North Beach was still predominantly Italian, family restaurants lining the length of Columbus Avenue and crowding the side streets, drawing tourists from all over the world. Many families had been there for generations, but many new tenants were kids out of college looking to rent in a neighborhood that had become hip simply by not trying to be.

Cape came to Broadway at Columbus, passing Frank Alessi's place on the corner. Frank was the local wiseguy, the self-proclaimed "don of North Beach." Cape had crossed his path a few times over the years, the meetings memorable if not always cordial. Frank was a successful businessman and major political contributor, but Cape knew his main enterprise was narcotics, moving all the product brought into the city by the Chinese tong gangs. Frank bought the bulk of each shipment and spread it across the Bay Area like a poison fog. If someone bought a dime bag off a dealer in the Mission district, a nickel found its way back into Frank's pocket. He'd built his distribution network as carefully as he'd constructed his façade of public respectability.

Within the borders of Chinatown, the tongs made their own sales. It was their turf and their product, after all. Even Frank's long arm couldn't reach across Broadway, the unspoken border between North Beach and Chinatown that Cape was crossing now.

At the corner of Stockton and Broadway, Cape became illiterate. The signs over every storefront, grocery, and restaurant were written in Chinese characters accompanied only occasionally by English.

The daytime crowds had long since gone home, but the street wasn't empty. Two old men sat at a small folding table outside a convenience store playing mah jong. Both were smoking, an over-flowing ashtray between their discarded tiles.

Farther down the block, four young men milled around the front of a restaurant that had closed for the night, puffy jackets and loose warm-ups incongruous in the mild weather. Cape wondered briefly if they were selling or buying, or just waiting for instructions from inside the restaurant. As he passed they did their best to give him the look, mouths set in straight lines, eyes hard. Cape smiled amiably and nodded at each in turn, making eye contact, and saw them buckle slightly, caught off guard by the warmth of his expression. They were still at the age where they needed to feed off someone else's fear or aggression to get their blood up. Cape knew they'd get the hang of it soon, change from kids trying to be hard to teenagers genuinely hardened by life. He guessed the oldest was twelve, thirteen at the most.

Another two blocks and Cape hung a right, subtitles on the signs disappearing altogether as he left the streets that welcomed tourists by day.

Sally's school and home were the same, a converted loft situated above a grocery that opened at five a.m. and closed by three every afternoon. The grocery made the rent by selling items not found in the local Safeway. During the day you could see ducks rotating on steel hooks through the front windows, their long curved necks looking like a grotesque series of question marks. Live eels swam in a metal tub just inside the door, while behind the counter you could find fresh ginseng, ginger, bamboo, and about fifty other spices and herbs Cape didn't know how to pronounce. It was rumored that if you knew how to ask, even powdered rhinoceros horn had a price.

Next to the grocery was a flight of wooden stairs that disappeared into the side of the building, leading to a landing on the second floor that served as an open foyer to Sally's loft. Cape took the stairs two at a time, anxious to see his friend and clear his mind.

Cape pulled up short as he landed on the top step. In front of him was a sliding wooden door that ran the entire width of the landing. Cape knew behind it lay another sliding door made of wood and paper, set into the wall at the rear of the landing. The door directly in front of him looked impregnable, its unfinished surface rough and scarred. Although he'd noticed this outer door in the past, hidden in the recess of the stairway wall, Cape had never seen it closed in all the years he'd known Sally. Its presence alone spoke volumes, and he didn't like what it was saying.

People in the neighborhood knew to stay clear of the school unless they had business there, and Cape had experienced Sally's approach to home security firsthand. It usually involved Sally dropping from the rafters behind you, unheard and unseen, with a knife or sword in her hand. Cape doubted if the Invisible Man could sneak up on Sally, even when she was asleep. And since you couldn't see if she was home from the landing, you took your chances by stepping inside. As a result, Sally had never bothered to shut the outer door. Until now.

Cape frowned, knowing the closed door meant one of two things:

Sally had left town and wasn't coming back any time soon. And that meant she'd left suddenly, without telling him.

The other option, that Sally was holed up inside, was a possibility that troubled Cape even more. As long as he'd known her, Cape never worried about Sally. Not once. He had seen her bleed, and he had seen her kill, but he'd never seen her afraid. He couldn't imagine who or what could make Sally hide behind this fortress door.

He raised his right fist and knocked, almost breaking his hand in the process. The door might be made of wood, but it felt like cement. He couldn't hear anyone moving around inside, and he seriously doubted they could hear him, even if he were using a sledgehammer.

Cape stood for several minutes staring at the faceless wooden surface, running through the possibilities again and again, liking them less each time. Tentatively, almost gently, he raised his right hand to the gnarled wood, his palm resting flat against the door. He stood that way for a long moment, as if he could divine Sally's whereabouts from the coarse surface. Finally, he exhaled loudly and turned toward the stairs, more frustrated than enlightened.

Sally knew how to take care of herself better than anyone. If she were inside, she'd come out when she was ready—*if* she was coming out at all. That door said *Do Not Disturb* louder than any sign. And if she had left, there must have been a good reason. Cape just had to find out what it was.

Head down, Cape descended the stairs slowly, lost in thought. As he reached the bottom he stopped, noticing a stain running across the top of the first step, down the side, and ending on the pitted cement of the sidewalk. In the dim light of the stairwell it was a dark reddish brown, maybe a water stain, a natural discoloration in the wood, or something more sinister.

Licking his index and middle fingers, Cape bent and ran his hand from the inside of the step toward the outer edge. Putting his fingers to his tongue, he frowned. Could he taste the faint copper tang of dried blood, or was it merely dirt mixed with his own anxious sweat that left such a bitter taste in his mouth? Reluctantly he admitted that he couldn't be sure without getting the proper equipment, and then what? The skeptic in him said he was wasting his time, that events were moving outside his control, while the hypochondriac in him said he'd just swept some serious germs into his mouth. Either way, he was fucked.

He started walking, trying to visualize the scene on the ship that Beau had described. He wanted to call it coincidence, not related to Sally's disappearance in any way, but Cape wasn't in the habit of lying, even to himself. He realized his visit to the loft had unnerved him, even though the only thing he'd found was a closed door.

As he walked toward the traffic sounds coming from the end of the block, Cape glanced again at the signs overhead, trying to discern a pattern in the characters. Even common Chinese characters seemed radically different as the typography and design changed from sign to sign, making an already foreign language indecipherable. Cape imagined the signs spoke of impending danger, only he couldn't understand the warnings. The silent faces of the closed storefronts mocked his ignorance as he passed.

At Broadway, Cape turned and looked back the way he had come. He had spent a lot of time in Chinatown over the years, and a few cases had taken him deep into the neighborhood. But he had never navigated the back streets and side alleys without Sally at his side, and he realized that without a guide, this world was as impenetrable as the names of the stores and restaurants he had just passed. Without Sally he was deaf, dumb, and blind. She might be missing, but he was lost.

Beau had been right. Sally was his partner in ways Cape never appreciated until now. Part of their relationship was taking each other for granted, trusting the other person would be there to watch your back. But now that Sally was gone, Cape found himself looking over his shoulder.

It was a feeling he didn't like.

Cape turned up the collar of his coat as he walked south on Broadway toward home. The wind off the bay had picked up and the temperature had dropped at least ten degrees in the last hour, but he felt colder still. He could feel Death in the clutch of the wind, but he couldn't tell if it was behind him or directly ahead.

He just knew it was close.

10

"STAY CLOSE, SALLY," CAUTIONED Li Mei. "The snakes are poisonous."

Sally wasn't listening. As Li Mei tried to navigate a clear path through the foot traffic on Bonham Strand, Sally squatted in front of a wooden cage. Inside a black cobra rose on its coils, its hood expanding like an open hand, beckoning. Sally met its gaze, neither the snake nor the little girl blinking.

Li Mei was halfway down the block before she realized Sally wasn't in tow. Scurrying back along the stalls and open-air restaurants, she passed cages and tanks holding cobras, lizards, turtles, and even a python. Though still early, Bonham Strand was crowded, the street slick with blood. People of all ages lined up to have their creature of choice slaughtered and freshly prepared. Snake's gall bladder wine was in great demand—the more deadly the snake, the greater the medicinal value.

Flustered, Li Mei tugged insistently at Sally's sleeve. The little girl grudgingly forfeited the staring contest with the snake. Blinking, she turned her green eyes on Li Mei and pointed at the cobra.

"I want one," she said simply.

Li Mei sighed and shook her head. "Come, Sally." She took the little girl's hand and resumed walking. "We mustn't be late, and we have two more stops to make."

They cut across Wing Lok Street and headed down Bonham Strand West, where ginseng wholesalers shared the street with banks made of chrome and marble. The street was a microcosm of Hong Kong, an endless juxtaposition of ancient customs and modern commerce. Throughout the city, East and West stood side by side but rarely came in contact.

A few minutes later came Central Market, a four-story structure where Queen Victoria meets Des Voex Road. Li Mei hurried Sally inside, where hapless turtles awaited a grisly end alongside sea cucumbers and salamanders, oblivious to their fate. As they passed through the meat section where tongues, intestines, and chicken feet lined the counters, Sally pointed to a collection of scrotums with a questioning look.

"What are those?"

Li Mei hesitated before answering. "Those," she said finally, "are the worst part of men." Never mind that they were dog scrotums and considered a delicacy, Li Mei had her own opinions. Before Sally could ask anything else, Li Mei grabbed the young girl's hand and dragged her down the aisle, finally coming to a stop at the fruit stands.

Reaching into a wooden crate, she grabbed half a dozen tangerines. She knew of a stall on the ground floor where they could buy some sweet pastries for the rest of their morning snack. She was standing in line to pay when she felt a tugging at her clothes. Sally was pointing at a spiky yellow-green fruit that resembled a medieval mace, roughly the size of a volleyball with triangular points jutting out from the center.

Li Mei shook her head. "That is a durian, Sally. You wouldn't like it."

Sally started to make a face when the woman behind the counter held up a hand. Li Mei smiled and nodded. The woman reached over and broke off a piece of the durian, holding it for Sally to take.

Sally wrinkled her nose and stuck out her tongue before the fruit even touched her lips, a smell like a gas leak permeating the air. Li Mei and the woman both laughed.

"It's called the stinky fruit," explained Li Mei. "Go ahead, try it."

Sally frowned at the fruit as she studied its custard yellow texture. Her expression made it clear she had lost any interest in trying this exotic and malodorous rarity.

"Don't be afraid, Sally," chided Li Mei. "It is only a fruit."

The gentle taunt got an immediate reaction. Turning her gaze to Li Mei, Sally shoved the fruit into her mouth. She almost gagged, but she kept chewing, her eyes locked on Li Mei the entire time. By the time she swallowed, her eyes were watering.

Li Mei chuckled and shook her head. "Next time let me pick the fruit, little one." She peeled a tangerine and handed it to Sally, who was clearly anxious to get a new taste into her mouth.

After Sally finished eating, Li Mei handed her another tangerine and told her to put it in her pocket. "One more stop before we reach your new school." They passed a series of apartment buildings, each tower more dilapidated than the previous one. Elaborate bamboo scaffolding covered the façades of most of the buildings, workers crawling overhead like spiders while tenants and pedestrians scurried below like ants.

At Hollywood Road and Ladder Street, tucked between two graying apartment towers, they came to a temple. The stone of the outer wall was pitted and crumbling, the path to the front door worn from the passage of generations of supplicants. Taking Sally by the hand, Li Mei led her inside.

Coils of incense hung like giant beehives from the ceiling, their cloying stench heavy in the air. Sally's nose twitched as she tried not to sneeze. The temple consisted of one large, crowded room. Minor Taoist and Buddhist deities lined the walls on either side of the entrance. Cats walked lazily back and forth, and fortunetellers sat cross-legged along the walls, tipping bamboo chim sticks from bowls onto the ground. At the far end of the room stood four larger statues, each wearing an elaborately embroidered jacket draped over its stone shoulders.

Pushing through the small crowd of people, Li Mei led Sally toward the heart of the temple.

"This is Man Cheong," said Li Mei, gesturing toward the first statue. "The god of writing—you see the pen?" She swept her arm toward the next figure. "And this is Kwan Tai, the god of war." Li Mei let Sally study each figure in turn before pointing to the third statue. "This is Shing Wong, who protects this part of Hong Kong from evil, and this—," she paused, wanting to make sure Sally was following her. "This is Pao Kung, the god of justice."

"Pao Kung." Sally mouthed the name silently to herself. She remembered the night they first arrived in Hong Kong, when Li Mei told her of the man who killed her parents and spoke of justice. She still wasn't sure exactly what Li Mei meant by justice, but she knew it was something she desperately wanted. And now they were standing in front of the god of justice, after Li Mei had said it was hard to find. Sally stared at the impassive figure on the altar, waiting for some kind of sign.

She jumped as a gong and drum were struck simultaneously, the combined boom echoing around the small space. Li Mei, seeing the shock in Sally's eyes, patted her on the head.

"Someone has made an offering, Sally." She pointed to the wooden boxes next to the statues. "When someone petitions the gods, the drum and gong are sounded."

Sally looked from Li Mei to the statue in front of her, her tiny brow wrinkled with thought. After a long moment, she reached into her pocket and took out the tangerine. Walking to the wooden box at Pao Kung's feet, she raised the lid and carefully placed the fruit inside. As she turned from the altar, an attendant at the back of the temple struck the gong and drum. As the base notes cascaded off the walls, Sally walked out of the temple, her mouth set in a determined line, green eyes bright with anticipation.

It took another half hour of walking before they were near the school. Turning down an alley lined with high stone walls, Li Mei slowed as if searching for an address, though none of the doors in this neighborhood seemed to be marked. Sally was beginning to suspect they were lost when Li Mei cried out and pointed to a solid oak door set deep into the wall and painted black. Carved into the center of the door were Chinese characters that had been painted red. Next to the door, set on a nail, was a hand-held gong and mallet.

Li Mei took the gong and struck it three times. In the enclosed space of the alley the sound carried, each new strike bringing another wave of energy to the summons.

They didn't have to wait very long.

The door creaked loudly as it swung outward, revealing a young woman of no more than fourteen. She spoke rapidly to Li Mei in Cantonese, too fast for Sally to follow. Sally spoke Cantonese well for her age, thanks to Li Mei, but was most comfortable with Japanese, her mother's language. English had been spoken whenever her father was home. Sally moved naturally in and out of each language depending on who she was with, not differentiating as an adult normally would. She just knew words, and which words went together to express her ideas, and that seemed to work fine. But when adults talked quickly, she sometimes found herself getting lost, only tracking every third word or so.

Whatever Li Mei had barked did the trick, because the young woman bowed before leading them to a small courtyard. With the door closed behind them, all sounds of the city seemed to disappear. As Sally looked around at the sandy ground of the courtyard, it felt as if Hong Kong was a world away. Small trees and bamboo lined the walls, effectively blocking any view of the city. At the far end of the courtyard stood another wall maybe ten feet in height with another heavy wooden door at its center, through which the young woman now disappeared.

Li Mei shifted nervously as they waited, looking from Sally to the closed doors, the one behind them as well as the one directly ahead. Sally had never known Li Mei to be antsy and wanted to ask why she was fidgeting, but just as Sally opened her mouth the door in front of them swung open.

A man was walking toward them. He wore black cotton pants bound tightly around his calves, his ankles exposed above thin black shoes. His black shirt was loose in the arms and the waist, held in place with a broad red sash. He was on the tall side, but Sally's impression was more of girth. Even from a distance he seemed thick, especially in the shoulders and chest.

He stopped a good twenty feet away, still partially covered by the shadow of the wall behind him, and gestured toward Li Mei, who made a cursory bow and then turned toward Sally.

"Wait here, little one."

Li Mei walked slowly toward the man, looking over her shoulder and forcing a smile. From where Sally stood, she couldn't make out the man's features, but she thought he was smiling at her, too.

Li Mei and the man stood close together, their voices soft and insistent. At one point, Li Mei pointed at Sally and raised her voice. The man took a small pouch from his belt and gave it to Li Mei. Days later, Sally would reflect on how strange it was for the school to be giving Li Mei money, and not the other way around, but she was too young to grasp what was happening. After almost ten minutes of discussion, Li Mei called to Sally and asked her to join them.

Sally bowed as she came upon them, as she had been taught. She kept her eyes on Li Mei, looking for cues to her behavior.

"This is Sally," said Li Mei. "She knows some Cantonese, Japanese, and even English." She smiled proudly, adding, "And she is a dragon." Sally had heard Li Mei say that before, referring to the year of her birth. Every child in Asia learned about their animal, compared its strengths and weaknesses with those of other children.

"A dragon, heh?" said the man, his voice like rolling gravel. "So am I, little one. Twenty-four years before you, but still a dragon." He reached out and grabbed Sally by the chin, turning her head toward him.

Sally gasped as she saw his face.

A jagged scar marred his features, starting above his right eye and running zig-zag across his cheekbone down to his jaw. As he smiled it jumped like an electric spark, the raised tissue livid in the morning light. Sally had the sudden urge to hide behind Li Mei, but she held her ground, twisting her head to free her jaw from his coarse grip.

"And what is it you want, little one?" the man asked, a mischievous or malicious light in his eyes, Sally couldn't tell which. "What is it you want when you grow up?"

Sally looked at the ground for a moment before turning to Li Mei. When she spoke, her voice was so soft that her aged guardian had to lean close to hear the question. Sally remembered the god in the temple, but she couldn't remember his name.

"What did she say?" demanded the man with the scar.

Li Mei glanced at Sally before answering. She knew her reasons for bringing the girl here, but she would be lying to say she had no doubts.

"Justice," said Li Mei simply. "She wants justice."

The man smiled broadly and barked out a laugh, the lightning scar jumping from his eye to his mouth. He bowed deeply toward Sally and waved his arm toward the heavy door behind him.

"Very well, little dragon," he said. "Time for you to go to school."

11

CAPE CALLED BEAU THE next morning and said he was hoping to see Sally later that day. He didn't mention that he'd already tried to see Sally the night before, so technically he wasn't lying. He really did hope to see Sally later in the day—he just didn't think he would.

"So why are you calling?" asked Beau. "To tell me you're gonna call later?" Cape thought he heard a mildly suspicious tone in his friend's voice. "Since when did you become so responsible?"

"I need someone to talk to," replied Cape.

"You want the name of my therapist?"

"About the case," said Cape. "I want to talk about the case."

"What case?" asked Beau. "I don't have a case anymore, remember?"

Cape sighed, realizing that asking Beau for help this week might be a bad idea. "The boat," he said. "I want to talk about the boat."

"You mean the *ship*."

"Whatever."

"OK, talk to me," replied Beau, suspicion turning to certainty. "But since you haven't talked to Sally, I'm not sure what there is to talk about."

"Look," replied Cape, "you're saying you have a hunch, that Sally might know something."

"Go on," said Beau, his voice noncommittal.

"So I'm checking it out," said Cape. "You already said there would be more leads than you and Vinnie could handle, not to mention the feds."

"Don't mention the feds," groaned Beau.

Cape ignored him. "So I want to get in front of this thing."

There was a long pause, and neither one spoke. Finally Beau broke the silence with a loud sigh into the phone.

"You're gonna talk to Sally," said Beau. A statement, not a question.

"Absolutely," said Cape. *Well, eventually, with any luck, if she hasn't left town, and if she's still alive.* "Fair enough," he said. "But will you help me?"

"What do you want to know?"

"I want to talk to someone who was on the ship," said Cape.

Beau paused again before answering.

"If I were you," he said, "I'd talk to a guy named Mitch Yeung."

"Who's he?"

"A cop," replied Beau. "A good one. He and I came up together at the Academy."

"I thought you started your career in L.A."

"So did Mitch," said Beau. "Transferred just a few months ago—wife's mom lives in San Francisco. He's been working Narcotics—my old division—but they've reassigned him for this investigation.

In case you missed his last name, Mitch is Chinese, first generation—he's helping the feds interview the refugees."

"And since he's new to the department ... ," began Cape.

"Right." Beau finished the thought. "Even if there is 'widespread corruption,' as the paper claimed today, it probably don't apply to a new guy like Mitch. So he's free of suspicion, as far as Management Control is concerned, which makes the feds a little less paranoid about having him around."

"What's *Management Control?*"

"Sorry," said Beau. "That's the new name for Internal Affairs—they're workin' on their image."

"You're kidding."

"They got new stationery and everything."

"My tax dollars at work."

"You bet," said Beau. "But no matter who you ask, Mitch is rock solid."

"Good enough," said Cape. "You'll call him?"

"Yeah," replied Beau. "But don't waste the man's time."

"I work fast."

"I hope so," replied Beau.

Me, too, thought Cape.

12

Sally was on her own.

Li Mei left her with the fierce-looking man, telling Sally she would visit her often. The old woman's voice caught as she said it, and Sally thought Li Mei's eyes looked wet, but Li Mei had already turned and walked through the front gate before Sally could think of anything to say.

As soon as Li Mei was gone, a young girl appeared at Sally's side. She was tall and lean, her black hair cropped short, almond eyes set wide in a pretty face. Sally guessed she was at least eight or nine, but it was hard to tell. Sparing only a cursory glance at Sally, the girl stood before the scarred man and bowed.

"This is Sally," he said, at which point the young woman turned toward Sally and repeated the bow. A smile flashed across the girl's face, disappearing so quickly Sally thought she might have imagined it.

"I am Jun."

Sally nodded in return but didn't say anything.

"Show Sally around," said the man. "Then bring her to me."

"Yes, Master Xan," said Jun, bowing again. Xan turned and walked across the packed earth of the open courtyard. When he was out of sight, the smile reappeared on Jun's face, but only for an instant, as if she feared someone would catch her having fun.

"How old are you?" asked Jun, looking down at Sally.

"Five," said Sally, adding quickly, "and eight months."

Jun nodded, then reached out and took Sally's hand. "Come and see your new home."

Your new home.

The phrase struck Sally with a sudden finality, as if the last few weeks had been a game, just a field trip with Li Mei. Now she was alone, standing with this girl she'd just met, who was reminding Sally that her parents were gone and never coming back.

———————

"Sally . . . Sally?" Jun was leaning over her. Jun's face appeared upside down, her inverted frown looking like a crooked smile.

"You fainted."

Sally blinked, wondering how long she'd been out. They were in the infirmary, Sally laying on a padded bench with a cold towel on her forehead. A stern-looking older woman dressed as a nurse gave Jun a warning look before leaving the room. Jun reached over and gave Sally's hand a gentle squeeze.

"Rest," she said, "and then we'll go for a walk. I'll show you the classrooms, the gardens, the pool—"

"A pool?" asked Sally, rising up on one elbow.

"Oh, yes," replied Jun, her eyes bright with mischief. "We have three pools."

The school grounds were enormous. Beyond the main courtyard, the rest of the block was revealed, a vast compound of wooden buildings, open courtyards, and gardens. Jun started the tour by leading Sally through a long one-story building that served as the school cafeteria. As they passed through the kitchen, Jun greeted three older women, who were obviously the cooks. Sally noticed all the young girls working with them, cutting vegetables, straining rice, and cleaning pots and pans. Some of the girls looked almost twelve, but many were barely older than Sally. They nodded as she and Jun passed, some flashing a quick smile before turning back to their chores.

Jun then led Sally across another small courtyard into a two-story square building.

"This is our theater," she said proudly, pointing across the room toward a low wooden stage. "We wear costumes and put on shows. We even wear makeup ... look!"

Behind the stage was a massive dressing room, the walls lined with dresses, capes, hats, even wigs and beards. Sally had gone into her mother's closet to try on her shoes, and she played dress-up with her dolls, but she'd never seen anything like this.

"We pretend," said Jun, taking a ragged shawl from one of the hangers. Wrapping it around her shoulders, she bent over and clasped her hands behind her back. "See? I'm an old woman!" She walked around in a tight circle, her lower lip extended in a mock frown, her tiny shoulders hunched forward in a pantomime of age.

Sally laughed, a sound more like an excited cough than a real belly laugh, but it managed to bring a smile to her anxious face. She walked to the wall and took a broad brimmed hat off one of the hooks. Jun came over and draped a coat over her small shoulders, laughing as the arms brushed the floor.

Sally turned to the older girl and smiled again, tentatively.

"Do you live here, too?" she asked.

Jun nodded. "Of course," she said. "We all live here . . . all the girls."

Sally looked at her but remained silent.

"My father died when I was four," said Jun, her voice suddenly quiet, making her sound as young as Sally. "Momma died the next year. I think she missed him."

"You came here, then?" asked Sally.

Jun shook her head. "Not right away, no. Me and my younger sister went to live with my aunt and uncle, here in Hong Kong. My uncle . . . ," Jun hesitated, her eyes suddenly unfocused and very far away. "He did things to me . . . that weren't very nice."

Sally didn't understand but felt bad just the same. "I'm sorry."

"That's OK," said Jun, "I'm fine now." Her smile reappeared for an instant, but her eyes still held that faraway look. "One night, when I was playing with my colored pencils, my uncle came to my room and tried to hurt me."

Sally wanted to ask a question but was afraid to interrupt.

"But I hurt him first," said Jun simply.

"How?"

"I took my pink pencil and put it here," said Jun, raising her small fist to her own throat. "I pushed it in . . . deep . . . and I . . . ," her voice trailed off for a moment. "Just kept pushing."

Sally gasped, her eyes wide.

"Pink was always my favorite color," said Jun. "But not anymore."

Sally watched the older girl's eyes come back into focus.

Jun shrugged. "Anyway, my aunt sent me and my sister here." She took off the shawl and placed it back on the hook, then turned and

65

walked across the stage. Sally stood alone for a few seconds, trying to grasp what Jun had just told her.

Sally was quiet the rest of the day as they toured the school, but Jun either didn't mind or didn't notice, never straying far from her narrative. And true to her word, there were three pools, but they looked more like ponds where you'd find koi fish than places for swimming. They were irregularly shaped and lined with plants and rocks, the largest of them almost twenty meters long and fifteen wide.

"They're connected by tunnels," said Jun, her voice a conspiratorial whisper. "So we can learn to swim underwater between the pools."

They passed through a series a connected buildings that Jun called classrooms, but which looked more like playrooms or gymnasiums. In one, a series of ropes hung from the ceiling, and Sally watched as girls of all ages climbed across the rafters like squirrels, then slid down the ropes like two-legged spiders. It looked fun to Sally, not what she thought school would be like.

In another room, girls Jun's age and slightly older practiced kendo, the Japanese martial art using wooden swords. Sally had been to an exhibition once with her father in Tokyo. The long wooden swords looked awkward in the little girls' hands, but they handled them gracefully, striking figures made of straw with surprising power.

Every room had at least one teacher, usually a woman but sometimes a man. They walked among the girls, giving instruction and encouragement, their voices low but firm. At other times they stood off to the side, observing as some of the older girls took on the role of instructor. Sally felt their eyes on her at every turn, even as she nodded or returned a smile from one of the other girls.

"The teachers are always watching," said Jun, as if reading Sally's mind. "By the end of the first week you'll feel like a koi fish in a bowl, someone looking no matter where you swim." She smiled, adding, "But by the second week you won't even notice."

The last part of the tour took them to actual classrooms, rows of wooden desks facing an old-fashioned chalkboard. Girls sat dutifully behind the desks, books open, eyes front. Jun led Sally to the doorway, but they stayed outside so as not to disturb the class.

"Language classes," said Jun.

They had been speaking Cantonese all morning. It never occurred to Sally to try to speak anything else.

"We can learn Japanese, Mandarin, even Russian when we get older," said Jun. "And English, of course."

"I speak English," said Sally proudly, thinking of her father.

Jun smiled mischievously. "Do you know any bad words?"

Sally shook her head.

Jun looked back through the door of the classroom before answering. "You will."

13

"THE SCORPIONS ARE QUITE deadly."

The Dragon Head stood looking down into the sunken room, a perfect cube twelve feet on a side. It was, in actuality, a room within a room, set in the floor of a much larger loft space like a racquetball court dropped into someone's living room, the ceiling removed so guests gathered around the square hole in the floor could look down and watch the game. The Dragon Head stood on the lip of the sunken chamber, his black eyes expressionless as he watched the fat man start to sweat.

The fat man's name was Lim, and if he heard the man standing fifteen feet above him, he was too preoccupied to answer. At the base of the wall on each side of the room was a gap maybe four inches wide, a thin line that looked like a drain. Scorpions were flowing into the room, small and incredibly fast, their legs clicking across the tile floor like castanets.

"A single bite is not typically fatal," continued the Dragon Head, his voice acquiring the cadence of a school teacher. "But this many, in combination, is sure to do the trick."

A wave of scorpions washed across the floor, their brown bodies clumping together and forming eddies in the deadly current that threatened to wash over Lim. As he scuttled toward the center of the room like a nervous crab, a heavy rope swung lazily back and forth above him, a promise of rescue just out of reach.

The lecture resumed.

"There are 1,300 species of scorpions worldwide, all easily identified by their elongated bodies, segmented tails, and, of course, stingers."

Lim shuffled his feet together and jumped, his fingertips brushing the end of the rope and knocking it away. He fell to his knees. A lone scorpion ran up his arm and he screamed, slapping it across the room before it could bite.

"They are technically arthropods of the class *Arachnida*, related to spiders. You'll notice they all have eight legs."

Lim shouted, a frenzied combination of anger and fear, as he hopped and kicked his way around the center of the room. The flow of scorpions through the drain had stopped, the vast army of legs, pincers, and tails seething back and forth less than three feet from where Lim stood. In reality they were as cautious of Lim as he was terrified of them, but in the close confines of the cell they seemed to lean forward, as if sizing up their prey.

Or awaiting instructions.

"Most people think of scorpions as desert creatures," said the Dragon Head, his voice almost soothing now. "But they have been found in grasslands, savannahs, caves, and even rain forests. Like any strong creature, they adapt to survive."

This last phrase got Lim's attention. Reluctantly he tore his eyes away from the floor and looked up at his captor, his lower lip trembling, his face covered in sweat.

"I told you," said Lim, gasping. "I haven't heard anything, I haven't seen anything. No one has tried to sell it—no one has even heard of it. And if it was being moved in Hong Kong, *I would know*."

The Dragon Head frowned, as if he resented having his lecture interrupted.

"That's why I asked you," he said simply.

"I can't help you, *lung tau*," cried Lim, tears welling up in his eyes.

"No," came the reply, the man's eyes cold and black. "You can't." Almost casually, he slid his right foot over a button set in the floor. A barely audible click was followed by a dull roar as the flood of scorpions resumed, the clicking and scraping sounds of the pincers and barbed tails filling the room.

The second wave flowed over the first batch of scorpions, pushing them forward, Lim hopping frantically around the room. He crushed several dozen in the first few minutes, but he was barefoot, and after another halting skip cried out as a four-inch-long tail whipped forward and found its mark.

"The venom is a complex neurotoxin." The voice from above droned on. "It causes rapid breathing—"

Lim fell to one knee as four scorpions scuttled up his right leg, stabbing as they climbed.

"—followed by shortness of breath—"

Lim's scream was cut short as a lone scorpion clambered up his back, the pincers opening and closing in anticipation, until it reached the exposed part of Lim's neck just above the collar.

"—then foaming at the mouth—"

Lim tried to stand but slipped, falling forward onto his hands and knees.

"—until, in the end, there is—"

The tail snapped forward, its stinger lodging in the thick flesh just below the skull.

"—total respiratory failure."

Lim's scream turned into a cough and he fell forward onto his chest, his arms waving spasmodically as the scorpions scuttled and jumped toward him. The Dragon Head watched dispassionately as the scorpions moved across Lim's body like water until he disappeared altogether.

Shaking his head, the Dragon Head turned his back on the spectacle and sat down heavily on a couch. Switching to English, he said:

"I feel like the *nefarious Doctor Fu Manchu*."

A voice across the room answered him.

"Traditions are important."

Sitting on another couch, set back from the edge of the sunken room, the man with the jagged scar smiled. His right eye seemed to disappear and then flash back into existence as the raised flesh of his cheek rose and fell with his expression. "And besides, I think it was the *fiendish* Fu Manchu."

"Whatever you say, Xan," said the Dragon Head, now in Cantonese. "But where did you get the scorpions?"

"Central market," replied Xan. "They have everything."

"So many?"

"They're prolific," said Xan. "The female scorpion can give birth to more than thirty-five young at a time."

"Really?" said the Dragon Head, raising his eyebrows. "I'll have to build that into the narrative."

Xan nodded. "Better than the snakes, I think."

The Dragon Head shrugged, then changed his tone. "Lim said it was no longer in Hong Kong."

"He said no one tried to sell it," replied Xan in a guarded tone. "We can't know for sure—"

"It's not in Hong Kong," said the Dragon Head definitively, their casual banter suddenly forgotten.

Xan nodded briefly, an understated bow. "Yes, *shan chu*. As you say."

"Don't patronize me." His father had preferred the more formal title, *shan chu*. Man of the mountain. He preferred Dragon Head. The older name might suggest wisdom, but the latter clearly said *power*. The power over life and death. And in the end, that was all that mattered.

"I mean no disrespect," said Xan evenly.

The Dragon Head said nothing, his black eyes staring at the pit. The scraping and clicking of thousands of feet and claws ricocheted off the walls as the scorpions finished their meal. Slowly he turned back toward Xan, his eyes blacker than the shadows behind him.

"Only those trained in the arts could have stolen from me," he said deliberately.

Xan narrowed his eyes but remained silent.

"And they would not be foolish enough to stay in Hong Kong."

Xan stood mute, his face expressionless.

"There is one who left," said the Dragon Head. "A long time ago."

"Yes, she did," said Xan, shifting in his chair.

"Go ask her what she knows," came the command. "The thief is someone who left the path."

"She is in America," Xan protested.

"Then bring a passport."

Xan breathed deeply before responding. "But your father—"

"*Don't* speak of my father," came the curt reply. "I am *not* my father."

And that is the problem, thought Xan, who merely said, "Yes, *lung tao*. I will leave tomorrow."

14

SALLY WAS DROWNING.

She had been underwater for well over a minute, kicking hard as she swam through the tunnel connecting the first two pools. The sky was overcast, which made the water murky, and Sally could not find the bend in the tunnel that led to the second pool. Koi fish swam past as she strained her eyes against the gloom, her small hands clawing the rough surface of the tunnel wall as she searched for the opening.

When she blinked, she saw spots and knew she was going to black out.

Instead of panic, the realization brought a sudden calm. Her mind drifted past the koi to thoughts of her parents, dead now three years. She opened her eyes wide and let the slight current take her, feeling utterly detached from her body, her mind lucid and clear despite the pounding in her ears and the burning in her lungs. She drifted silently, holding fast to the silent wish that she would see her parents again very soon.

The water pushed her backward toward the left side of the tunnel wall. The bend in the tunnel had always been on the right, but Sally was beyond caring. As she turned slowly in the current, she realized the koi were moving in the same direction, and as she watched, they disappeared one by one. A large gold and black fish with bulbous eyes darted past, its tail fins brushing her cheek before it swam toward a shadow on the wall and vanished.

Sally blinked as she drifted closer and realized the shadow might be an opening, a subtle curve in the tunnel wall. She was jolted out of her morbid reverie, her senses suddenly alive with blood rushing through her ears, the stale taste of water in her mouth, and adrenaline coursing through her arms and legs. She kicked frantically toward the spot where the koi had disappeared, half expecting to slam headfirst into the wall.

Light exploded through the water and Sally broke the surface with a loud cry. Sucking in air, she swallowed some water and started coughing violently, sinking back under the water as adrenaline fled her exhausted arms and legs.

An iron hand snatched her by the wrist and yanked her out of the water in one strong pull, dropping her unceremoniously onto the embankment. Coughing and spitting, Sally looked up to see Xan staring down at her, a grim smile on his ruined face.

"Well done, little dragon," he said. "You learned to see without trusting your eyes."

Sally could barely talk, her lungs wracked with pain. "The tunnel . . . ?" she began, faltering. Turning her head, she saw a small group of girls standing some ways off, watching. Jun was with them, as was her sister Lin, anxious looks on their faces.

Xan bent closer to Sally and smiled, the electric scar jumping with delight. "The tunnel moved, neh?" he said. "You have been here almost three years—I thought it was time you learned some of our secrets, so I gave you a little test."

Sally sat up with some difficulty, the color returning to her face. "But if I had failed?"

Xan's smile broadened, his black eyes as hard and bright as obsidian.

"Then you would have died, little dragon," he said matter-of-factly. "Now get dressed—it is time for your next lesson."

15

MITCH YEUNG LOOKED LIKE a guy you could trust.

Most of the refugees had been taken to a temporary housing facility on Treasure Island, a small patch of land bisected by the Bay Bridge on its way from San Francisco to Oakland. The island was man-made, part of a WPA project from the thirties to build the first airport for the San Francisco area. Back in the days of water-landing planes like the Pan Am Clipper, an island in the middle of the bay was the perfect location, so the navy built one by dredging mud from the bay and the Sacramento Delta. Memories of the California gold rush from decades before were still fresh enough to start rumors that silt dredged from the bay contained untold riches, so the name Treasure Island was an inside joke among the men who built it.

Part of the island housed an old naval base, shut down after Pentagon budget cuts several years back. The low white buildings remained largely unused while city officials on both sides of the bay argued about what to do with the land. But this week no one was arguing, thankful to have a temporary home for two hundred refugees who had none.

Mitch had asked Cape to meet him inside the main building, a long white rectangle set back from the road by a short lawn of brown grass. Cape heard the undercurrent of human voices as he approached, but once he stepped inside, the din was overwhelming. At least a hundred people inside a single long room with exposed rafters, the floor lined with cots, chairs, and the occasional desk. A corner had been draped off, doctors and nurses milling about on this side of the curtain. Cape assumed they'd taken those needing immediate medical attention to one of the many hospitals around the city, but the white lab coats were on hand in case anything new cropped up on the island.

Men and women wearing a variety of uniforms and suits were scattered around the area, most holding clipboards, a few carrying tape recorders, most of them Asian. The men, women, and children from the ship sat on their cots, on the floor, and stood around in small groups. Cape noticed that the refugees talking with various officials looked very serious, even worried, but those chatting amongst themselves looked happy and relaxed. It was as if they knew their journey was almost over, the promised land just beyond that door, if only the men and women with the clipboards would promise not to send them back.

Before Cape could get his bearings, a tall Chinese man with broad shoulders walked toward him, wearing khaki slacks and a navy blazer with no tie. As he approached, Cape took note of his short black hair, salted gray near the temples, and dark eyes sitting high on an open, friendly face. His wide mouth curved into a smile as he extended his hand.

"Cape Weathers?" The man's grip was firm, his hand dry and callused.

"Mitch," said Cape, shaking his hand. "How'd you know who I was?"

Mitch broadened his smile. "Beau said you dressed like you were still in college." His gaze moved from Cape's running shoes, past his jeans, and over a black T-shirt covered by an old white dress shirt, unbuttoned and untucked. "Or a reporter," he added.

Cape shrugged. "Saves on dry cleaning."

"He also told me your nose was broken," added Mitch. "Several times."

Cape touched the bridge of his nose lightly, where it took a slight left turn before resuming its course. "Not for at least a year."

Mitch nodded, then looked over his shoulder before gesturing toward the door. "Let's go for a walk." He took off his jacket and draped it over a chair, rolling up his shirtsleeves. As he turned the cuff of his left sleeve, Cape noticed a dark tattoo at the edge of his wrist, but Mitch had stepped outside before Cape could catch the design.

The view across the water toward San Francisco was distracting, the morning sun having burned through the fog. A few sailboats followed in the wake of a tanker moving slowly under the bridge, close enough to reach with a brisk swim. They walked for a couple of minutes before talking, both men squinting from the glare off the bay. They stopped beside a stone bench but neither sat down.

Mitch said, "You mind my asking, what's your interest in the ship?"

"I don't mind you asking," replied Cape.

"But you're not gonna tell me," said Mitch, nodding as if he already knew the answer. "Beau said you were a *very* private detective."

Cape shrugged.

"But he said he doesn't hold that against you," added Mitch, "and that neither should I."

"Guess we're off to a great start."

"Your client involved in this?"

Cape thought of Sally, realizing he didn't have a client. "That's what I'm trying to figure out."

Mitch nodded, looking out toward the water. After a moment he seemed to make a decision, gesturing toward the bench. He took a seat on one side.

"You'll tell me what you find out?"

Cape thought about it before responding. "If I think it will help the case and not hurt my ... *client* ... yeah. I'll tell you, or Beau."

"But not the feds?"

Cape shrugged. "I'll tell anyone I think can help, you want the truth."

Mitch nodded. "What do you want to know?"

Cape looked over his shoulder toward the main building. "Where did those people come from?"

"Fuzhou," said Mitch, his intonation shifting as he said the name. "It's on the northeast coast of Fujian province in China. A lot of human smuggling starts in Fuzhou."

"Why?"

"That's where the major smuggling rings are based," replied Mitch. "Quite a few used to be in Changle City, but there was a brief government crackdown, so they moved."

"Just like that?"

"You have to understand, smuggling humans is big, big business," said Mitch. "One of the feds I'm dealing with told me it's now a billion dollars annually, with some smugglers making as much as thirty mil a year."

Cape let out a low whistle. "That's a lot of *yuan*."

"That's right," nodded Mitch, "especially since it's almost eight yuan to the dollar these days—so bribing local officials doesn't break the bank. Neither does moving your base of operations. Plus, there's prestige involved."

"Prestige?" Cape wasn't sure he'd heard correctly.

"If someone makes the journey, then their family back in China gains in stature," explained Mitch. "And if they can send money back to their family, even better. So these smugglers aren't necessarily regarded as criminals, at least not by the people they're smuggling."

Cape wanted to ask Mitch more about that—about China—but he forced himself to stay on track.

"How's it work?" he asked.

"Say you make your way to Fuzhou," said Mitch. "Or you're from Fuzhou to begin with. You save up sixty bucks for a bus to Guangzhou, where you're put on a freighter bound for Hong Kong, or the U.S. directly. You're smuggled into the country, then you're put in a safe house until you can find work, or get papers, or contact family, depending on the situation."

"How much?"

"The folks back there," said Mitch, jerking his chin toward the barracks, "were on the hook for thirty grand."

Cape almost gasped. "Each?"

"You bet," said Mitch, adding, "I told you it was big business."

"How can they possibly come up with that kind of money?"

"One of two ways," replied Mitch. "Family that's already here, who borrow against everything they have to bring other family members over, one at a time. That's option one."

"And option two?" Cape feared he already knew the answer.

"You become someone's property."

"Property," said Cape, the word as cold and dispassionate as the concept itself.

Mitch chewed his lower lip before giving Cape a cynical smile. "You didn't think China was the only place with sweatshops, did you?"

"So they work as slaves," said Cape, "getting room and board, until their debt is paid off?"

Mitch nodded. "Keeps the prices down in Chinatown," he said sarcastically. "Good for tourism."

"Why do they do it?" asked Cape. "I thought things were getting better in China."

"Better is relative," replied Mitch. "But you're right, it's easier to emigrate legally from some cities today, depending on how much *guanxi* you have."

"What?"

"Connections," said Mitch. "You know an official you can bribe, or you're related to an inspector, then maybe you can get papers. But with no *guanxi*, the only way to get here is inside the baggage compartment."

"Do they really know what they're getting into?"

"No, they don't," said Mitch. "And in most cases, the journey isn't that bad. Refugees are flown by plane to South America, then sail up the coast. And they're generally treated well, considering. But ships like this, with people crammed in the hold like animals ... it still happens."

Cape stared at the bay, trying to imagine being that desperate, wanting to escape something that badly.

Mitch seemed to read his mind. "You know what they call the United States in China?"

Cape shook his head.

"*Meiguo*," replied Mitch. "That's Mandarin for 'beautiful country.' America might have lost sight of the American Dream, but these people are praying for it every night of their lives. You have no idea what life is like over there, even on a good day."

Cape detected an undercurrent in Mitch's voice, some subtext to the narrative.

"This is personal for you," he said simply. "Isn't it?"

Mitch turned from the water, his right hand raised to block the sun. "Yeah," he said, meeting Cape's eyes. "My parents came over on a ship like this one. Lucky for me, they got asylum."

A long minute passed as Cape held Mitch's gaze. "What will happen to these people?"

Mitch shrugged. "Depends on who they are, in large part. Things are a little funny with China right now, as you probably noticed in the papers. We're asking for help with North Korea, trying to play nice. So these people might get asylum, but they also might get sent home."

Cape cringed at the thought, thinking of the derelict ship, trying to wrap his head around making a voyage like that twice. "But they'll keep trying, won't they?"

"Oh, yeah," said Mitch. "Once you get it in your head you're leaving, most people find a way. And there's enough people waiting to help them, or prey upon them, depending on your perspective."

"You going to find out who's behind this?"

"Not me," said Mitch, "though I'd like to. That's for the feds to figure out. The INS and FBI, mostly. Me, I'm just a narcotics cop who speaks Chinese."

Cape suspected Mitch was much more than that, but he kept the thought to himself. "What if I wanted to find them?"

Mitch smiled, his mouth a little crooked. "You have to go hunting for the snake."

"Snake?"

"The person behind this is called a 'snakehead,'" Mitch replied. "There's a *little snakehead* and a *big snakehead*."

"What's the difference?" asked Cape.

"The little snakehead is probably in China. He or she—women are involved sometimes—arrange for the transportation and handle logistics on that end."

"And the big snakehead?"

"That's the one you want," replied Mitch. "He or she is probably here, in the States. The big snakehead is the main investor—the one that fronted the money, and the one that gets the big payoff. Without them, none of this would be possible."

"You think the feds will find them?"

"Not a chance," said Mitch, his cynicism audible. "They'll probably find some of the handlers—the middlemen who took the money, set up the safe houses, that sort of thing. But the real power behind it…those guys are almost never caught. Too many layers between them and the actual crimes."

"What kind of person am I looking for?"

Mitch shrugged. "Could be anybody. An anonymous business-man, a well-connected financier, or some guy you never heard of, working in the shadows. They may not even be Chinese."

Cape's surprise must have registered, because Mitch continued.

"The old days of Chinese-only crime are over," he said. "Now the tongs and their gangs are in bed with the Russians, the Italian Mafia, even the Chinese government. If they can make money, they'll call you brother—at least until they cut out your liver."

Cape caught the edge in Mitch's voice and gestured toward the tattoo on his arm.

"Were you in a gang?"

Mitch smiled, rubbing the back of his hand as he spoke. "Beau said you were smarter than you looked."

"I'm even smarter than *he* looks," replied Cape.

"A long time ago," said Mitch. "The Flying Dragons in L.A. took me in, along with my younger brother. I got out before it was too late."

Cape wanted to ask about the brother, but Mitch's expression made it clear the subject wasn't open for discussion.

"OK, smart guy," said Mitch, "what else do you want to know? I should get back inside."

"Fair enough," said Cape. "Two more questions?"

"Shoot."

"If you were looking for a snakehead, where would you start?"

"I'd try to find the tail," replied Mitch. "Find someone lower on the food chain, and take it from there."

Cape nodded; no surprise there.

"And the second?" asked Mitch.

"The people who were on the ship—what have they said about what happened onboard?"

"You mean what killed the crew?" asked Mitch.

"Don't you mean *who* killed the crew?"

"Not if you ask the people who were onboard," replied Mitch. "I've talked to almost forty men, women, and children, and practically every one says the same thing, with maybe two exceptions."

"Yeah?"

"They say there were *yaomo* onboard," replied Mitch. "That's what killed the crew."

Cape raised his eyebrows but remained silent.

"Demons," replied Mitch. "Evil demons. They told me a demon killed those men."

Cape frowned. "Is that the Chinese equivalent of *'officer, I swear I didn't see anything'*?"

"That's part of it," Mitch replied. "It's bad enough they got caught trying to slip into the country—these people do *not* want to be witnesses in a murder investigation. But remember, a lot of these people come from rural China—they can be very superstitious."

"You said there were two exceptions," said Cape.

Mitch nodded. "An older woman and her daughter. I think the daughter might have been raped by the crew."

"What did they say?"

"That the crew was killed by *tianbing*," replied Mitch. "A 'heavenly soldier.'"

Cape squinted into the sun but said nothing.

"The English equivalent would probably be 'angel,'" added Mitch, shaking his head. Cape frowned, but Mitch didn't seem to notice, adding, "So we're looking for someone who is part demon, part heavenly spirit—sound like anyone you know?"

"No," said Cape, lying through his teeth for the second time that day.

16

"You are not thirsty," Sally muttered to herself.

Summer in Hong Kong was a cauldron, and the girls had been training outside all morning. The noon sun beat down like a hammer, bending the air into visible waves that flowed across the packed earth of the courtyard. Sally squinted and tried to concentrate on what Master Xan was saying, his form distorted by the shimmering air.

"You have all been here five years." His voice boomed off the walls of the enclosure as he turned and faced the perfectly straight line. Twenty girls ranging in age from nine to fourteen watched as he moved down the line, pausing to make contact with every one of them. "And soon, you must choose a path."

Sally stuck her tongue out, trying to catch some of the sweat dripping off her brow. As she concentrated on a promising bit of moisture at the end of her nose, her eyes crossed and she momentarily forgot about Xan. The drop smacked dead center on her tongue just as she realized everything had gone very quiet, as if the girls standing next to her had stopped breathing. Looking up she saw Master Xan had reached her spot in the line, only to find Sally crossing her eyes and sticking out her tongue.

Sally turned her head slowly to her right, looking to her best friend for guidance, but Jun's eyes were twice their normal size, her eyebrows so high they practically floated above her head. Whether in shock or fear, she was useless.

Sally took a deep breath and locked eyes with Xan. With a somber expression firmly in place, she bowed her head slightly, keeping her gaze steady. Neither coy nor defiant, just respectful.

Barely eleven and Sally already understood the power in a woman's eyes.

Xan's scar seemed to jump even though his face didn't move, a signal that usually meant he was angry or about to burst out laughing. Sally could never tell the difference. But today Xan merely held her gaze, his eyes boring into Sally as if he could read her mind. After a moment that seemed a lifetime, Xan nodded once and looked away, apparently satisfied with what he had seen. As Xan turned his back on the line of girls, Jun reached out and squeezed Sally's hand tightly. Sally squeezed back and released the breath she'd been holding.

Xan pointed directly in front of him.

"At the end of this courtyard is an exit." He gestured toward a small wooden door. "Six months from now, you may leave."

Sally snorted under breath. And go where? All of the girls were orphans, this school the only family they'd had for five years. Most of them had never known the outside world, even as children, and certainly not the streets of Hong Kong. Sally couldn't think of a single girl who had talked about leaving.

Xan motioned to the right and the girls turned as one, looking at a massive circular door set into the high stone wall of the inner courtyard. The door was ten feet in diameter, made of red lacquered wood elaborately carved, dragons and tigers intertwined with butterflies and cranes. The carvings became progressively more complex and dense as you neared the center of the circle, creating a sense of movement that bordered on vertigo, as if the door were some sort of vortex pulling you to the other side. At the exact center were two door handles, each one a half-circle painted black. Two Chinese characters had been carved deeply into the wood, one on each handle.

"This is the path of joy and sorrow," said Xan, naming the characters. He paused before continuing. "Beyond this door awaits a life of pleasure and servitude."

Sally leaned closer to Jun and whispered. "The path of hair and make-up."

"Intimacy and deceit," intoned Xan solemnly, his back to them.

Jun whispered back. "Kissing and telling."

"Spying and screwing," added Sally, both girls suppressing a giggle.

Xan turned to face the line again as both girls forced a frown and looked straight ahead.

Xan gestured to the red door again. "This is the path of consorts and concubines," he said, his voice suddenly quiet. "Some of you may think the life of a concubine is exotic, and you might be right. But do not think of it as a romantic life." He paused and looked meaningfully at each of the girls. "If you choose to go down that path, you will be chosen by someone." He paused again for effect. "But you will not get to choose that someone in turn."

The girls shifted uncomfortably, staring at the ground between their feet.

"And you might find yourself living with one person," Xan continued, his voice even more quiet but no less clear, "yet working for another. A consort hears many things. Many secrets."

Xan looked up at the sun and squinted, sweat beading on his forehead. The girls remained silent.

"If you choose the path of joy and sorrow," he said, as much to himself as the girls in front of him, "one day you will be called. And you will have to answer."

Sally turned to look up and down the line. Everyone already knew which girls would choose that path. Whenever a class was given time to themselves, certain girls would break off into pairs or small groups and run to their favorite part of the compound. For Sally and Jun it was always the obstacle course or the dojo. For some girls it was the theater and the room full of costumes. For others, the kitchen or music hall. After five years each girl had mapped out her future, whether she realized it or not.

And Sally knew the instructors saw everything. This speech was part of the tradition of the school. A ritual, nothing more.

Xan turned his back again and raised his left arm, gesturing toward the opposite side of the courtyard. Set into the wall was another circular door, this one painted black with red door handles forming the inner circle, once again marked with Chinese characters. Equally elaborate carvings covered its surface, the tigers and dragons intertwined with swords and symbols that looked like shuriken, or throwing stars. The same optical illusion of the carvings made the girls lean forward unconsciously as they studied the door. Sally felt herself pulled by the gravity of the images.

"This is the path of life and death," Xan said, his voice regaining its previous timbre.

Sally felt herself tremble with excitement.

"Beyond this door is a life of power and control," Xan continued.

Sally and Jun held their breath.

"Discipline and despair.

"Judgment and justice."

Sally gasped at the last word.

Xan turned, locking eyes with her as he finished. "If you choose this path," he began, seeming to speak directly to her, "you will come face to face with your darkest self."

Sally met his gaze, her face expressionless.

"You will have control over how you do things," he said deliberately, "but not over why you do them."

Again he looked up and down the line, unblinking despite the sweat in his eyes. "Your life may be your own, but your conscience will belong to someone else."

Sally's nostrils flared as she breathed in deeply. She felt lightheaded and thought she might faint. Xan's words seemed no more than whispers, as if Sally were hearing his thoughts instead of his voice.

"If you choose the path of life and death," he said, "there is no turning back."

Sally stared at the black surface of the door and felt herself being drawn inexorably to the other side, the undertow pulling at her as she welcomed its embrace. She had already turned her back on any other door a long time ago.

Xan's final words seemed to reach her from far away as they echoed around the courtyard.

"In six months, you will have to choose."

17

Cape was pleased to find himself surrounded by pancakes.

Mama's Restaurant had been a fixture in North Beach for almost thirty years. They served one of the best breakfasts in San Francisco until three p.m. daily, except for Mondays, when they were closed. Cape had noticed all the good breakfast joints were closed on Mondays and suspected some sort of collusion, a concentrated effort by the forces of evil to prevent him from starting the week off right. He made a mental note to conduct a thorough investigation, if only to ease his neurotic mind and justify a sampling tour of all the pancakes made in the Bay Area.

Mama's was cafeteria style, with only a handful of tables squeezed into a space smaller than most studio apartments. Seating was allocated based on the number in your party or the size of your order, and based on the plates surrounding him now, Cape had obviously given the impression that four or five more people were coming. He had secured the much coveted corner table, behind which he waited patiently for Linda to arrive.

In front of him on the table, bracketed by plates of food, headlines from the local paper jumped up at him. *Mayor versus Mayor* covered the front page, with two facing photographs—one of the current mayor of San Francisco, who was colloquially referred to as "da Mayor," and the other of Harold Yan, whom the paper called "the Mayor of Chinatown." Yan was accusing the mayor of dragging his heels investigating the refugee ship, saying the people of the city deserved answers. Yan referenced a trip the mayor had taken to China the previous year as a member of a goodwill committee from West Coast cities to encourage trade with the Pacific Rim.

Yan never accused the mayor of corruption or undue influence from his "new Chinese friends," but by suggesting the mayor turn to them for help, the insinuation was all too clear. And coming from a man who was himself Chinese, it was irrefutable, at least from a political standpoint.

Cape studied Yan's face in the picture. He had black hair with occasional hints of gray slicked back from a high forehead, dark eyes, a strong nose, and an easy, confident smile. Even on newsprint there was something charismatic about the man, and reading the article, there was no question he knew how to work the press. By contrast, "da Mayor" looked tired and angry, like he'd been at this game too long. Cape knew the newspaper trade well enough to know these photos were selected to create just such a contrast, but he couldn't shake the feeling that it wasn't that far from reality.

The hanging bell chimed as the door swung open, and people in line made way for another hungry soul to enter the crowded space. Linda Katz wasn't immediately visible over the shoulders of the other patrons, but her hair was.

Dark brown and omni-directional, Linda's hair added a good four inches to her height and considerably more to her attitude. People standing nearby eyed it warily, not sure if angry hornets would emerge or if the hair itself would strike without provocation.

Linda eschewed blow dryers, curlers, or anything involving electricity that might tame her unruly tresses. Convinced that electromagnetic radiation was a real and present danger to her and every other life form, Linda was very particular about where she went. Linda would only spend three hours a day indoors, unless she was at home, so they'd usually meet in a park or along the water, careful to stay at least fifty yards from any telephone poles or cell towers. Fortunately, Mama's was sufficiently earthy for Linda to make an appearance.

Since she used the phone only when necessary, it usually took two or three tries to track her down, but Cape had been lucky and caught one of her co-workers who knew where she was. Despite her quirks, Linda was a damn good reporter, one of the best when it came to background checks and research, as far as Cape was concerned. He'd met her when he was still working as an investigative reporter, too brash to get along with the editor, but too talented to get fired. Linda had taken him under her wing and taught him some manners; he'd forgotten most of them, but he always remembered the gesture.

As she approached the table, he watched her eye the overhead lights suspiciously, then smile at him before sitting down, the lines around her hazel eyes running deeper than he'd remembered. He'd never asked her age, but Cape guessed she was ten years his senior.

"Are more people coming?" she asked, perusing the table. Arranged around the points of the compass were three stacks of pancakes and, directly in front of Linda, a bowl of granola.

"They're short stacks," Cape insisted. "That's what it says on the menu."

"They're not that short."

"Breakfast is the most important meal of the day," Cape added defensively.

"It's two o'clock in the afternoon."

"I haven't eaten anything since breakfast," said Cape, regretting it as soon as it was out. "Besides, I thought you'd like some pancakes with your granola."

Linda's hair lurched backward at the suggestion. "Sugar is a killer," she said defiantly, pulling the bowl of granola closer.

Cape shrugged and transferred one stack of pancakes onto the other before ladling a generous amount of syrup onto the plate. "Here's to a sweet demise."

Linda sighed in dismay. "Is your client paying for this?"

Cape shook his head. "Don't have a client."

Linda put down her spoon as Cape told her about the ship and his conversation with Beau. Although the two women didn't interact and couldn't be more different, Linda and Sally were connected through Cape. While Cape might only feel good about himself when he was saving someone, both women were committed, in their own way, to keeping Cape from getting lost in the process. Linda had always considered Sally a kindred spirit, another woman looking after this errant knight that sat across the table, stuffing his face with pancakes. Neither relationship romantic, and both the stronger for it.

When Cape finished his story, the deep lines around Linda's eyes looked like permanent scars. "You don't think Sally was on the ship?"

Cape frowned before returning her anxious gaze, his eyes darkened, blue turning gray with doubt.

"I'm alive today because Sally has killed," said Cape, knowing he could never lie to Linda. "Without hesitation."

"But never without cause," said Linda, unnerved at her own ability to rationalize so quickly.

Cape cut her off. "You don't have to convince me," he said. "I'd be a hypocrite to say I don't approve, but I'd be a liar if I didn't admit Sally has a different set of values from normal, law-abiding citizens. Hell, even from me, and I'm not very normal or very law abiding."

"There's nothing wrong with a woman defending herself," said Linda half-heartedly. "Or others, for that matter."

"I agree." Cape held up his hands. "But let's be honest—her school of self-defense believes in the pre-emptive strike. It's more like a school of offense."

Linda shook her head. "But if it *was* Sally, then she must have had a reason."

"Absolutely." Cape nodded. "She might be the most dangerous person I've ever met, but she's not a sociopath. Like I told Beau, she's one of the good guys. Sort of like Dirty Harry in a leotard."

Linda frowned at the image. "But if she had a reason, wouldn't she have told you?"

Cape had thought about that, too, and kept coming up with the same answer. "Not if it was personal."

Linda didn't say anything right away. They sat for a few minutes, alone in their own thoughts. Finally Linda raised her eyes and caught Cape looking at her.

She said, "You're going to find her."

"Hopefully, before anyone else does."

"Have you thought about talking with Freddie Wang?"

Freddie Wang was the local big man for the tongs, a genuine Chinese gangster who touted his connection to the Triads like some men bragged about the size of their dicks. He ran most of the gangs in Chinatown, acting as point man for the heroin smuggled in from Asia. He was also the bag man for the Triads' distribution deals with the Mafia, but according to Sally, Freddie wasn't the real power in Chinatown, just the face. Cape had crossed Freddie's path before on another case, but he had Sally along as an interpreter. Even with her watching his back, the meeting had not gone well. If Freddie knew something about the refugee ship, Cape had no way to get him to talk.

Cape shrugged. "I might end up talking to Freddie, but I can't start there. I need some kind of leverage."

"Like what?"

"Like information," replied Cape. "How's the granola?"

Linda scowled. "Are you asking because of a genuine concern for my well-being, or was that a less-than-subtle attempt to remind me that you're buying breakfast in return for a favor?"

Cape did his best to look wounded. "I'll take that as a yes."

"What do you need?"

"That's the problem," said Cape. "I don't know where to start, so I want you to dig into anything you think might be relevant. The ship's registry, for one. The containers onboard—what was in them, and what was supposed to be in them, according to the ship's manifesto."

Linda nodded as she pulled a small pad and pen from her purse. "What else?"

"The cop I talked to said these people came from Fuzhou," said Cape. "That's in the Fujian province of China."

"So?"

"So what goes on there?" asked Cape. "If you live in that part of China, what do you do, and why would you leave?"

Linda looked up from her notebook. "This is gonna get pretty broad, as searches go," she said. "You want me to get the Sloth involved?"

Cape smiled at the nickname. His friend Barry hadn't used his given name for over a decade. Sloth was a genius trapped inside a body that could barely respond, only connecting with the world around him through computers. He could use them to talk, see things invisible to others, and go places forbidden to all but a select few. There wasn't a network he couldn't hack or security system he couldn't breach without leaving a trace. And with Linda asking the questions, Sloth could tell you things about yourself even your own mother wouldn't remember.

"Tell him I'll come by," said Cape. "As soon as I come up with more questions."

Linda nodded, her hair waving back and forth. "Where will you go next?"

"I think there are answers in Chinatown," said Cape, "but without Sally I'm half-blind."

"Is that like being half-dumb?"

"*That* I'm used to."

"So?"

"I need a guide," said Cape. "Someone who knows Chinatown from the inside."

Linda raised her eyebrows. "You have someone in mind?"

Cape finished the last bite of pancakes before answering, bringing his empty fork down onto the newspaper that lay between them. The silver tines landed neatly on the bridge of Harold Yan's nose, his dark eyes staring up from the front page.

"Why not ask him?" said Cape.

Linda shook her head in disbelief, thinking of all the reasons why not, but instead saying, "You think he'll talk to you?"

Cape looked hurt. "Wouldn't you?"

"I'm not running for mayor," Linda replied.

"Too bad," said Cape as he glanced at the check and put some bills on the table. "I would have voted for you."

Linda smiled. "Want me to check him out, too? Maybe I'll find a way in."

Cape shrugged. "I think I'm going to try the direct approach and call Yan's office, but sure—go ahead. It's always nice to know who you're dealing with."

Linda stood to leave. "Thanks for breakfast."

Cape nodded absently, his thoughts already somewhere else.

He was wondering what the hell he was going to say to the Mayor of Chinatown.

18

"WATCH HIS LEFT FOOT," whispered Sally. "He drags it to the left before he strikes."

Jun nodded, wiggling her toes as she watched the kendo instructor take his position in the center of the floor. He and the girls were barefoot, their wooden sandals lined up outside the open door of the dojo. Sally could see other girls in the exercise yard in groups of ten or twelve. Some sparred while instructors shouted at them, sometimes stepping between two girls to show them how to strike or block a kick. Others practiced balancing on wooden poles eight feet high and four feet apart.

Sally unconsciously rubbed her right knee as she watched, remembering the fall she had taken the week before. Master Xan had kept her on the poles for four hours, long after the other girls had gone to supper, making her practice until she could finish the course without falling. Sally had collapsed on her bed afterward, too exhausted to eat or change her clothes, but pleased with herself for not failing.

The next day Xan made her lead the class.

Three days later he made her do it blindfolded.

"Su Quan!" yelled Xan from across the room, breaking Sally out of her reverie. "Come forward."

A girl with short black hair jumped up and ran lightly to the nearest wall, where long wooden swords hung on racks next to several life-sized figures made of bound straw. Selecting one of the swords, she crossed the hardwood floor and approached her opponent.

The teacher was a young man named Yuan, whom Sally guessed was maybe eighteen, only a few years older than the girls. His hair was cut very short, looking almost spiked, making his forehead seem too big for his face. His eyes looked dull and flat as he studied Su Quan, meeting her nervous gaze as they faced each other and bowed.

The sudden crack of wood against wood was like a gunshot in the enclosed space as Yuan lunged forward, his sword coming down like a scythe toward Su Quan's head. She parried the blow but it cost her balance, and she staggered backward. Before she could regain her footing, Yuan sprang forward and swung his sword low, knocking her feet out from under her. Su Quan landed hard on her side, her sword clattering across the floor.

Xan came forward as Yuan stepped back into a neutral position, a self-satisfied look on his face.

"Yuan is stronger than Su Quan," Xan said matter-of-factly. "He is taller, and he is faster. Does this matter?"

"No, Master Xan," replied the ten girls as one. "Strength does not matter. Not if you are cunning."

Behind Xan, Yuan smirked at the girls, clearly confident that they were not cunning enough. Sally fought the urge to stick out her tongue— getting caught once by Master Xan was plenty.

"The sword is not a weapon," said Xan, his eyes running up and down the line. "You are the weapon. The sword is merely a tool." He paused for effect. "Remember this."

Xan turned just as Yuan adopted what he hoped would pass for a humble expression. As Xan passed him and approached the open door, Sally noticed a figure standing just outside, looking in their direction. The figure looked male and older, but he was too near the building, his body largely in silhouette beneath the eaves, his face in the shadows. Although slightly stooped and shorter than Xan, there was something in his bearing that convinced Sally he was not just another instructor. Watching Xan approach him, Sally could tell this was someone important.

When Xan bowed deeply, she almost stood to get a better look.

"Jun!" Yuan called, bringing Sally's attention back to the floor. "You're next."

Sally squeezed Jun's arm as she stood. "Remember the foot!"

Jun flashed Sally a quick smile as she ran to the wall and selected a sword.

Yuan bounced lightly on his toes as he waited, clearly not intimidated. Sally gritted her teeth as her best friend took her position. Xan stood in the doorway, his arms crossed, his head cocked to one side as he listened to his guest.

Yuan and Jun bowed, their eyes betraying nothing. As Yuan stood and raised his sword, Jun leapt forward and swung low at Yuan's left leg, catching him below the knee. Crying out, he staggered but remained standing, catching himself with his sword and using it as a crutch. But before Jun could press her advantage, Yuan reached with his left hand and grabbed her sword, a move that would be impossible if they were using real blades. Before Jun could stop him, Yuan wrenched the sword from her grasp and jabbed it back at her, catching her in the solar plexus and knocking her down.

Jun lay on her back gasping, eyes watering as she struggled for breath. Yuan cursed as he hopped over to her and raised his sword, looking as if he would crack her skull open. Ten girls jumped to their feet, Sally at the front of the pack.

"Enough!" shouted Xan, his voice echoing around the chamber. The man next to him remained motionless.

Yuan sneered at Jun and lowered his sword, turning his back as he limped to his mark. Sally and Su Quan lifted Jun off the floor and carried her back to the line.

"Sally!" called Xan. "Choose a sword, little dragon."

As Sally walked slowly toward the wall of swords, the figure next to Xan spoke, his voice too low for anyone but Xan to hear.

"Is she the one?"

"Yes, shan chu," replied Xan.

"And she is ready?"

Xan hesitated. "She is barely fifteen, shan chu."

"That wasn't the question."

Xan sighed. "She speaks three languages," he said deliberately. "She can tell jokes or curse in any of them, better than you or me. She knows math, music, and some art. She excels at disguises—she can dress up like an old woman, and you would swear she is an old crone. She has studied the martial arts of the samurai and the Shao Lin."

"But is she ready?"

Again Xan hesitated. "It is difficult to judge, shan chu. She is young."

The figure nodded, as if considering the wisdom of Xan's words. When he spoke again, his tone was milder, as if he had grown bored and changed the subject.

"My son is getting older," he said idly. "And so am I."

Xan took a deep breath. "With all due respect, shan chu, your son—"

"My son," came the stern reply, "is pak tsz sin—the position of White Paper Fan is a serious one, equal in rank to your own."

"I know, but—"

"But you think he is not ready to ascend further, is that it?"

Xan tried to control his breathing. "I think all of the society's money flows through his fingers," he said carefully.

"That is his job," said the man. "That is his duty."

"I understand duty, shan chu," Xan said slowly.

The man turned slightly and nodded. "I know you do, Xan." He gestured idly toward the room, where Sally was still looking over the swords. "Who is the instructor?"

Xan shrugged. "Just one of the 49s," he said. "A sze kau—one of our foot soldiers."

"He is a good swordsman."

"He is fast," agreed Xan, "but he is impetuous."

Sally looked over her shoulder. Yuan was looking toward Xan, probably wishing Xan would yell at her to get moving. By the time she faced him, Sally wanted Yuan to be impatient at the very least, and ideally mad. Glancing at Xan she saw he was still talking to the older man, but they were both looking her way. It was time to fight.

Walking slowly across the floor, Sally smiled sweetly as she held Yuan's gaze. As she came closer, his sullen look transformed into an angry sneer, but Sally only increased the voltage of her smile. By the time they were facing each other, Yuan looked as if he were about to scream and Sally looked as if she'd just been asked to dance. She held her sword tightly in her right hand, her eyes never leaving Yuan's face.

They bowed and Yuan came up quickly, raising his sword before he had even stood upright, his legs sliding apart as he prepared to lunge.

Sally never even stood up. Bent forward from her bow, she swung her sword across her body, catching the tip in her left hand and holding it like a staff. As Yuan started to crouch, Sally somersaulted forward, her hands holding the sword and pushing down against the floor, sending her into a spring-loaded handstand. Yuan started to jump and Sally lunged upward feet-first, her right heel connecting with his crotch.

Sally's classmates gasped as Yuan choked on his own scream, the force of Sally's legs sending him flying backward. By the time his back hit the floor and he curled into a fetal position, Sally had landed on her feet.

She stood over him, her sword inches from his face.

"I am the weapon," she whispered fiercely.

Yuan yelped and curled tighter into a ball.

Xan coughed, as if stifling a laugh, then clapped his hands to signal the end of class.

The man next to him blinked, stunned at how quickly the match had ended. Turning to Xan, he spoke quietly but firmly, making it clear there would be no further discussion.

"She is ready," he said. "In one month, Xan, give her to me."

19

A BLOCK FROM THE retail madness of Union Square, two red columns entwined with golden dragons stood at the entrance to Chinatown. All the San Francisco guide books told you to walk the length of Grant Avenue, starting at the dragons and ending where Grant intersected Broadway and spilled out into North Beach.

Cape had walked from the Broadway side, passing storefronts catering to tourists and offices and groceries that were exclusively Chinese. When he reached the address he'd been given over the phone, he stepped back onto the street, looking up at the two-story building he was about to enter. It stood to the right of a grocery and to the left of a restaurant with *Hunan* in the name, which applied to every other Chinese restaurant in the city. The first floor housed a print shop, and through the plate glass to the right of the door Cape could see three men talking to a woman behind a counter, the woman pointing to samples of paper tacked to the wall behind her. Just to the left of the front door was another door of plain wood, held open by an iron doorstop cast in the shape of a traditional Chinese dog. A stairway leading to the second floor started just past the threshold. Set into the wall alongside the door was a bronze plaque:

CHINATOWN MERCHANTS BENEVOLENT ASSOCIATION
HAROLD YAN, PRESIDENT

Cape took the stairs two at a time, pausing on the second floor landing to straighten his jacket. He wore a black sport coat over jeans and a white dress shirt but no tie. The pair of New Balance trail runners he'd worn earlier in the day had been traded for black dress shoes. He may not be ready to work at a bank, but at least he looked professional. A grown-up, if not an adult.

The woman in the reception area was young, Chinese, and very pretty. Cape put her at twenty-five, tops. She took his card with a pleasant smile and told him to take a seat, then picked up the handset on her phone and talked quietly to the person on the other end. Cape took one of four straight-backed chairs clustered around a square table littered with magazines and newspapers. In addition to the usual coffee-table clutter of the *Chronicle* and *Examiner*, Cape saw several Chinese-language newspapers and a few magazines, as well. Grabbing the nearest one from the pile, he saw that Harold Yan adorned the cover.

The phone buzzed and the young woman said something into the receiver that sounded like *shur-dur*, then hung up. She smiled warmly as she gestured toward a door in the wall behind her desk.

"Mister Yan will see you now," she said. "The last office at the end of the hall."

Cape thanked her and opened the door. The hallway was short, maybe twenty feet long, with two offices on each side and a door at the very end. He could hear voices coming from behind the doors on each side, but as he stepped onto the thick red carpeting of the hallway, his attention was on the photographs lining both walls.

The first showed Harold Yan shaking hands with the mayor in front of the elementary school located just around the corner. The second photo featured Yan with the president from the previous administration, standing with a group of ten men and women on the White House lawn. With the exception of the president, everyone in the photograph was Asian. The next two had Yan talking to the chief of police and the governor, respectively, both of whom appeared to be listening intently to something Yan was saying. By the time Cape reached the end of the hallway, he'd been given a walking tour of who's who in politics.

The door opened before he could knock, Harold Yan smiling at him across the threshold. He was taller than Cape expected, with squared shoulders under a nicely tailored suit jacket. His handshake was firm, his smile relaxed. His eyes were large, the overhead fluorescents dancing around their edges as he turned and gestured toward a chair in front of his desk.

"Have a seat, detective," said Yan. The office was fairly spartan. There was a beige love seat set against the left wall, above which a window looked out over Grant Street. Cape stood in front of a desk made of dark wood, its surface cluttered with papers, a phone, and a stack of file folders. In front of the desk sat two red chairs, their backs high, the seats themselves cushioned. On the right wall was a bookcase; Cape scanned the titles, noticing several books on politics and a few on religion and philosophy before he sat down and faced his host. Yan was already seated, his eyes friendly but inquisitive.

"Thanks for seeing me," said Cape.

"Always glad to be of service," replied Yan. "But before we begin, which precinct are you with? I didn't recognize your name."

Cape had expected this. "I'm not with the police," he said. "I'm a private investigator. Sorry if that wasn't clear when I called." People naturally made assumptions when they heard "detective," and Cape saw no percentage in clearing things up until he was through the front door. He took his license from his jacket pocket and slid it across the desk.

Yan's eyes flashed for an instant, but he didn't miss a beat. "How interesting," he said pleasantly. "And what are you investigating?"

"The refugee ship," said Cape.

Yan leaned back in his chair, studying Cape for a minute before saying anything. "Could you be more specific?"

"I'm looking for someone," Cape began, choosing his words carefully. "Someone who may have been onboard the ship."

"And you think I might know them?" asked Yan, frowning.

"That hadn't occurred to me," replied Cape truthfully.

Yan raised his right eyebrow quizzically. "You have me at a disadvantage," said Yan. "Do I know your client?"

Cape hesitated before responding. "That hadn't occurred to me, either," he said. "I'm here looking for advice, if you want to know the truth."

Both eyebrows went up as Yan said, "Advice?"

Cape leaned forward. "I'm looking for someone in a place that I can't navigate on my own."

"Chinatown," said Yan knowingly.

Cape nodded.

"And you're not Chinese," continued Yan.

"You noticed."

"A lucky guess," replied Yan, smiling. The lines around his eyes revealed his age—Cape guessed Yan had ten years on him—but the rest of his face was smooth and unlined. His voice was resonant, with just the slightest edge to the consonants. He was better in person than in the newspaper, and he already came across pretty good in print. *If I was the current mayor*, thought Cape, *I'd be nervous.*

"Are you from the Bay Area?" asked Yan, seeming genuinely curious.

Cape shook his head. "East Coast, originally, but it's been almost twenty years since I moved out here."

Yan nodded. "Practically a native, as far as San Francisco goes."

"Long enough to call it home, anyway," said Cape, shrugging. "You?"

"Ten," replied Yan, a note of pride entering his voice. "I came over from Hong Kong, after fleeing mainland China with my brother."

Cape had read the story about Yan in the local papers, how he spent his first few years in San Francisco working for less than minimum wage, taking classes at night to learn about his new home. Four years later, he passed the California State Bar and opened a small legal practice. The next year he ran for District Supervisor and got elected, and had been in the office ever since. It was the great American success story, still pursued in earnest by almost every man, woman, and child living in Chinatown.

"You've done well," said Cape, stating the obvious but sensing Yan wanted the acknowledgment.

Yan nodded. "I've been lucky," he said. "But I'm the exception, not the rule."

Cape stayed quiet, sensing a soapbox was being added to the conversation.

"Do you know how many people in Chinatown speak little or no English, Mister Weathers?" asked Yan.

Before Cape could answer, Yan added, "Fifty percent." He leaned forward in his chair, putting both palms on the desk. "And do you know how many Chinese work for less than the minimum living wage in this city?"

Cape shook his head.

"Almost thirty percent," said Yan, a look of disgust crossing his face. "Some have good jobs, and they're treated fairly, but many others are taken advantage of; these are not illegals, you understand. They're simply isolated because they don't know the language. They are totally dependent on the community in which they live. A community that exploits them."

"The Chinese community," said Cape simply.

"Sad, isn't it?" said Yan. "But it's worse in China," he added. "Much worse."

"That's why people try to leave," said Cape, trying to steer the conversation off the campaign trail.

"Yes," said Yan, nodding absently.

"That's why a ship full of refugees ran aground on Alcatraz."

Yan took the hint. "Yes ... yes. You wanted to talk about the ship."

"If you don't mind."

Yan nodded.

"The people onboard," began Cape. "Where would they have gone if the ship had docked the way it was supposed to?"

"You mean if they hadn't been caught?"

"Yes."

Yan hesitated, so Cape forged ahead. "I know they would have been taken to some sort of safe house," he said, watching Yan for a reaction. "Maybe several houses in Chinatown. And they would have stayed there until they worked off their debt."

Yan raised his eyebrows again. "You've done some homework."

Cape shrugged. "That's my job."

"And who did you say your client was?"

"Does it matter?"

"It might," said Yan, his eyes cautious.

"Didn't you say the refugee ship was 'a crisis affecting not only Chinese, but every taxpaying resident of San Francisco'?"

Yan's mouth twitched, as if he had started to frown, before managing another smile. "Was that in the *Chronicle*?"

Cape nodded. "Right on the front page."

Yan pursed his lips. Cape knew what was going through his mind. He looked directly at Yan, making sure he had full eye contact before he spoke.

"Look," he said, "I'm not a reporter—I used to be—but I'm not here to burn you. You're in the midst of a political campaign—I understand that."

Yan smiled briefly, his body language more relaxed. "Are you saying this is off the record?"

"There is no record," replied Cape. "You didn't have to see me in the first place, and I appreciate that. You want me to leave, just say the word."

Yan looked out his window before turning back to face Cape.

"Ask your questions," he said.

"You're putting a lot of heat on the mayor," said Cape.

"He deserves it," said Yan matter-of-factly.

"There's a rumor he'll step down," said Cape. "Maybe not run against you, but nominate someone in his place."

Yan shrugged. "There are a lot of rumors in this town," he said, noncommittal. "Like charges of police corruption."

"You saying the charges are bogus?" asked Cape.

"I'm saying it's quite a coincidence," said Yan. "I've suggested the current administration is corrupt, and yet the only scandal making the headlines has to do with *Chinese* police officers."

"Which reflects on the entire Chinese community," said Cape, finishing the thought. "So the politics are about race."

Yan shook his head. "Not exactly," he said. "The current mayor is black, so it's not as simple as racial innuendoes or exploiting hidden bias in the voters. That only works when one of the candidates is white, at least in this city."

"So?"

"It's about reinforcing a perception that the Chinese in this city are somehow *them*, while everyone else is *us*. You set up a strong enough *us versus them* dynamic, and that could carry the election. The Chinese are isolated, different ... many don't even speak English ... you get the idea."

"So even when there's a scandal in the current administration," said Cape, "it somehow hurts *your* campaign, not the mayor's."

"The mayor is a smart man," said Yan admiringly, his eyes bright with either envy or ambition, Cape couldn't tell.

"With the Chinese cops sidelined during the investigation," said Cape, "it makes it kind of tough to get a handle on the refugees, and the ship."

"I was going to ask if you already talked to the police," said Yan.

"Some," replied Cape. "But I wouldn't be here if they had it all figured out."

Yan chewed on his lower lip. "You look honest."

"It's the blue eyes," said Cape.

Yan laughed. "All right," he said. "I won't pretend Chinatown is a utopia. Most of our residents are hard-working, honest families, doing what we must to survive. But I would be lying if I didn't acknowledge that some of our residents are less law-abiding than others."

"Like Freddie Wang," suggested Cape.

Yan laughed again. "It seems you know more about Chinatown than you've let on, detective."

Cape shrugged. "I'm ignorant, but not naïve. Freddie hasn't kept the lowest profile over the years."

"True," said Yan. "Wang is a local gangster, plain and simple. He deals in drugs, among other things. But I imagine you know all that."

"Rumor has it Freddie heads a *tong*," said Cape, "that controls all the heroin coming in from Asia."

Yan snorted. "Tong?" he said scornfully. "Do you know what a tong is, Mister Weathers?"

Cape shook his head. "Just what I've read—Chinese organized crime."

"Indeed," said Yan. "That's very true, in some cases. But 'tong' simply means chamber—a meeting place. It's a blanket term to refer to any large organization, fraternity, or business association."

Cape recalled the plaque outside. "Like the Chinese Merchants Benevolent Association?"

"Exactly," said Yan, nodding. "A group of local merchants joined together to pool resources. They share business contacts, legal services, and make loans to members at favorable rates. The association allows Chinese businesses to become competitive. There are many such associations in Chinatown—ours has been in existence almost one hundred years."

"I don't think Freddie Wang is making loans at favorable rates," replied Cape.

"Neither do I." Yan smiled, a cynical look on his face. "But he's got his own organization—he's not a member of ours."

"But why do you tolerate him?" asked Cape. "It can't be good for the community, for that legitimacy you want."

Yan spread his hands. "Our resources are limited," he said. "That's like asking why the Italian community tolerates the Mafia, or why the city police can't stop prostitution."

"OK."

"We have an understanding with the tongs," said Yan. "We have to live in the same neighborhood, after all."

"But if someone in the Chinese community was involved with hiding the refugees—," began Cape.

"It would be Freddie Wang," said Yan. "That's my guess."

"I was hoping you'd point me somewhere else," said Cape, frowning. "I've talked to Freddie before, and it wasn't what you'd call a cordial conversation. I don't think he'll talk to me."

"He will if I tell him to," said Yan confidently.

"Is that part of your understanding?" asked Cape.

Yan shrugged. "I'll tell him what you told me—you don't want to cause trouble, you just want some information. It could be much worse for Freddie if you just started knocking on doors in the neighborhood, asking questions."

"That was my next step," replied Cape, "if I wasn't able to talk to you."

"I'll talk to Freddie," said Yan definitively. "And he'll talk to you. Beyond that, I can't make any promises."

Cape stood. "Mister Yan, I've taken enough of your time."

Yan extended his hand. "Good luck."

They shook hands. "Thanks," said Cape. He started to turn, but Yan held his hand a moment longer than expected.

"You know, Mister Weathers," he said, turning to look out his window, "your answers might not be in Chinatown."

"What do you mean?"

"Do you know what was onboard that ship?" asked Yan. "Or what those people were doing in China?"

"No," said Cape. "I don't." He thought about telling Yan he'd already asked that question of someone else, but for some reason didn't. "Do you?"

Yan shook his head. "I just thought it might be relevant."

Cape nodded. "Thanks again. If you think of anything else," he said, handing Yan his card.

"There is one more thing," replied Yan, reaching behind him. He extended his right hand and pressed something into Cape's palm. "Wear this in November, if you don't mind."

Cape looked down to see a round button emblazoned with *Yan for Mayor*. He smiled and dropped it into his coat pocket. "Good luck in the election."

Cape turned and walked down the hall, passing through Yan's gallery of photos. Waving to the pretty receptionist, he let himself out and took the stairs down to the street. The air was crisp, a hint of fog in the chill wind coursing down the street.

He stood for a moment on the curb, reflecting on the meeting. It was still early and the street was crowded, pedestrians of all ages moving around him like water. Yan was a politician and a law-yer, which normally meant two strikes against him, but there was something disarming about the man. Cape reminded himself that he didn't really know Yan, but he suspected that he'd like him if he did. And if nothing else, he'd given Cape a reason to move forward.

Cape moved to cross Grant and was knocked sideways by a young Asian boy with orange hair carrying a large backpack. The boy muttered something under his breath as he brushed past, step-ping up onto the curb without looking back. Cape started to say something but caught himself, watching as the boy rounded the corner. Looking both ways before resuming his walk, he crossed the street and turned right toward Broadway.

He walked two blocks before reaching into his right jacket pocket to fish out his cell phone. He wanted to call Linda and see if she'd found any background on the ship. His fingers brushed against something that wasn't his phone, something with a hard, thin edge to it.

Cape pulled a card out of his pocket, a rectangular piece of cardboard about an eighth of an inch thick. Written across the top were the words *One-eyed Dong*. Below was an address just a few blocks from where Cape stood, in the heart of Chinatown.

Cape turned the card over in his hands. On the back was a tri-angle, the three sides carved into the card with blood-red clarity. Below the triangle were three Chinese characters that meant noth-ing to him.

Cape thought of the boy with the orange hair and looked again at the card. He wondered if he'd been followed on his way over here, or maybe the entire day.

Either way, he didn't like looking over his shoulder.

20

"NUTS?"

Lucy cranked up the wattage on her Tennessee smile as she proffered the small cup of mixed nuts, but the big Chinese fella wasn't having any of it. He looked at her like she'd just shit on the tray table.

She didn't think he spoke English, but it was pretty damn clear what she was saying. She was holding the nuts in her hand, after all.

Part of being a flight attendant was meeting all sorts of interesting people, but the flipside was dealing with folks who just couldn't see the sun for the clouds. This boy'd clearly had a tough life, just from the look of him. That scar was as long and crooked as an interstate highway. Not even a mother could love that face.

But this was business class, and she wouldn't become *positive employee of the month* for backing down from a challenge. (The airline used to have awards for plain old *employee of the month*, but the constant squabbling with the unions made the flight attendants so surly that management had decided to get specific.) The award came with a free trip to Hawaii including lodging and two hundred bucks cash, so Lucy wasn't about to let some grouchy Chinaman knock her off her game.

She bent down to show some cleavage and gave it another Tennessee try.

"Nuts?"

"Yes," came the reply, and Lucy almost yelped in surprise, his English crisp and clear, the voice so deep. Then the big man turned away and closed his eyes, never reaching for the small cup in her outstretched hand.

Lucy wondered if maybe he didn't understand her after all, or if he thought she was asking him a personal question. That last thought gave her a little shiver.

Lucy walked back to the galley and checked her watch. They'd be landing in San Francisco pretty soon. She decided to keep to herself for the rest of the flight. Pulling out the folding seat next to the lavatory, she absently chewed on a Macadamia from the cup in her hand.

It was only the middle of the month, she told herself. Still plenty of time to win that trip. Better to conserve her energy so she could charm the shit out of the passengers on the way back to Hong Kong.

21

Xan leaned forward and stared at the two girls in disbelief, his thickly muscled forearms pressing against the edge of the table. It was three o'clock in the morning, and Jun and Sally had just returned to the compound.

"You stole his watch?"

Both girls nodded.

"And his wallet," added Sally.

"And his passport," said Jun.

"And his car," they said in unison.

Xan's scar jumped imperceptibly.

"Your assignment was to follow and observe," he said slowly, hammering the last three words as if driving stakes into the ground.

"We did follow," protested Sally.

"And observe," added Jun.

"And then?" demanded Xan.

"We engaged," came the reply, in stereo.

"On whose initiative?" demanded Xan.

Sally and Jun exchanged a glance and then pointed at each other. "Hers."

Xan breathed deeply through his nose. "He is a senior official of a rival clan," said Xan. "We could be exposed."

Sally shook her head. "Not a chance," she said definitively before catching herself. She nodded once out of respect and added, "I don't think so, Master Xan."

"And why not?"

Jun spoke next. "He thinks we're prostitutes."

Xan looked at the two teenagers before him as if noticing for the first time their short black dresses, hair, and makeup. Though Xan was still getting used to seeing this group of girls in a different light, scheduled trips into Hong Kong were a regular part of their training now. After all, you couldn't blend in with your surroundings unless you had experienced them, if only while playing a role.

"Prostitutes," Xan repeated.

"Underage prostitutes," corrected Sally. "We told him we were only seventeen."

"You're only fifteen," replied Xan. "Jun is seventeen."

"That's not the point," said Sally, almost but not quite dismissively.

"And what is the point?" asked Xan, raising his eyebrows.

"He's married," said Sally.

"And he knew we were not yet eighteen," added Jun.

"But he bought us drinks," said Sally.

"Which we spilled when he wasn't looking," added Jun.

"But he drank."

"And drank."

"And drank."

"Then he fell asleep."

"Or passed out."

"Then we took off."

Both girls nodded, obviously pleased with themselves.

"So he won't tell his wife, because she would divorce him," said Jun.

"And he won't tell his mistress, because she would kill him," added Sally.

"And he won't tell his associates, because he would lose face for being so careless," said Jun.

"So we were not exposed, Master Xan," said Sally, a little more contrite this time. "We were very careful."

Xan sighed again.

"This man was second to the pak tsz sin of another society," he said. "He is an accountant and, as you have so clearly demonstrated tonight, he is a buffoon."

Xan paused as he looked deliberately at each of the girls.

"But tell me," he continued, "what would you have done if this man turned out to be something other than what he appeared to be? What if he did not drink? What if he had been a Red Pole or a sze kau who intended to capture you or inflict damage on our clan in some way?"

Both girls leaned forward in their chairs, but Sally answered first.

"I would have killed him," she said simply.

Xan met Sally's gaze, her bright eyes almost unnaturally green, her pupils dark and wide. In that instant it seemed as if the young girl in front of him was older than Xan himself. Somewhere in the dark undercurrents of her eyes swam a vengeance unfettered by the shackles of remorse. Those eyes could kill a man, he thought.

Xan looked at Sally for a long moment before saying anything.

"As you say, little dragon." Then he turned to Jun and nodded.

"Leave us."

Jun stood and bowed, shooting a quick glance at Sally.

Once Jun had closed the door, Sally turned back to Xan.

"Am I in trouble?"

Xan shook his head. "This does not concern Jun."

Sally nodded her understanding, even though she suddenly felt anxious. She was usually paired with another girl, and almost always it was Jun. They were roommates. They trained together, ate together. Sally wondered what could possibly concern her and not Jun.

"Sally, do you know why all of your instructors are men?" asked Xan.

"We have many female instructors."

Xan nodded. "Of course," he said quickly. "For language training and music."

"And acting," said Sally. "And math and science."

"Yes," agreed Xan. "I wasn't thinking of your morning classes."

Sally understood. "You mean our instructors for the martial arts."

Xan nodded but remained silent. Sally thought for a moment before answering.

"We used to have female instructors," she began, trying to remember when she had stopped sparring against women. "Until I was twelve."

Again Xan nodded. "When you were no longer a girl."

Sally knew what he meant, though she still thought of herself as a girl. But that was the year she first got her period, and also the year she was sent into Hong Kong by herself.

"'If you know the enemy and know yourself, you need not fear the result of a hundred battles.'" Xan spoke in a voice that suggested to Sally he was quoting from something. Probably from The Art of War.

No matter what class you were taking, the instructors were always throwing Sun Tzu in your face. The girls often joked that without Sun Tzu, they wouldn't have any homework.

Xan saw the look on Sally's face and pressed on. "The clan is a male organization," he explained. "Much like the other societies. White Lotus, Heaven and Earth, Phoenix and Dragon. They are all run and staffed by men."

"I understand," said Sally tentatively.

"Naturally, this makes them suspicious of other men," said Xan. "To penetrate another organization, therefore, we must sometimes use cunning."

"'Attack him where he is unprepared, appear where you are not expected,'" said Sally confidently. "Sun Tzu."

Xan smiled. "Well said, little dragon. There is no mystery, then, as to why you are here."

"No, Master Xan," replied Sally. "None."

A life without mystery, thought Xan, studying Sally for the second time that night. Such a life begins here.

"Very well," he said, as if to himself. Reaching behind him, Xan produced a folder of heavy brown paper, its texture and weight suggesting it had been handmade. Sally had seen folders like it before, always containing photographs and backgrounds of men she was supposed to follow in the city.

"The shan chu wanted me to give you this," Xan said simply, sliding the folder in front of Sally.

Sally looked up from the folder. The shan chu was the head of the school. No, the head of the clan. The Master of the Mountain. The Dragon Head.

Sally knew she wasn't going to just follow a man around Hong Kong. This was something more important. She opened the folder, not sure what to expect.

The first thing she saw was a photograph, black and white, taken with a long lens. The man in the picture looked Japanese. He was standing next to a white delivery truck on a busy city street with a cigarette in his right hand, his eyes screwed up against the smoke. Sally guessed he was maybe forty-five. Even from a distance, his features looked coarse and unfriendly. Sally was about to look at the rest of the file when she felt a sudden and unexpected revulsion.

"Who is he?" she asked, looking up to find Xan staring at her with an odd expression on his face. If she didn't know him so well, she would have sworn it was one of concern.

Though their eyes were locked, Xan seemed to be looking somewhere far away when he finally answered.

"Little dragon, he is the man who killed your parents."

22

Of the countless Chinese restaurants with *Hunan* in their name, only one served tourists by day and gangsters by night.

Located in the middle of Grant Street, Freddie Wang's restaurant was a known haunt for criminals, but since Freddie routinely swept the place for bugs and never handled transactions on the premises, he managed to keep the place open despite its questionable clientele. The trick was convincing law-abiding citizens to clear out before the conversations in the dining room turned to drugs, gambling, and prostitution.

So Freddie started giving away fortune cookies with very special fortunes inside. The cooks and waiters studied each table, then ran back to an old man crouched in the kitchen who wrote custom fortunes. A young girl on a date might get a fortune warning her that the young man sitting across the table was in the midst of an outbreak of genital herpes, while a family of nervous tourists from the Midwest might open their cookies to find a prophecy of an impending earthquake. There were no lucky numbers or promises of wealth and happiness at Freddie Wang's place.

Cape took a seat in a corner booth, where he waited for almost an hour, watching the tourists clear out one table at a time, some engaged in heated arguments about what they'd just read about each other. By nine o'clock he was alone in the dining room, sipping Tsingtao from a bottle and watching the waiters clear the tables. When the last of the tablecloths had been removed, a lone waiter walked across the room and set a small plate in front of Cape, a single fortune cookie resting on its plain white surface. Cape cracked open the cookie and let the crumbs fall out of his hand as he read the small slip of paper.

Come upstairs, gwai loh.

Cape suppressed a smile as he made his way to a narrow stairway beside the entrance to the kitchen. His last time here, he had been with Sally, and his fortune was part threat and part insult. He was moving up in the world, now rating a simple invitation laced with disdain. The call from Harold Yan had done the trick. Freddie may not like Cape, but at least he'd talk to him.

At the top of the stairs, a thick-waisted man named Park waited impassively next to a door, wearing dark glasses and a suit that cost more than Cape's car. Park spent all day, every day searching people, and he was getting sick of it. His name meant *cypress tree*, and recently he'd been having dreams that roots were growing from his feet from standing around so much. With a brusque gesture, he indicated Cape should raise his arms, then pushed him roughly against the wall and patted him down. When he got to Cape's waist he hesitated, feeling a strange bulge on his right side. Reaching under the tail of Cape's sport coat, he pulled a wad of yellow rubber from beneath Cape's waistband. He took off his sunglasses and screwed up his face as the thing unfolded in his hand.

It was a rubber chicken.

"I brought that as a present to Freddie," said Cape over his shoulder. "Figured the guys in the kitchen could do wonders with it, especially with the right sauce."

The guard threw the chicken back at Cape but caught himself before following through with his fist. He'd clearly been given orders.

"Should I have brought cat instead?"

The guard grabbed him by the collar and turned him to face the door, then twisted the knob and shoved him forward. Cape raised his hands in time to avoid opening the door with his face.

It was dark inside, the only light coming from an old lamp with a green shade sitting on a desk. The cloying smell of incense filled the room, and thick tendrils of smoke curled in the subdued light. Behind the desk sat Freddie Wang, his long gray hair sprouting from a high forehead, his dark eyes squinting through the smoke as Cape stepped forward.

"I hear you died last year," said Freddie, his voice like dry reeds cracking in the wind.

Cape shrugged. "I heard that, too," he said. "Turns out I just had a bad case of food poisoning... I think I got it at this restaurant, as a matter of fact."

Freddie cackled, which quickly turned into a wracking cough. A gnarled right hand moved into the pool of light and snatched a lit cigarette from a carved wooden ashtray, then scuttled back out of sight like a cockroach. As the tip of the cigarette glowed red in the darkness, Freddie's cough subsided.

"If you got food poisoning here," he said slowly, "you'd stay dead."

Cape nodded but didn't say anything, moving to sit in one of the two straight-backed chairs in front of Freddie's desk. As he turned to sit, Cape noticed a stolid-looking man lurking in the shadows behind him and to the right. He had long black hair pulled tight into a ponytail and hands that looked too big for his body, jutting out from the sleeves of his suit like oven mitts. Although they came in all shapes and sizes, Freddie always had protection.

"So what you want?" asked Freddie testily.

Cape noticed Freddie's accent came and went depending on his mood and realized taking a seat without being asked had irked his host. Freddie didn't like visitors.

"I want your wisdom," said Cape pleasantly.

"Fuck you," said Freddie. "You think you kiss my ass, tell a joke, I tell you stories?"

"Nah," said Cape. "I think that if you tell me stories, then I leave you alone."

"You make threat?" Freddie leaned into the light. His face stretched painfully as he stared at Cape, the wrinkles unfolding like a broken accordion. His left eye was droopy and faint, its inner light all but extinguished, but his right eye glowed like a black sun. Cape caught himself leaning forward unconsciously, as if he were getting sucked into Freddie's gravitational pull.

"I want to know about the refugees on that ship," said Cape evenly.

"*Fah*," spat Freddie in disgust, leaning back in his chair. "You talk to cops?"

"I have," said Cape, "but I won't talk to them about you, if that's what you're worried about."

Freddie's half-lit face contorted again, revealing a mole on his right cheek sprouting three prominent hairs. "I look worried, *gwai loh*?"

Cape shook his head, smiling. "No, Freddie. You look great— you look like a lingerie model. They say aberrant facial hair is all the rage this year."

Freddie coughed violently in response, then gagged before summoning a wad of phlegm from the back of his throat. Leaning forward, he spat it expertly into the center of his ashtray. Running the back of his right hand across his mouth, he took another drag on his cigarette before his breathing returned to normal. Cape sensed the bodyguard moving closer but Freddie waved the man off. When he spoke again, his voice crackled as if a fire had started somewhere deep in his chest.

"You talk to cops about me," he wheezed menacingly, "I eat your eyeballs."

"So that's what's in hot-n-sour soup."

Freddie squinted through the smoke, his baleful right eye unblinking.

Cape shrugged. "Deal."

"You know what's on boat?" asked Freddie. "Besides dead Chinese?"

"Nope." Cape shook his head. "You?"

Freddie shrugged but didn't answer, looking from Cape to the bodyguard, then back again. Freddie loved playing the part of the Asian gangster, and Cape sensed this was one of those obtuse conversations in which Freddie spoke in half-truths and riddles, as if

131

the constant threat of surveillance hung over him like so much ciga-rette smoke. Few professional crooks had stayed in power and pub-lic view for so long, so maybe the paranoia was justified.

"You think that's important?" asked Cape, trying to keep the conversation going. "The cargo?"

"Not to me," replied Freddie. "But many people lost money when ship crash."

"On the cargo, or the passengers?" asked Cape.

"Cargo insured," replied Freddie. "Passengers, maybe not."

"Did *you* lose money, Freddie?"

"Me, I have plenty insurance." Freddie smiled broadly, his teeth yellowed from smoke.

"So you're saying the refugees' families paid for their transport, or they did themselves, and that money's gone," said Cape, want-ing to spell it out. "But someone like you keeps your share no mat-ter what."

"What you mean, like me?" asked Freddie defensively.

"The *snakehead*," replied Cape, trying out the word and watch-ing Freddie for a reaction.

Freddie shook his head, a series of popping sounds like hiccups coming from his throat. Cape realized he was chuckling.

"You get lesson in smuggling?" asked Freddie.

Cape shrugged.

"Too bad you not get lesson in *thinking*," said Freddie causti-cally. "No snakehead here, *gwai loh*."

It was what Cape expected him to say. Freddie may have to talk to him, but he didn't expect to get a full confession. "My mistake," he said amiably. "So what were you saying about the cargo?"

"Had to go somewhere," replied Freddie. "Maybe people on boat headed to same place as cargo."

Cape nodded but remained silent. This was probably as far as Freddie was prepared to go, at least on the record.

"We done here?" asked Freddie pointedly, confirming the suspicion.

"Sure," said Cape. "If you say so, Freddie." He stood but didn't move away from the desk.

"You used to live south of Market Street," said Freddie. A statement, not a question, maybe reminding Cape he knew where to find him.

"Yeah."

"Lots of warehouse space there," said Freddie idly.

"Some," said Cape, noticing how Freddie had leaned back into the light so he could read his expression. "Some have been turned into lofts, though. You know, residential space."

"People living in warehouses," mused Freddie.

Cape met his gaze and nodded. "Imagine that."

Freddie chuckled softly, then faded back into the shadows.

Cape turned to leave, suddenly realizing the bodyguard that had been standing behind him was no longer there. The hairs on the back of his neck stood up as he heard Freddie cough behind him.

"Last time you here," Freddie called out, "you came with friend."

Cape turned at the door. They both knew whom Freddie was talking about. Cape had only seen Freddie before with Sally at his side for protection. Even Freddie wouldn't mess with a girl raised by the Triads.

"Lots of people killed on that boat," added Freddie, his voice charged with an undercurrent of satisfaction.

"You have a point, Freddie?"

"You alone now, *gwai loh*," said Freddie, chuckling. "Better watch step."

"You making a threat, Freddie?" asked Cape evenly. "You did your favor for Yan, and now that we've had our little chat, I'm fair game—is that it?"

Freddie stayed in the shadows, saying nothing, his claw of a hand reaching for the ashtray.

"Or are you just worried about me?" added Cape.

"I look worried?" asked Freddie, the red tip of his cigarette glowing in the darkness.

"No, Freddie," replied Cape. "You look fuckin' great." He turned the doorknob, half expecting it to be locked, but it swung open with a rush of cool air. The smoke from the office billowed into the short hallway, making him realize how claustrophobic he was feeling. Cape descended the steps two at a time, thankful for the cool of the night fog as he left the restaurant behind him.

His car was where he'd left it, without a ticket on the windshield. A minor victory in the scheme of things, but at this point Cape wasn't taking anything for granted. The neon from the restaurant reflected off the side panels of the old convertible, colors twisting in a lurid dance along the contours of the car. It looked like it was riding low, and as he crossed the street Cape noticed something behind the left rear wheel. Squatting down, he picked the object up and studied it in the murky light.

It was roughly the size and shape of a Walkman, except without the outer casing. Wires ran from a red interior to a blank LCD screen and AA battery. Squinting, Cape saw that the red area looked soft and malleable, like Play-Doh, and behind the battery was a thin wire that looked like it could be an antenna. Next to the battery was a small switch, which Cape decided not to throw, but he did move the box closer to his car to test a hypothesis. Feeling the pull of the magnetic base, he had absolutely no doubt about what he was holding.

It was a bomb.

Cape glanced back at the restaurant, but the front door was closed and the lights on the first floor turned out. The rest of the street was just as quiet, save for the occasional car cutting across a block away. Taking one more look behind him, Cape slid his key into the trunk, popped the lid, and saw right away why the car was sitting low.

The bodyguard with the oven mitt hands stared at Cape with a surprised look on his face. It was an expression that wouldn't be changing anytime soon, since his eyes were dead and unblinking, the face locked in a rictus of shock. The angle of the head reminded Cape of a marionette. He wasn't a pathologist but was pretty sure the guy had died from a broken neck.

Cape blew out his cheeks and stood for almost a full minute staring at the corpse in his trunk. One half of his brain told him to call the cops while the other half made a compelling argument for kicking in the door to the restaurant and demanding answers from Freddie.

Instead he shook his head, trying for a moment to embrace the madness that had taken over his world. Cape tossed the bomb onto the body and closed the trunk, then walked around and got behind the wheel. As he pulled away from the curb he glanced in the rear view mirror, but the fog had grown so thick it was impossible to see more than a block away. He pulled his collar up and muttered to himself as he drove deeper into the fog, Freddie's rasping taunt chasing him down the street.

"You alone now, *gwai loh*."

23

"HE IS YAKUZA."

Sally's eyes never left the photograph. When she finally blinked, the picture distorted, and Sally realized she must have tears in her eyes. Yakuza. The word seemed to reach Sally from very far away, as if she were swimming under water and Xan was calling to her from the shore. Only when Xan repeated himself a third time did Sally tear her eyes away long enough to return his stare, giving him a look of pure defiance.

"He's in the Japanese mob," said Sally. "So?"

"So," replied Xan patiently, "that is something you should know. This folder was not given to you lightly, little dragon."

Sally gritted her teeth and nodded, forcing herself to breathe through her nose. She'd waited ten years for this opportunity; she could wait another ten minutes.

"I understand," she said. "Please continue, Master Xan."

"He is not very important," replied Xan, "but his uncle is—that's why we know who he is—and also why he didn't go to jail after his truck collided with your parents' car."

The room started to spin and Sally closed her eyes and tried to concentrate on her breathing, ten years of training and discipline struggling against a lifetime of pain and longing.

"We have an understanding with the yakuza," explained Xan. "Sometimes we do business together, and other times we compete for the same business."

Sally opened her eyes and nodded, not saying anything.

"But we do not attack them directly."

Sally felt her heart stop.

"Then why did you show me this folder?"

Xan looked almost paternal. "I said directly, little dragon," he said. "That means your task is to watch this man for one week, take photographs of his meetings—we are interested in one meeting in particular. And then..."

"And then?" Sally held her breath.

"Then this man means nothing to us," said Xan, "or to anyone else." He paused, watching her carefully as he spoke. "Then you must make a choice, little dragon."

Sally didn't hesitate. "I already made that choice," she replied, "when I stepped through the black gate."

Xan nodded. "We always have choices, Sally. Remember that."

Sally bowed her head, her thoughts rushing by too fast to register.

"There is one more thing."

Sally looked up, worried by the change in Xan's tone. "Yes?"

"You have mastered most of the fighting arts," said Xan. "But many will not be at your disposal on this trip."

Sally remained silent but looked puzzled.

"The bow, throwing darts, even poison." Xan's tone was one of warning. "These all leave a signature, Sally, for those who know the signs."

"What are you saying?"

Xan leaned across the desk. "If you want to kill this man, little dragon, you will first have to get close to him. Closer than you would like."

Sally swallowed hard and stared at Xan for a full minute before answering, her eyes now completely dry. When she spoke, her voice was hoarse, as if she had aged a hundred years since this meeting began.

"When can I leave?"

24

"I'd like ten bags of ice, please."

Cape had stopped at the Safeway in the Marina district, which was open twenty-four hours even though most people finished their grocery shopping by eight. At nearly eleven o'clock, Cape was one of five people in the store.

He smiled pleasantly at the young man behind the checkout aisle, who had been reading one of the tabloid newspapers they kept near the registers. Apparently Oprah had gained weight again and Martha Stewart was doing hard time.

The young man nodded at Cape, the beads woven into his hair jangling with the motion. His name tag said *Rex*.

"Havin' a party?" he asked as he tapped the keys on the register.

"Something like that," said Cape, glancing at his car through the glass front of the store.

"You want some beer?" asked Rex, his purple fingernails paused above the keys. "Maybe some chips? We got these sour cream 'n onion chips you wouldn't believe, man, especially after you been partyin' for a while."

Cape turned back from the window, his smile evaporated. "They pay you on commission, Rex?"

Rex backed up a step, then snorted. "No, dude, just tryin' to help you out."

Cape nodded, grabbing a pack of gum from the rack beside him. "Just this," he said, trying to keep an edge out of his voice. "And ten bags of ice."

"Whatever," said Rex, punching buttons. "You got a club card?"

Cape shook his head. "No, I'll just pay cash."

"It's not a credit card," replied Rex. "It's a *club card*. You type in your phone number, and you get all sorts of free shit. Like, tonight, you might even get a discount on the ice."

Cape stared at him, wondering if he should go back to his car and get the gun from his glove compartment. Rex stared back, confident in the flawless logic of his suggestion.

"Thanks, anyway," said Cape evenly. "Just the ice."

"You still want the gum?" asked Rex. "'Cause I already rang it up. I could void it, but then I'd have to call my manager, and—"

Cape held up his hands. "I want the gum," he said emphatically, picking it up off the conveyor and handing Rex a twenty before he could say anything else. "Thanks for reminding me."

Rex smiled and shrugged, pleased at his catch. "No sweat," he said, handing Cape his change. "You need help out to your car?"

"No," replied Cape—a little too quickly, he thought. "I'll manage."

"Peace," said Rex, turning back to his tabloid.

Cape used a cart to move the ice to his car, then did a quick scan of the parking lot before opening the trunk.

The expression on the dead bodyguard had not changed. He looked just as surprised that Cape had bought ice as he had looked when Cape first found him. The bags almost filled the trunk, and Cape figured they'd keep things under control for at least a few hours.

Getting behind the wheel again, he fished his cell phone from his jacket and made a short call, then turned out of the parking lot and headed toward Golden Gate Park.

—

25

IT WAS RAINING HARD by the time Hideyoshi Kano left the night-club.

Lighting a cigarette as he stepped under the awning, his face was lit by the blazing neon sign across the street. Fifty feet of blue neon twisted to form two giant characters in kanji above a red neon sign in English, which read "Happy Donuts."

The donut shop occupied the ground floor of an office building, unremarkable except for the European style of the architecture. While most buildings in Tokyo were glass and steel, this was only ten stories tall and built almost entirely of stone, complete with gargoyles lining the edge of the roof. Kano had never paid much attention, and tonight was no exception. He always had a few drinks before he took off, since this club was the last stop on his collection run.

Kano liked making the rounds, squeezing the local businesses for protection money, then taking a piss on their floor after having free drinks in their bar. He got off on the looks of hatred and fear when they saw him coming—they knew who his uncle was, and they knew they couldn't do shit. Some nights he'd slap someone around just to make a point, then watch them shit their pants when he pulled out a gun.

It made him hard just thinking about it.

Kano adjusted himself and turned his collar up, stepping off the curb into the waiting town car. Since he never looked up, Kano never noticed that one of the gargoyles was moving.

Sally shook the rain from her eyes as she crouched on the roof, a single step between her and ten stories down. Dressed entirely in black, with a hood obscuring her face, she was a silhouette against a murky night sky.

She stared at the empty street where the town car had been moments ago, her knuckles white as she gripped the edge of the roof in silent fury. Slowly she rocked back and forth as if she were about to jump, counting out the minutes. She watched as the bartender locked the place up and turned east to walk home.

It was raining even harder now, the sounds of traffic and sirens from a few blocks away drowned by the staccato thunder of the storm. When she was sure the car was out of earshot and the street was again empty, Sally stood and bellowed in rage, her voice a guttural cry of agony that echoed off the surrounding buildings. Had someone been watching, it would have looked as if a gargoyle had come to life, a demon from the underworld come to take its revenge.

Sally tore off her hood and let the rain wash over her, stepping back from the edge of the roof. Every night she fantasized about soaring across the night sky and tearing his heart out, and every night she forced herself to remain perched on the roof. Then she looked into the chasm and thought about jumping, thinking that would be easier than enduring the agony of waiting.

She had been in Tokyo for almost three weeks. The day she arrived, a young man not much older than Sally met her at the harbor, giving her some yen, keys, and an address printed on a slip of paper. Then he turned and ran away, as if terribly late for another appointment.

It had never occurred to Sally that he might be afraid of her.

At the apartment there were three fake IDs and a closet full of clothes suitable for any occasion. On a small desk she found more photographs and a map, along with a list of known haunts and addresses that Kano frequented.

Kano. Even saying his name made Sally want to retch. She was fluent enough in Japanese to know that the name meant masculine power.

We'll see, she thought, clenching and unclenching her fists.

Kano was a thug, plain and simple. Sally had followed him as he visited local businesses and bars, sometimes stopping at a tall glass building that Sally soon identified as a drop-off point for yakuza muscle. Although the busy office building was filled with smartly dressed men and women, Sally also noticed rough-looking men like Kano coming and going. Most did a poor job hiding full-body tattoos under ill-fitting suits.

Sally was certain when she saw Kano stop outside and light a cigarette. As he cupped his left hand to shelter the flame, Sally saw that he was missing his little finger. The next few days she noticed several men with maimed hands, running four fingers through their hair, holding a briefcase, or opening the door.

The yakuza believed mistakes should have consequences, and most members made at least one mistake on their way up. The offending clan member was required to sever his own finger, then wrap it in a white cloth and present it to his master. Always portrayed as a stoic ritual in books and movies, Sally had heard that many cried and screamed in agony, sometimes being held while their yakuza brothers did the cutting.

Sally smiled grimly as she thought of the ceremony, taking solace in the thought that Kano had already suffered once during his miserable life.

But I bet he knew his parents.

Each day in Tokyo peeled a layer of doubt from her heart.

On the sixth day, she followed Kano to a park, a small patch of green bordered by cherry trees with a stream running through it. A small wooden bridge arched over the water, allowing visitors to admire the koi swimming back and forth in their outdoor aquarium. It was a glimpse of nature, squeezed into a square plot of land and landscaped for observation, placed carefully in the heart of the financial district.

There were maybe a dozen people scattered around the park, including a few sitting on benches and several young professionals striding purposefully across the park on their way to their next appointment. Kano walked directly to the footbridge to stand alongside another man his age, at which point both men deliberately faced the water and assumed postures of men idly watching fish. Sally knew that Tokyo was just like Hong Kong, where no one did anything idly.

Straightening the pleats of her Japanese schoolgirl skirt, Sally casually removed the camera from her purse and started taking pictures of the park.

The other man looked Chinese. He had longish hair and hunched shoulders that jerked up and down while he talked. The two men clearly knew each other by sight but their postures were slightly con-

frontational. Sally couldn't hear what they were saying, but she had been trained to study body language since she was ten.

He belongs to a Triad.

The thought struck Sally as if it had always been there and just came to light. Why else would Master Xan know or care about someone meeting with a yakuza? The man moved aggressively, his gestures abrupt and impatient, so like the mannerisms of men Sally had followed before. She knew, just looking at him, what he did for a living.

He's a gangster.

Sally walked lazily through the park, a young girl more interested in her new camera than getting to school on time. By the time the men finished their meeting, she had several pictures of the fish and the trees, and almost half a roll of the bridge and the men standing on it.

That night Sally started frequenting the club that was Kano's last stop. In a short black dress with her hair down, she looked almost as old as her forged ID said she was. The bouncer didn't care—a few choice words convinced him Sally was an underage prostitute working the neighborhood, willing to give him a cut of any tricks she picked up in the bar.

The world beyond the soundproofed doors was an assault on her senses. Neon and strobe lights sliced through air heavy with sweat and smoke. Sally felt like she was underwater, and it took a few minutes to adjust her breathing. A square bar ringed with blue neon sat along the inside wall, a tiny island of calm in the vast club, but even there the bass from the speakers rattled glasses and pounded against Sally's chest like a sledgehammer. That first night she sat in a dark corner of the bar and listened while men and women shouted for drinks until they were hoarse.

Sally knew how she looked in her dress. She could feel the eyes of the men boldly crawl across her body as she turned her back, then dart away in cowardice as soon as she turned to face them. It took all her will to keep her features soft and her smile warm.

Kano usually arrived maybe an hour before closing time and then hung around until the club was empty. Her first night in the club, Sally left before he arrived, flirting a little with the bartender before saying goodnight. When she had walked a block north, turned right, and then doubled back to the building across the street, she changed her dress for the black cotton pants, shirt, and hood she had squeezed into her purse.

The next night she stayed in the shadows, watching.

It was well after midnight when Kano strode across the club like he owned it, heading straight for the bar. The bartender looked nervous as Kano slid next to a well-dressed young man and his date, nonchalantly putting his hand on the woman's ass. Before the man could react, Kano shoved him backward over the barstool. The woman yelled something, but the pounding music drowned her out. Nearby patrons barely glanced over, either not hearing the commotion and thinking some drunk just fell off his stool, or not wanting to get involved.

Kano grabbed the woman's wrist as she threw her drink in his face, realizing too late that the hand clutching her only had four fingers. Her eyes went wide with fear as Kano punched her full in the nose, then strode away, laughing, toward the men's room.

The whole incident had lasted maybe ten seconds.

The couple had fled by the time Kano returned to smile at the bartender as if nothing had happened. Pulling up a stool, he threw back a shot, slamming the empty glass onto the bar and gesturing for another.

Submerged in the darkness at the back of the club, Sally watched, uncertain if the deafening roar came from the pounding bass or the blood rushing through her ears. Her eyes were red from smoke and staring, and her hands were cold as the grave.

But as the white noise of music and rage devoured her, Sally devised a plan.

26

CAPE PULLED ALONGSIDE THE curb directly across from the park, only a block from the house where Sloth lived. Linda was waiting at the door when he arrived, her hair moving despite the lack of wind.

"Thanks for meeting me here," said Cape.

Linda gave him a noncommittal smile. "Learn anything new?"

"I think someone wants me dead."

"That's new?" asked Linda. "I'll bet plenty of people want you dead—ex-girlfriends, their ex-husbands or fiancés from before you came along, their therapists, who are probably sick of hearing about you—"

Cape cut her off. "I think someone is *trying* to kill me—note the use of the present tense."

"Oh," said Linda, her hair shifting in apology. "That's different. I guess that means you're making progress, huh?" She smiled encouragingly and turned to enter the house.

"You find anything?"

Linda's hair nodded but she didn't turn around. "I think so."

Cape followed her through the short foyer, wondering if any of her other friends thought of her hair as a separate person, a fuzzy third wheel that wouldn't leave you alone.

Sloth had designed his home around his affliction. Born with a rare neurological disorder, the Sloth didn't get his nickname from how he looked, but for how he moved. Far slower than the world's slowest mammal, it could take him an hour to cross the room, minutes to finish a single sentence. Until he came into contact with his first computer, the Sloth was trapped inside a frozen body that could only move at a glacial pace.

A large living room dominated the first floor, an open kitchen off to the side separated from the living area by a short counter. In the living room sat small islands of furniture, each arranged by function, none more than three feet apart. A television, DVD player, and amplifier sat off to the left, surrounded by a set of chairs and a small couch. Filing cabinets and a desk sat a few feet away, clustered together in a pattern that seemed quite deliberate but entirely unconventional, as if someone wanted to decorate their house with the furniture equivalent of crop circles.

In the center of the room were the computers. Box-shaped servers lined the carpeted floor beneath a wide desk shaped like a crescent moon, above which were mounted four plasma screens. Sloth sat behind the desk, his face bathed in iridescent light.

Computers had revealed Sloth's curse to be a mixed blessing, for while his body steadfastly refused to speed up, his brain was faster than a laptop on steroids. He saw patterns in data invisible to cryptographers, heard music in equations that spoke only to mathematicians. The screens in front of him flowed like rivers, numbers and bit streams scrolling downward at a dizzying rate, Sloth's hands shifting spasmodically across the top of the desk. A liquid crystal square was directly below his fingers, a touch-sensitive screen he designed himself. A butterfly landing on the desk could activate it, and the Sloth could play it like a piano. As Cape watched, words and symbols appeared and disappeared from the surface of the desk like stray thoughts, a holographic code only understood by the pale, stoic man behind the desk.

"Hello, old friend," said Cape warmly.

Sloth's watery eyes blinked slowly behind his glasses and his mouth twitched, an expression that would have looked pained on anyone else but was somehow full of affection. A lurch of his right hand and the second screen from the left went blank. As Cape watched, words appeared in large black type on the glowing surface.

WANT TO KNOW WHAT WAS ON THE SHIP?

Cape nodded and sat down next to the Sloth, while Linda, always cautious about anything emitting too much electricity, paced back and forth behind them. The room was lit by halogen lights set directly above each cluster of furniture, except the computers. The screens cast a bluish pall over Cape's face, the words appearing as if conjured from the depths of a crystal ball.

BLUE JEANS.

Cape glanced at the inscrutable Sloth, then gave a quizzical look over his shoulder at Linda.

"That's it?" he said. "Blue jeans?"

Linda nodded. Her hair shrugged.

"No drugs?" asked Cape. "No heroin?"

"Nope," said Linda.

"No guns?"

Linda shook her head.

"Uranium?"

"Uh-uh."

"Plutonium?"

"None of that," replied Linda. "But there were several dozen refugees onboard—in case you forgot."

Cape frowned. "No, I didn't forget. But Mitch Yeung told me it was fairly common for refugee ships to be smuggling operations of another kind. Since they've already taken the risk of getting searched, why not double the profits?"

"Does that matter?" asked Linda.

Cape shrugged. "Not necessarily."

Linda nudged him. "But … ?"

"But if there was heroin onboard," said Cape, "then it would be easier to tie the ship to Freddie Wang, since he controls the smack trade in the Bay Area."

"Why so anxious to tie the ship to Freddie?" asked Linda.

Cape told them about his visit to Freddie Wang's restaurant and the bomb he'd found beneath his car. When he told about his stop at the grocery store, Linda's eyes went wide and her hair became agitated and seemed ready to leave without her. The corner of Sloth's mouth twitched repeatedly as if he were laughing.

"There's a corpse in your car?" asked Linda, as if she hadn't heard correctly.

"It's OK," said Cape. "I told you—I bought ice."

"Isn't that against the law?"

"No," replied Cape. "Ice is perfectly legal in the state of California. It's one of the few things that is anymore, unless you want to count medicinal marijuana."

"That's not what I meant," snapped Linda. "And you know it."

Cape held up his hands and shrugged.

Linda crossed her arms. "I have no interest in getting arrested as an accessory to … to … to whatever it's called when you drive around with a corpse in your car."

"It seemed like a good idea at the time," Cape said simply.

"What are you going to do with him?" demanded Linda. "I mean, with it?"

"I haven't decided," said Cape matter-of-factly.

Linda made a noise that sounded like *harumph*.

Cape smiled hopefully. "Can we talk about the ship?"

Linda didn't answer right away, but she turned her frown toward the plasma screen, which Cape took as a conditional "yes."

"Where was it registered?"

The words materialized on the screen, each new phrase causing the previous one to disappear.

REGISTERED IN HONG KONG …
PICKED UP CARGO IN FUZHOU.

"Who is it registered to?" asked Cape.

KOWLOON IMPORTS.

Linda cut in. "But Sloth thinks that's a dummy corporation."

Cape looked at the Sloth while asking Linda the question. "How come?"

"He hacked their network and checked their balance sheet, then compared it with other Hong Kong shipping companies, including two that work the same trans-Pacific routes."

"And?"

The screen on the right resolved into four quadrants, each filled with a series of columns and numbers. At the top of each square was a company name, with Kowloon Imports in the lower right quadrant. The amount of detail on the screen made it difficult to read, and Cape didn't know where to look. As he watched, a blue rectangle flashed across the screen, stopping at certain figures in each quadrant before jumping back to the top and beginning a new course through the data.

"The cash flow doesn't line up with actual dates in port," explained Linda. "We checked the records from the harbor masters in Fuzhou, Hong Kong, and San Francisco."

Cape knew the answer to his next question but asked it anyway. "You have access to that kind of data? I thought only the feds could plug into those records."

Linda smiled sheepishly as the Sloth's mouth twitched.

Cape shook his head. "And you're giving me shit for driving around with a dead guy in my trunk," he said. "Talk about a double standard."

"That's not the point," said Linda defensively.

"What *is* the point?" asked Cape.

**THE COMPANY GETS PAID FOR
SHIPMENTS THAT AREN'T MADE.**

"By whom?" asked Cape.

Linda answered before any words appeared. "We don't know yet," she said simply. "The money trail is complicated, but you'd think the companies expecting shipments would notice."

"Unless they were part of the scam themselves," mused Cape.

Linda nodded, her hair bobbing excitedly. "That's what we thought."

"So who owns the blue jeans?" asked Cape.

Linda nodded toward the screen.

GASP

"*Gasp?*" said Cape.

"That's what everyone calls them," said Linda, "but you're supposed to say the letters: G-A-S-P. It's an acronym."

"For what?"

GREAT ASS, SEXY PACKAGE ... G-A-S-P.

Cape looked from Sloth to Linda. "Unbelievable."

"So are midriff shirts that look like they got shrunk in the dryer," replied Linda, "but all the young girls are wearing them."

"They're the new designer jean, right? Supposed to go up against Diesel, Levi's, and the GAP?"

"Except they cost over a hundred dollars a pair," replied Linda.

"Are they selling?"

"They did at first," said Linda, "but sales have slowed considerably. They're not the kind of jeans you'd wear every day of the week."

"Is the company publicly traded?"

Linda nodded vigorously, her hair threatening to take flight. "GASP went public right before the crash a couple of years ago— their stock is in the toilet."

"And they're made overseas?"

Linda nodded. "Just like everything else."

"In China?"

"In Fuzhou, to be specific," said Linda. "Same place the ship came from."

"Well, well." Cape looked back at the screen. "Where are their headquarters?"

"Right here in San Francisco," replied Linda. "Actually, they're on the Embarcadero, right next door to the new headquarters for the GAP."

"Butting up against their competitors," said Cape.

Linda groaned. "Was that an attempted pun?"

"Couldn't resist," said Cape. "I don't suppose GASP Jeans has any warehouses in town?"

An address flashed onto the screen. Cape recognized it as south of Market Street.

"Interesting."

"What?" asked Linda.

Cape didn't respond. Freddie Wang had basically told him to check some warehouses south of Market Street. That was fine, but he also told Cape to go fuck himself, if not in so many words. Freddie spoke in half-truths, and Cape had no way of knowing which half was bullshit. But the address on the screen was too much of a coincidence to ignore.

Cape put his hand on the Sloth's shoulder and squeezed. "I'd be lost without you," he said gently.

YOU STILL MIGHT BE LOST.

Cape nodded. "You're probably right, but at least I've got somewhere to go." He turned to Linda. "You mind doing one more thing?"

"What?"

"Who owns GASP?"

"Michael Long," replied Linda. "Chairman and CEO. Used to work for Disney and, before that, the GAP. Rumor has it, he used to manage strip clubs in Vegas before coming to California."

"That would explain his fashion sense," said Cape. "Can you get me on his calendar tomorrow?"

Linda shrugged, her eyes narrowing. "What do you want as cover?"

"Tell him I work for your paper," replied Cape. "And we're doing a story on local fashion icons—Levi's, the GAP, and him—he should love that. Tell him I'm the fashion editor."

Linda gave him a deliberate once-over, stopping at the running shoes.

Cape shrugged. "I'll be presentable," he said. "I promise."

Linda looked skeptical but nodded. "Just don't wear jeans," she said, "unless they're his."

"Got it," replied Cape. "And thanks."

Linda smiled, her eyes just visible beneath her shifting hair. "Anything else?"

Cape glanced at his watch. "Yeah," he said, looking past her toward the kitchen, then over his shoulder at Sloth. "Can you spare some ice?"

27

SALLY HAD BEEN SITTING at the bar for over an hour when she saw the bartender's eyes go wide with fear.

Kano had arrived.

It was the same expression Sally had noticed the other night, when Kano brutalized the young couple. Now Sally sat alone on a barstool, her black skirt hiked up as far as it would go, letting the pounding bass from the speakers override her heartbeat and protect her from what was about to happen.

She felt Kano's hand on her back.

Swallowing bile, Sally turned and smiled, nonchalantly knocking his hand aside.

"I'm working," she said.

For an instant, Kano's face twisted into a mask of rage, but he quickly recovered, showing Sally a smile that was half sneer, full of bravado and male posturing.

"You're new, heh?"

Sally smiled prettily and shrugged, turning her attention back to her drink.

Kano pressed on, his tone gaining confidence.

"You must be."

Sally nodded absently at the bartender, saying nothing. He took her empty drink and replaced it.

Kano grabbed Sally's arm before she could raise her drink to her lips. She noticed he'd made it a point to reach across the bar and use his maimed hand, his shirtsleeve pulling back to reveal the elaborate tattoos on his arm.

"If you're working this bar," said Kano, his eyes flashing with broken light, "then you're working for me."

Sally smiled again, not flinching under the cruel squeeze of his hand. Letting her eyes move lazily across his tattoos, she looked at him coolly. Reaching out with her free hand, she put it on Kano's chest, her fingers outstretched. She felt him jerk involuntarily from the warmth of the gesture. She laughed lightly.

"Fine," she said, removing her hand. "But buy me a drink first."

Kano blinked as he released her and barked out a laugh. "You have some steel in you, baita." He gestured at her new drink. "But you already have one!"

Sally took her drink and swallowed it in one gulp, her eyes never leaving Kano's face. As she lowered the glass to the bar, she jerked her chin at the bartender.

Kano laughed again as he threw some money on the bar. "This will be the first time I paid for a drink in this bar," he said smugly. He smiled at the bartender as if they were best friends. "Tequila."

Sally nodded her approval. "A man's drink." She raised her glass, reflecting on the advantages of arriving early. At this point the bartender knew she was drinking cranberry juice and soda water, which looked exactly like the vodka drinks so many young girls in Tokyo favored. So while she and Kano kept asking for another drink, he was getting drunk and she was getting more sober by the minute.

Three drinks later Kano asked Sally her name.

"Miko," she said. She bit her tongue until it bled, forcing a smile. It was her mother's name.

The next hour lasted forever, a purgatory of flashing lights, smoke, and the incessant throbbing of the bass in her skull. When Kano finally started to slur his words and his hand slid lazily off her thigh, Sally made her move. She leaned across the gap between the stools and put her lips close to Kano's ear. It took all her will not to scream.

She pointed toward the ladies' room. "When I come out," she said sweetly, "I want you to take me home with you." She squeezed his thigh as she stood up, then ran her hand across his cheek. Kano had a drunken, lopsided grin on his face as she turned and walked briskly across the club.

Silence.

The door to the ladies' room was padded, and suddenly Sally found herself in a cocoon, her ears ringing, the bright fluorescent lights making her blink. Walking over to the nearest sink, she looked at herself in the mirror. The short black dress, the makeup, the silver locket around her neck. The dead, flat look in her eyes.

Sally turned away suddenly, rushing to the closest stall. She dropped to her knees and retched, the drinks from the last two hours and what little food she had eaten spilling out into the bowl in a swirl of loathing and pain. Closing her eyes, she rocked back and forth on the cold tile.

"Not much longer," she whispered. "You can do this. You must do this."

Coughing, she went back to the sink and washed up, forcing herself to look in the mirror one more time. Her eyes seemed to absorb all the light in the room, green dark seas with no bottom and no shore.

Kano was drunk but not drunk enough. The ride in the limo was the hardest thing Sally had ever done. She needed him sober enough to keep him interested, but that came at a price. She found the strength to smile once or twice, playfully batting his hands away, letting her fingers wrap around his leg or arm. But the ride took too long, and Sally felt part of her soul break away with every passing minute. She closed her eyes as his hands slid across her legs, bit her cheek as his coarse lips drooled their way down her neck. By the time the car stopped, the only sensation Sally had left was the taste of her own blood.

Kano was talking to her, telling her to get out of the car, but Sally couldn't hear the words, the music from the club still with her, filling her body with a rhythmic drumbeat that kept her heart from stopping.

Sally had been to Kano's apartment building before, when he was out making rounds. Thirty stories tall, it looked like a sewing needle thrust into the sky, its tip obscured by low clouds mixed with smog. The limo pulled into an underground garage and let them off at an elevator, then pulled away down a ramp. Her arm around Kano's waist, Sally stepped into the elevator and held her breath.

Kano leaned close, his breath foul with cigarettes and drink.

"I've got something to show you upstairs."

Sally smiled and let her eyes move down to his belt.

"I'll bet."

Kano blinked and gave a short laugh, his reaction time a few seconds off. "That, too," he promised lasciviously, leaning closer. "But something else."

"I can't wait," replied Sally. It was the first time all night she had told the truth.

The apartment was huge, the kitchen bigger than the room Sally shared with Jun back at school. Black leather and chrome, halogen lights. A large modern painting of a samurai warrior filled one wall, slashes of color and abstract shapes surrounding a classic image of a lone warrior with drawn sword. A large television and stereo dominated the opposite wall. The far wall was made entirely of glass.

Neo-masculine yakuza-chic, Sally thought to herself.

"It suits you," she said, smiling.

Kano grunted absently, then led her through the open kitchen and across the living room toward the glass wall.

"Now I'll show you something," he said, pulling open a sliding glass door.

Sally stepped onto a curved balcony that wrapped around the apartment. By Tokyo standards, the entire place was huge, but the balcony alone was larger than many families' apartments. There could be no doubt that Kano's uncle paid the rent.

Kano stepped over to the railing and gestured down, reaching out with his other hand to pull Sally closer.

"Take a look," he said, obviously pleased with himself. "Not bad, huh?"

Looking straight ahead, Sally could see the soft glow of other skyscrapers penetrating the clouds, fixed constellations for the rich and privileged to gaze upon. Looking down, a dark ring encircled the building, a wide swath of landscaping that looked black in the night. But just beyond were the streets of Tokyo, a maze of headlights, neon, and reflections in the clouds that looked like rivers of light. Sally gasped despite herself, thinking of pictures she had seen of volcanoes, rivers of molten lava coursing down the mountainside.

As she stared at the shifting lights, Sally sensed Kano move closer, his hand grabbing her ass and pressing her against the railing. "Turn around," he commanded. "Now I've got something else to show you, bitch."

Taking a deep breath, Sally felt the fires from below seeping into her. She turned slowly, her smile warm and inviting. "Now that's no way to talk," she chided. "Come here, I want to show you something first." Grabbing his belt with her right hand, Sally pulled Kano closer, her left hand moving up toward her breast.

Kano's eyes were glazed with lust and alcohol, and the smell of tequila and sweat oozed from his pores. As he pressed closer, Sally could feel him stir beneath her right hand.

Kano licked his lips, his eyes following Sally's left hand as it swept across her body and stopped at the locket around her neck. As he watched, she deftly opened it and spread the two halves apart, revealing a photograph on each side.

"I wanted to show these to you," said Sally. The warmth was gone from her voice, taken by the wind, burning somewhere in the streets below.

Kano's eyes blinked as he tried to focus on the two images. A man on the left and a woman on the right, the man smiling broadly, his American features strong and friendly. The woman was Japanese and looked more serene but no less friendly, her long black hair shining even in the small photograph. Kano's eyes narrowed as if in sudden recognition or fear. His body stiffened as he started to say something, but Sally cut him off.

"These are my parents," she said simply. "And you killed them."

Kano looked up at Sally and then again at the pictures, his eyes narrowing. Before he could react fully, Sally pulled at his belt, holding him close.

If you want to kill this man, you will first have to get close to him. Closer than you would like. Master Xan's words echoed in her thoughts as Sally spoke again.

"I wanted you to see them again," she said, her eyes locked on Kano's. "Before you died."

Kano's face twisted as he tried to jerk away from Sally, his right hand up as he prepared to strike.

Kano was a bully, used to men and women shrinking from a blow before it landed. But Sally stepped forward as he stepped back, her right hand still grabbing his belt. Before he could start his punch she slid her hand under his belt and into his pants.

As Kano clenched his fist, Sally squeezed.

Kano buckled as Sally dug her nails deep into his scrotum. He screamed as she twisted her wrist, first to the right and then the left.

Kicking wildly, he caught Sally in the right knee, causing her to lose her grip momentarily, which gave him an opening. Kano desperately backhanded her across the face, catching her in the nose and snapping her head back. As Sally fell, Kano dropped to his knees, gasping.

Sally caught herself on the railing. She tasted blood, which flowed freely from her nose, and her eyes were watering. The lights from below were a jumbled blur, and as she blinked she saw stars. She heard Kano's feet scraping on the cement behind her, the sound punctuated by the noise of metal against metal.

Sally looked down and saw the locket clanging gently against the metal railing just as she felt Kano's hand grab her hair from behind.

Blinking the tears from her eyes, Sally stole a glance at the two smiling faces around her neck as Kano pulled her head back.

When Kano tensed his arm to bash her head against the railing, Sally closed her eyes and relaxed.

Kano's arm thrust forward and Sally's foot thrust down, her heel crashing onto his instep and shattering the small bones there. Kano bellowed in rage as Sally spun like a dancer to face him, her hand already a blur. She bent her fingers and struck Kano's nose with the heel of her hand.

Blood sprayed across the balcony as Kano screamed, both hands clutching his ruined face. He fell on his back, head hitting the cement hard as Sally jumped lightly and landed next to him, her right foot coming down to press against his neck, holding him.

Kano coughed and spat, his hands flopping around the floor as if he were being electrocuted. Sally held him in place for several minutes before his eyes focused again.

"You fucking bitch!" His tongue was thick with blood, his voice ragged. Sally stood calmly over him, not even hearing the words. The music from the club had returned, coursing through her veins and pounding in her ears, turning everything else to white noise. As Kano's lips moved, she pressed down slowly with her foot.

"You can't kill me," Kano coughed defiantly. "You know who my uncle is?" Kano said his uncle's name as if it were a magic spell. "You're fucking dead. A fucking dead whore, that's all you are."

Sally remained silent, her attention turning again to the locket around her neck. She looked at the gentle smiles and loving eyes, then stared silently at the blood on her hands. She adjusted her balance and eased the pressure of her foot.

Kano assumed the mention of his uncle's name had the desired effect, and he spoke with renewed bravado.

"Now let me up and maybe I won't have you killed," he demanded.

Sally absently took her foot off his neck.

Kano sat up and spat. "You want to know something?" he taunted, a bloody sneer on his face. "I probably enjoyed killing your fucking parents."

Sally's eyes refocused. The music from the club faded and died, swept away by the night air. She could hear herself breathing. The patter of Kano's blood as it sluiced past his ears onto the cement. Her own blood as it dripped off her chin onto her dress. The susurrus of traffic thirty stories below.

"Now help me up," said Kano, extending his hand with the missing finger.

Sally looked at his hand and then at her own, the blood on them turning black as it dried. With her left hand, she shut the locket without looking at the pictures, hearing the soft click as the latch closed. Extending her right, she bent down and grabbed Kano's hand in her own and pulled him to his feet.

Kano started to say something, a smug expression forming on his battered face, but Sally kept pulling him forward, accelerating his upward momentum. Bending her legs, she grabbed Kano's belt with her left hand as she pulled his arm forward with her right, turning her body as she lifted. Before he could get his footing, Kano was already hurtling forward. Sally pushed up against his stomach and dropped her right shoulder, rocketing Kano over her head.

Kano didn't even start to scream until he cleared the balcony, a high-pitched wail of terror cut short when he hit a flagpole ten stories down.

As Sally watched, Kano's body spun through the clouds toward the burning lights below. A dead leaf taken by the wind. A damned soul on its way to hell.

She couldn't hear the body hit the park below, but she watched until it disappeared into the ring of blackness. Then she stood, immobile, at the railing. It was several long minutes before she even blinked.

Holding the locket in one hand, Sally closed her eyes and willed herself to cry, but no tears came. She thought of her parents and the fading memories of a five-year-old, the life she never had and never would. She thought of Kano and realized she felt absolutely no remorse. No guilt. Nothing.

She thought of Jun and the long trip home.

Home.

Sally took one last look at the lights below, then turned and left, never looking back.

28

THE PROBLEM WITH FINDING a dead body in your trunk is deciding where to put it. As Cape drove through the night fog with the top down, he ran through his options.

He briefly considered leaving the corpse at the house of Richard Choffer, his pretentious ex-client. But since Richard was probably going to sue him, Cape figured depositing a dead body on Richard's lawn was a bad idea, even if the thought did make him smile.

His responsible side told him to drive straight to the nearest police station, calling Beau on his cell phone on the way. Beau might help him cut through the red tape and stay out of jail, but the fact remained that Cape fled the scene of a crime with a body in his car. The interrogation alone would take the rest of the night. When it came right down to it, Cape didn't believe Beau could help him on this case, so he drove on.

He was frustrated and angry by the time he crossed Broadway and headed into Chinatown. He was groping for leads, working with none of the resources of the feds and no real connections of his own. He felt more like a pawn in someone else's chess game than a detective, and it pissed him off.

It was well past midnight, and the street was deserted, tourists and tenants alike having gone inside and turned off the lights. Cape slowed the car as he neared Freddie Wang's restaurant, scanning the second floor for lights or open curtains.

As he pulled up to the curb, Cape checked the rearview mirror and caught a glimpse of himself, his hair tangled from the wind, the crow's feet etched around his blue-gray eyes. Taking another quick glance at the restaurant, he smiled, pulling away from the curb without stopping. He shook his head at his own reflection in the rearview, realizing he'd crossed a line and didn't care.

Taking a right and then another, Cape drove slowly down Grant Street with his lights off until he came to the front of the building where he'd first met Harold Yan. The brass plaque for the Chinatown Merchants Benevolent Association glowed dully in the light from the lone streetlamp half a block away. Twisting in his seat to look the length of the street, Cape put the car in park but kept the engine running.

The corpse was heavy, cold, and a little moist. Cape saw that one of the bags had burst open, the half-melted ice scattered across the bottom of his trunk. With a series of muffled grunts and curses, he managed to get the body out of the trunk and onto the curb. Two minutes later and it was propped next to the front door, directly under the plaque.

Rigor mortis had started to set in, but the body was still fresh enough for Cape to position the arms and legs. He crossed the legs at the ankle and laid the arms to the sides, the man's enormous hands jutting out awkwardly. The head was twisted at an odd angle, and

Cape knew he was pushing his luck as it was, so he left it sagging to one side. The expression on the dead man's face hadn't changed—he looked shocked to be there.

"I don't blame you," muttered Cape. "I'm a bit surprised myself."

Cape turned and reached into his car, popping open the glove compartment and fishing out a digital camera. Glancing down the street and up at the windows one last time, he quickly fired off a shot, the flash throwing everything into stark relief for an interminable moment.

"It's been fun," he said to the corpse, tossing the camera onto the passenger seat and putting the car in drive.

Freddie Wang couldn't—or wouldn't—help him, whether Freddie knew his bodyguard was dead or not. And neither could the police.

Cape needed someone of influence to help, and that meant he needed to make his problem *their* problem. Harold Yan got him an interview with Freddie, so he obviously had influence in Chinatown. And Yan had told the press he wanted answers on the smuggling case. That sounded great as a press release, but Cape needed someone with juice like Yan to take an interest.

A personal interest.

Cape didn't know what would happen, other than Yan calling the cops. But since he was fishing without any bait, he figured he might as well stir up the water and see what surfaced.

And in the meantime, he'd print out a copy of the photo and send it to Beau, just to make things more interesting. As he hit Broadway, he flicked on his lights and gunned the engine, knowing deep down he still had no idea where he was headed.

29

It had been almost a week since Sally had thrown a man off a roof.

The return to Hong Kong took longer than expected, an extra two days while the Japanese freighter waited out a tropical storm. She arrived in the middle of the night, but Master Xan was waiting in his office, fully awake and dressed, as if he'd known the precise moment she would return.

Sally wondered, not for the first time, if Xan ever slept.

"Welcome home, little dragon." His dark eyes studied her as she bowed. Sally met his gaze, her green eyes hard and clear, as she extended her right hand and dropped a roll of undeveloped film on his desk.

"Here are your pictures," she said.

Xan took the film in his left hand but kept his eyes on her the whole time. "Thank you."

Sally turned to leave but Xan raised his hand.

"Is there anything else?"

Sally hesitated before answering. "No, Master Xan. I would like to go to my room."

Xan nodded. "Jun will be happy to see you," he said. "She has also been away."

At the mention of Jun's name Sally felt a surge of something—excitement? Fear? She caught herself and blinked before answering.

"I'm just very tired."

"Of course," said Xan. "We can talk in the morning."

As Sally turned toward the door, Xan spoke again, his voice so soft that Sally wondered if she were hearing his thoughts.

"You went to Japan looking for something, little dragon," he said.

Sally turned to face him, her green eyes going gray, dark storms clouding deep green seas. She nodded, her jaw muscles tight as she spoke.

"Justice."

Xan nodded. "And what did you find?"

Sally held his gaze for a minute, then looked down at her hands.

"Revenge."

Xan nodded again as she looked up at him. "Sometimes, little dragon, the two are not so different."

"But they're not the same," said Sally diffidently.

"No," replied Xan. "They're not."

Sally remained silent.

"Tell me," asked Xan, "if I asked you to travel to Tokyo again tomorrow for the same reason, would you still go?"

"Yes," replied Sally unhesitatingly.

"Would you do anything differently?"

"No."

Xan smiled, his features softening. "Then you should sleep well, little dragon."

But Sally didn't sleep well.

She had gone to bed without waking Jun, who slept ten feet away on a simple bed against the far wall of their room. A small part of Sally wanted to tell her everything, but the rest of Sally didn't want to speak of Tokyo, or her parents, ever again. She was different now, and as she closed her eyes, she made a silent wish that Jun would still recognize her in the morning.

An hour later, the nightmare came for her.

If you want to kill this man, you will first have to get close to him.

Xan's words rolled across thunderheads on the horizon as Sally, her arms heavy and useless, struggled in Kano's embrace. She could feel him stir as he pressed his hips forward, his right knee forcing her legs apart. His scent was a cloying mixture of musk, booze, and sweat that filled her nostrils, his unshaven cheek sandpaper against her skin. As his right hand grabbed her breast and his left pulled her closer, her arms grew heavier, and Sally realized she wasn't strong enough. She wouldn't be able to fight him off.

Kano could take her, and there was nothing Sally could do about it.

As his mouth pressed against hers, she saw the horror on her parents' faces and knew that she had failed. From beyond the grave they called out to her, their voices merging into a single, plaintive wail of despair.

"Sally! Sally, wake up!"

Light from under the door and Jun shaking her, the darkness retreating to the corners of the room.

Sally shuddered as her eyes focused, her body slick with sweat, suddenly cold in the night air. Jun held her at arm's length, watching her eyes to see if the dream still possessed her. Sally exhaled and forced a smile.

"Sorry I woke you."

Jun smiled back, her hands still resting on Sally's shoulders. Wordlessly, she leaned across the bed and hugged Sally. After a long moment she pulled back enough to kiss Sally lightly on the cheek.

"Welcome home," she said.

Tears started pouring down Sally's cheeks. Tears she had never found. Tears for her parents. Tears for the last remnant of innocence she threw over the balcony in Tokyo. All the tears that she couldn't find for more than a decade.

Jun held her and they both cried silently, the tears running down their faces and chests, flowing together on the bed between them, pooling their sorrows. The two girls sat crying for what seemed like a year, the sheets soaking up all the pain and doubt the world had given them.

When there were no more tears left between them, Sally and Jun looked at each other. Their eyes were red but they both smiled, neither shy nor embarrassed.

Without saying anything more, Jun leaned forward and kissed Sally again, this time on the mouth.

Sally gasped briefly, then returned the kiss. Jun tasted of salt and something else, tears mixed with emotions too subtle and complex to put into words.

Sally closed her eyes and felt Kano's coarse hands fade away. His scent dissipated in the night air, and his twisted mask of lust and hate shrank to nothingness as he fell, plummeting endlessly from her consciousness into oblivion.

The rest of the night until the dawn Sally stayed in Jun's arms. Looking back, years later, Sally would remember that night as the last time she had a nightmare.

She knew Death would be her constant companion, but she no longer feared or hated him for what he brought and what he took away. She considered Death an ally, if not a friend, the only one she could count on besides Jun.

30

MILFRED P. JAMES DECIDED the guys running the union were nim-rods.

Milfred, or Mill, as he liked women to call him, was tired and more than a little pissed off. Working customs for six hours straight was brutal, even wearing orthopedic shoes and the back brace his ex gave him last Christmas. Some genius in the union figured longer shifts gave them more leverage on the pension plan.

Mill would like to see the union bosses stand for six hours at a time, bending to open people's bags, standing up again to scan the crowd, bending over again to open the next set. He'd been to union meetings and seen the beer guts on those guys, the tans from playing golf with their politician buddies every Friday. He'd give anyone five-to-one odds those chicken-fuckers would be in traction if they tried to do his job for a day, let alone a week.

Six hours was a bitch.

Mill looked at his watch. Ten minutes to go. Then another five minutes to change his clothes in the locker room, then twenty minutes to drive home to South San Francisco. Ten more minutes to walk to the bar down the street, then another ten to throw back a shot of bourbon and finish off his first beer of the night.

A family that looked like they were coming home from vacation was headed his way, the mom looking exhausted, two kids talking nonstop—a boy and a girl, both teenagers—and the dad looking pissed. Early in his shift Mill might fuck with them just to pass the time, watch the woman get all crazy and blame the husband for looking so angry that he looked like he had something to hide.

But Mill was tired, and the clock was ticking. He unzipped two of the wheely-bags and lifted the flaps a few inches, then waved them off. He called it the *quick-zip*, when you knew there was nothing inside, just going through the motions.

"That's it?" asked the dad. "Not much for security around here, are you?"

"Stan, don't argue with the man," said the wife.

"Don't start, Judith."

"*I'm* not the one who—"

Mill raised both hands, palms out. "Judith."

Judith whipped her head around, knocked off balance by the customs guy saying her name like that. She looked at Mill like he was a talking dog.

"Yes?"

"Give it a rest, Judith," said Mill.

The husband jumped in with both feet. "What did you—"

Mill's hands were still up as he pivoted toward the man. "Stan, put a sock in it."

Stan's head snapped back like he'd been splashed with cold water. The two teenagers started giggling.

Mill looked deliberately from Judith to Stan. "Been on vacation?" he asked pleasantly.

Judith was the first to find her tongue. "Well, yes. We took the kids to visit friends in Hong Kong." She smiled pleasantly, back on firm ground, reflexive answers to simple questions.

"Swell," said Mill.

"Excuse me?" said Stan.

Mill let his hands drop to his sides. "You got a choice, folks. You zip up your bags and go home, or you continue irritating the fuck out of me and I recommend you for a cavity search."

"I don't have any cavities," said the teenaged boy, revealing a set of braces that looked like barbed wire.

Mill shook his head. "One ... two ... three ..."

Stan and Judith got the bags off the metal table and the kids through the doors before Mill counted ten. He watched them scurry away, then screwed up his face and spoke in a nasal whine.

"*Not much for security around here, are you?*"

God, did he hate this fucking job.

He looked up to see another wave of passengers flowing toward him, a tall Chinese guy in the lead. He was big, broad in the chest and shoulders, and he moved like he was gliding across the carpet. Must be a dancer or something.

As he came closer, Mill got a look at his face. Jesus, what a scary motherfucker. His eyes looked flat and lifeless, his mouth a straight line, but the first thing you noticed was that fucking scar, a black diamond ski slope running down the guy's face. Mill felt his palms sweat just looking at the guy. He noticed the man scanning the tables, checking out the lines. He was probably just looking for the shortest one, but Mill wondered if he was giving all the customs guys the once-over.

Sure enough, he was coming to Mill's table.

Mill looked at his watch. Two minutes to go. He looked back at the Chinese dude and tried to imagine himself telling the guy he'd have to stand for a search. Mill looked over his shoulder to see if Jeremy, his replacement, was headed this way.

Of course not. Jeremy was always late.

Mill looked back at his watch and made a decision.

"Welcome to San Francisco," he said casually as he unzipped the black nylon duffle bag. Mill was halfway through the *quick-zip* when he caught a glimpse of metal. *Shit.* Sighing audibly, he pulled the zipper the rest of the way and revealed . . . a snow globe?

Amidst a bundle of shirts, underwear, and socks sat a snow globe six inches in diameter, a bright silver key sticking out from the bottom. Inside the globe two small figures of Chinese girls stood facing each other, one holding a fan, the other a sword. Before Mill could say anything, the scary guy reached out and turned the key.

A plaintive tune filled the air as the two girls circled each other, the one with the fan keeping the girl with the sword at bay. After an awkward minute during which Mill stared studiously at the snow globe while the man stared at him, the song ended and the two little girls seemed to tilt forward, an awkward mechanical bow. It was the strangest fucking snow globe Mill had ever seen.

"It's for my niece," said the man, his voice as deep as a well.

Mill smiled and nodded, feeling the sweat roll down his back. He zipped up the bag and waved the man forward, not saying another word.

He had to find another job. One without any unions.

Xan smiled as he walked through the glass doors and shouldered past the waiting families. He shouldn't need any weapons for this trip, and he could always acquire them in Chinatown, but he liked to travel prepared for anything. He had made the snow globe himself. The gears were *shuriken*, throwing stars with razor tips. The flanges of the music box were metal darts. The wire spring coiled around the key had a finger-sized loop at each end and made an excellent garrote that could cut through a man's windpipe in seconds.

Xan had not wanted to take this trip, but now that he was here, he planned on enjoying himself.

31

"YOU'VE KILLED SIX MEN *in as many months.*"

"*You asked me to.*"

Xan walked the length of the office and turned, hands behind his back. It was almost summer in Hong Kong, and he could feel the humidity on his back and neck as he paced. He looked down the long wooden table at Sally, who sat impassively watching him.

"*As a graduate of the school, you sometimes get to choose your next*"—*Xan paused, searching for a word*—"*field trip." He breathed through his nose and nodded, satisfied with his choice.*

"*Many of the girls go on field trips," replied Sally, putting even more emphasis on the euphemism, her voice just this side of mocking. "They follow men, they take photographs, they infiltrate other clans. All very important work, no?*"

"*True," Xan nodded. "But you, little dragon, always volunteer for the most dangerous assignments." He studied her again before adding, "You and Jun, of course. You have more kills between you than all the other girls combined.*"

Sally shrugged but didn't say anything.

"You've killed six men," he said.

"You mentioned that already," replied Sally. "Is there a prize when I reach ten?"

Xan stopped and studied Sally for some sign of emotion, but she betrayed nothing. No anger, remorse, or even grim satisfaction could be found on her face or in her voice. Xan shook his head. They might as well have been talking about the weather.

"It's humid today," he prompted.

"I noticed," replied Sally, her voice pleasant.

"How do you feel about it?" asked Xan.

"The humidity?"

Xan exhaled loudly. "No." Realizing that Sally might be playing with him. "The men you killed."

"They were only men." Sally shrugged and looked away, thinking this wasn't something she wanted to discuss with Xan. The question wasn't as simple as "how do you feel about it?" Sally didn't want to tell Xan that she saw Kano's face in the eyes of the men she killed, his expression frozen in that moment when arrogance had turned to fear. Or that part of her felt stronger for killing these men, and she was never afraid, and she never felt alone.

Sally didn't want to tell Xan any of this, because then she'd have to admit to herself that those feelings never lasted. Death had kept her company these past six months, but his companionship hadn't made her feel any better.

But it hadn't made her feel any worse, either.

Xan had been studying her face. "Not all men are bad, little dragon," he said quietly.

Sally looked up at him with a calm expression, her eyes making it clear she thought Xan was incredibly naïve.

"I'll have to get out more," she said simply. "Meet a better class of gangster."

Xan sighed, wondering why he felt compelled to ask this girl about anything. Was she not a perfect weapon? He had learned over the years to kill without hesitation and had taught Sally well. So why did this girl always fill him with a sense of... what?

The sense that you are looking in a mirror, he told himself, shutting his eyes as he walked toward the back of the room.

From behind his closed lids, a young woman smiled at Xan. Standing on a dock cradling a child in her arms, a baby girl. The woman's face open and smiling, her eyes bright. The young mother waved at Xan, her dark hair swept sideways by the wind off the harbor. As she moved down the dock toward Xan, she never saw the powerboat come up behind her.

The boat's engines roared to muffle the sound of the automatic weapons as bullets tore through the woman's back, rocking her forward onto her knees, her arms still clutching the baby. As she stared at Xan with her mouth open, blood-red constellations appeared on her blouse, forming in slow motion on her chest, along her arms, and across the baby's blanket.

Xan opened his eyes and blinked away the memory before turning back toward Sally. *We cannot choose our fate. We can only choose which path we take when fate arrives.* Sally had made her choice when she walked through the black door, and it was her path to follow. Xan knew that he, of all people, was in no position to question her now.

Sally seemed to read his mind. "Master Xan, why did you want to see me?"

"I didn't," he replied. "But the Master of the Mountain did."

Sally sat straighter in her chair. She had never met the Dragon Head, even after her trip to Tokyo. In fact, she had never been told the result of that trip or what had become of the man in the pictures she'd taken. Sally got her instructions from Xan, who told her just enough to motivate her and provide the necessary background for her assignment. According to Xan, any more information could put her at risk. When Sally had asked, "At risk for what?," Xan had looked at her with an expression much like the one she had just given him, letting her know that she was still young and very naïve. "Not all our enemies are outside these walls," he said simply. Sally tried to ask questions, but Xan cut her off, saying, "Remember that, little dragon."

Sally jumped as the phone rang, her thoughts snapping back to the prospect of meeting the head of the clan. Xan picked up the receiver and listened for a few seconds before nodding and hanging up.

"Time to go upstairs," he said.

The room was large and square, maybe thirty feet on a side. Banners with family crests and carefully drawn characters hung on the walls—dragons, fish, flowers, and an occasional phoenix staring out from the yellowed fabric. In the far corner of the room was a folded wooden screen with a painted battle scene, one of thousands of images throughout the school of Chinese warriors fighting the Mongol hordes.

In the exact center of the room was a dark wooden desk set adjacent to a short cabinet of matching wood with two chairs set before them. As Sally entered the room behind Xan, she noticed the hardwood floor was entirely covered by rice paper, its beige surface torn in some places but otherwise undisturbed. A primitive security system recording the comings and goings in this room. Xan's feet left small wrinkles and tears that belied his weight. Looking back at Sally for an instant, he nodded once in satisfaction at the unbroken paper in her wake. A team of forensic experts would never know she had stepped into this or any other room.

"Welcome, Master Xan."

The man behind the desk gestured toward them without standing up. Sally noticed his eyes first, luminous black suns that surprised her with their warmth as they tracked her progress across the paper. His face was long and elegant, his hair slicked back from a high forehead. Only the wrinkles around his mouth and eyes betrayed his age, which Sally guessed to be around sixty. He smiled as she came to a stop before the desk.

"Sixty-eight," he said, his voice deep and resonant.

Sally remained silent but her eyes widened.

"You were guessing my age," the man said pleasantly. "Everyone does, you know."

"You look younger, shan chu," replied Sally, bowing her head slightly.

"Ah, but I feel older," came the reply. "What do you make of that?"

"The weight of your office must be a heavy burden," said Sally.

The man nodded. "One I am tired of carrying by myself," he said, moving his gaze toward Xan, who stared back at him in silence, a neutral expression on his face.

Both men let the moment pass as the Dragon Head turned his attention back to Sally.

"My name is Zhang Hong," he said simply. "Did you know that?"

Sally shook her head.

Hong sighed and shifted in his chair. "My loyal friend Xan does not always approve, but I get bored with the protocol of this office. So before you called me Master of the Mountain again, I wanted to let you know that I, too, am just a man."

Sally could tell his phrasing was deliberate and assumed he'd been listening to her conversation with Xan. For some reason it neither surprised nor offended her. It seemed somehow ... consistent with her surroundings. She looked back at Hong and nodded in acknowledgement, careful to look him in the eye when she spoke.

"We all have our shortcomings, shan chu."

Xan coughed uncomfortably as Hong barked out a laugh, slapping his hand on the desk.

"She is indeed formidable, Xan," he said, chuckling softly. "With that tongue alone she could start a war with another clan."

Xan looked at Sally with vague disapproval before responding. "We can only soften the steel so much as we forge the weapon, shan chu."

Hong nodded, still smiling, and gestured toward the two chairs.

"Sit down, Sally," he said. "Master Xan has told me of your accomplishments."

Accomplishments, thought Sally. Field trips. I live in a world of male euphemisms.

"Did you know I recommended you for the assignment in Tokyo?" asked Hong.

Sally's eyes snapped into focus. "Thank you," she said simply.

Hong waved his hand distractedly. "It was unfortunate the film was ruined," he said, frowning. "That was an important lead. But you distinguished yourself in other ways, as you have over the past few months."

Sally wanted to look over at Xan, ask what had happened to the pictures she'd taken. She had tested the camera in Tokyo with another roll of film before she went after Kano. But there would be time later to ask her teacher. For now she kept her attention on the man sitting behind the desk, the man—she suddenly realized—who controlled her fate.

Hong glanced idly at the cabinet next to the desk before continuing.

"You have defended the society's honor bravely," he said. "So I wanted to show you something." Hong reached under his collar and pulled a gold chain from around his neck, on the end of which dangled a black key. Leaning over to the cabinet, he inserted the key and turned it two revolutions to the right before twisting it again to the left.

"This cabinet is really a safe, bolted to the floor," said Hong, turning the key one more time. "This key allows me to turn a combination lock. If the wrong combination is dialed more than once, it automatically triggers an alarm." Hong used his free hand to gesture toward the ceiling. "The alarm sounds in my personal quarters, and poison darts shoot from holes in the wooden beams overhead." He paused as a loud click sounded somewhere inside the cabinet. "A single dart would kill a man instantly."

"How many are there?" asked Sally.

"Two hundred." Hong looked up at her, amusement in his eyes. "There is a cloud of death, ten feet in diameter, hovering directly over this desk. A comforting thought for someone in my position."

Sally watched as Hong lifted the top of the cabinet toward her and Xan—the back obviously hinged—and reached inside with both hands. The object Hong placed upon the desk met Sally's gaze with a dozen eyes of its own.

It was a three-legged bronze urn standing almost a foot high, with a hinged lid and two ornately carved handles. But what commanded Sally's attention were the eyes, deep-set and fierce, intricately carved into the faces of dragons adorning every square inch of bronze. The three legs of the urn emerged from dragon's mouths, the legs themselves smaller dragons twisting their way toward the clawed feet of a larger dragon visible from above. The lid was a swirling cloud of dragons, some holding glowing suns in their talons, others swallowing their own tails. Everywhere Sally looked, another dragon looked back at her.

"You know something of our history," said Hong, smiling across the desk, his own eyes betraying his excitement. "Surely you have studied the origins of the Triads in your classes."

Sally nodded. "The five ancestors," she replied by rote.

Hong nodded. "Exactly. It was the sixteenth century, although some say it was the fifteenth. The throne of China had been stolen by a Manchu warlord. He neglected the people and the land. He had forfeited the mandate of heaven."

Sally remained silent. She knew the story but suspected it might have a new ending.

"But he was still the emperor," continued Hong. "So one day, when a rebellion occurred, the emperor turned to the monks at the Shao Lin monastery, who were trained in the martial arts. The monks agreed to help the emperor if he would help the people of China. The emperor agreed, promising the monks of Shao Lin he would return to the path of righteousness."

Hong set his hands on either side of the urn as he continued.

"One hundred monks defeated ten times their number in battle, defeating the rebellion and returning the emperor to power. Then the monks returned to their monastery, reminding the emperor before they left of the promise he had made. But the emperor did not keep his word. Instead, he declared the monks a threat to the kingdom because of their superior military skills. He ordered that their monastery be destroyed. So while the monks slept, agents of the emperor sealed the entrance and burned the monastery to the ground."

Hong moved his hands to the front of the urn and slid his fingers under the edge of the lid. "Only five monks managed to escape. They were the original five ancestors, vowing to avenge their brethren and fight the corruption of government for generations to come."

Sally shifted in her seat but said nothing. She had no illusions about the business of the Triads and doubted Hong did, either, yet all their ritual and history characterized the members as rebels, not thieves. Men are always brave in the stories they tell each other.

"But the five ancestors did not escape so easily," said Hong, his eyes fixed on the urn. "The emperor sent soldiers to capture or kill the monks. The soldiers chased them to the ocean, where the monks found themselves surrounded, outnumbered, and with no means of escape."

Hong looked over the urn at Sally, his eyes bright.

"All was lost," he said, pausing dramatically, "until a three-legged incense burner appeared on the beach before the five monks. Within the incense burner, the monks found something that gave them strength beyond their numbers. Something that made them invincible in any contest." As Sally and Xan looked on, Hong slowly lifted the lid.

"That something," said Hong, "was this." As his hands cleared the lid, Sally gasped.

At first she thought it was a human heart, with the same asymmetrical curves and roughly the same size, mottled green and blood red in patches. But in the next instant she saw it as a dragon, the scales so precisely carved and the eyes so clear she could have sworn it just emerged from an egg. As Hong moved it between his hands, the dragon seemed to glow faintly, as if it were breathing.

"This is the heart of the dragon," said Hong proudly. "Passed on from the original five ancestors. It has kept our house strong for generations. It is, quite simply, our most valuable possession."

Sally stared at the object for several seconds before speaking.

"What is it made of?"

Hong smiled. "Everyone asks that," he said. "Bloodstone and jade, with some other elements mixed in—the blood of our ancestors, to be sure. Do you want to hold it?"

Sally hesitated for a moment before reaching across the desk, then stood as she took the object in both hands. It was heavier than she expected but even more compact, no bigger than her own fist. The dragon stared back at her with blazing red eyes, the trick of light making the stone seem to glow from within. And it was warm—there was no denying it—but whether from Hong's touch or the rock itself, she couldn't say.

Xan cleared his throat behind her, and Sally realized she'd been holding the object for a while. Tearing her eyes away from it, she carefully handed it back to Hong.

"It's lovely," she said respectfully. "But why show it to me?"

Hong nodded as he set the heart back inside the incense burner, closing the lid with both hands. "Why indeed?" he asked. "Because you are one of us, a direct descendant of our five ancestors, the monks of Shao Lin. You are stronger, smarter, and more formidable than our opponents. And you, too, have the heart of a dragon."

Sally bowed her head respectfully but said nothing.

"And one day," continued Hong, "someone else will be sitting in this chair. So I wanted you to understand your connection to the clan. To the Triads. To your own place in history, and the history we will make together."

Sally nodded again, forcing a smile. She was moved and intrigued by Hong's words but also trained to mistrust flattery in all its forms. She heard a slight scraping on the rice paper and sensed Xan shifting his weight. Xan didn't like where this was going.

"I am an old man," said Hong, lifting the incense burner and returning it to the cabinet. "And one day will leave this middle kingdom for the next journey. But they say a man lives on through his sons, and I have two."

Xan's feet shifted again on the rice paper. This time Sally heard a slight tear.

"I want you to meet them," said Hong. "So that you will recognize them, when they call upon you as I have."

Hong moved his right hand under the desk as if pushing a button, and Sally heard movement at the far corner of the room. From behind the wooden screen two men approached, both in their thirties, the paper under their feet tearing with every step.

The man in front had the blackest eyes Sally had ever seen, pools of ink that seemed to draw light from the air around him and cast the rest of his face in shadow. He was clean-shaven, his hair slicked back from his forehead, his body trim in an expensive suit. He walked directly up to the desk, obscuring Sally's view of his brother. His cold gaze moved past Sally and landed on Xan, where it held for a long minute before turning back toward his father.

"This is Hui, my eldest," said Hong proudly. "He is our White Paper Fan."

Sally nodded in greeting, thinking Hui didn't look much like an accountant.

"And this," said Hong, gesturing behind Hui, "is Wen. He is the Grass Sandal."

Public relations, thought Sally. Bribing reporters, threatening editors, then smiling for the cameras. A man with two faces—I wonder what he looks like?

As Hong finished his introduction, the younger brother stepped to the side, moving past Hui into Sally's line of sight. She breathed in sharply as he looked back at her, his expression one of polite disinterest. He had longish hair and slightly hunched shoulders, and Sally had seen him before.

In Tokyo, standing on a bridge, talking fast and moving his hands as he berated the man next to him, a yakuza. She was sent to Tokyo to find a traitor, and she had found him. And now he stood before her, untouched. Sally realized that the film she took in Tokyo hadn't been ruined, after all.

It had been buried, along with the truth.

32

THE WAREHOUSE LOOKED LIKE a mausoleum.

Unlike most of the corrugated boxes that lined the streets south of Market, the GASP warehouse was a converted federal building, a former courthouse from the days when the city could afford to provide some form of justice in every neighborhood.

The unadorned gray concrete of the exterior had all the charm of Tiananmen Square, but the heavy doors were flanked incongruously by ornate columns that gave the effect of pomp with no circumstance. The building was so big and unattractive, it had only been used as a warehouse since the courthouse closed. Other buildings had been constructed around it, and the spaces between them were dark and littered with trash and empty boxes.

Cape couldn't stop yawning, even though the temperature outside had plummeted and he was shivering inside his coat. It was the middle of the night, only a few hours till dawn, but he felt as though he'd been awake for days.

One of odd things about San Francisco was how quiet the streets became after dark. Unlike New York, where the apartments were squeezed among the restaurants and businesses, everyone living right next to each other, San Francisco had an almost suburban feel about it. Many neighborhoods were either entirely commercial, in which case they shut down at night, or mostly residential, in which case the streets stayed busy after dark.

But not long after. At three in the morning south of Market, there was nothing to do unless you were up to no good. Cape had to admit he fell into that category.

Taking a crowbar from his car, Cape walked to the side of the GASP warehouse, looking for a service entrance or window. The warning stickers on the massive front doors assured him that the building was guarded by a state-of-the-art alarm system. An image of a snarling Doberman added menace to the claim. Cape had found that most companies were too cheap to spend a lot of money on state-of-the-art alarms and preferred to spend a little money on stickers. And the ones that did install security systems tended not to advertise the fact, preferring to catch the thieves red-handed or just scare the crap out of them.

Cape was counting on the fact that GASP was in financial trouble, but he needed something to test the integrity of the alarm system.

He chose a rock.

He found one in the alley between the GASP building and the warehouse next door. It was roughly the size of a softball. A series of windows were placed six feet off the ground on the right side of the building, their smoked-glass surfaces thick and opaque, the kind of windows you see in public high schools and hospitals.

Taking aim at the nearest one, Cape hurled the rock overhand and prepared to run like hell.

The rock tore through the ancient glass with a solid *thunk*, making a hole twice its size but leaving the rest of the window intact. Cape peered through the opening for any sign of flashing lights, cocked his ears for any echo of barking Dobermans, but there was nothing. Walking quickly but quietly back to his car, he listened for sirens as he pulled away from the curb.

If it was a silent alarm, the typical response time was ten minutes or less. Cape drove around until he found a Wendy's drive-through near the highway that was still open. He ordered a fried chicken sandwich, fries, and an iced tea, then added a chocolate shake to the order as an afterthought. Cape told himself the calories would keep him awake, but his subconscious wasn't buying it. He just wanted the chocolate.

Twelve minutes later, Cape drove past the warehouse and saw nothing had changed. Five minutes later, he drove past again and decided to stop procrastinating. Parking the car down the block, he reached into the glove compartment and pulled out a pair of unlined leather gloves. Then he jogged to the side of the building and worked his way toward the back.

As Cape rounded the corner of the building, he saw what he was looking for: two sets of double doors, rear exits from the courthouse days. Wedging the crowbar between the first set, he threw his weight against it until he heard a satisfying crack. Shifting the bar lower, he repeated the move, then shifted the bar again until the right-side door was half off its hinges. An old bicycle chain was looped ineffectually between the two doors, but Cape was able to duck under it as he squeezed through the opening.

Pulling a flashlight from his pocket, Cape stepped inside.

The space was cavernous. The building had been gutted, the old walls removed to make way for the boxes and containers that would take the place of jurors and judges, benches and galleries. Cape's light dissipated into the gloom.

Boxes were everywhere, heavy wooden crates four feet high, labeled with letters and numbers, presumably inventory codes for the jeans. The boxes were stacked, four or five together, forming a series of barricades twenty or more feet high around the warehouse.

Using the crowbar, Cape tore off the face of the nearest box, the wood wrenching away from the nails with a tortured squeal. A pile of jeans spilled lazily onto the floor at Cape's feet, the rivets and buttons glinting in the beam of his flashlight. Turning the light to peer into the box, Cape saw a piece of paper and reached in to grab it.

It was a computer printout of the shipment, detailing the style and quantity of jeans. Nothing about it looked out of place until Cape noticed the date, almost a year ago. Cape looked at the jeans on the floor. According to this piece of paper, they should have been in stores months ago, adorning the backsides of young men and women shortly after that. If Michael Long was carrying inventory for this long, his company was in big trouble. And if he wasn't selling jeans, how was he keeping the company afloat?

Cape found a gap between two of the stacks and made his way deeper into the warehouse. Finding another opening in the next wall, he stepped through, expecting to find yet another stack of boxes. Instead, he found a boarding house.

Hidden within the perimeter of boxes was a vast open space filled with rows upon rows of cots. Cape was reminded of images from the national news during hurricane season, when high school

197

gymnasiums along the Florida coast were converted to shelters. To the left was a row of portable toilets, the type seen at construction sites, and to the right were a handful of rolling tables holding a television, VCR, small hot plates, and a microwave. Power cords snaked through the gaps in the wooden crates to a wall outlet thirty feet away.

Cape took a step forward, doing a quick count of the rows. There were easily enough cots to house the refugees from the ship, maybe more. Cape played the flashlight across the makeshift beds, straining his eyes against the gloom.

That's when he realized someone else was in the warehouse.

Near the center of the sea of beds, a man sat alone, his back propped up by a stack of pillows, his legs outstretched on a cot. His face was lost in shadow, his body a silhouette against the darker black of the warehouse. Cape couldn't tell if the man was facing him, watching him, or sleeping. He clicked off the light and stood stock still, trying to hear past the pounding of his own heart and the blood rushing in his ears.

As his eyes adjusted to the darkness, Cape could still see the outline of the figure on the bed and, as far as he could tell, the man hadn't moved. That meant he hadn't seen Cape, or he was asleep. As he moved forward on the balls of his feet, Cape considered a third possibility but hoped he was wrong.

Cape was unarmed and exposed, a feeling he didn't like much. As he got within ten feet of the cot, he raised the crowbar with his right hand and readied the flashlight with his left. When he stepped within five feet he flicked the light on, aiming for the man's face.

At first Cape thought the man was smiling like a lunatic, so bizarre was his expression, until Cape blinked and his eyes adjusted to the light, telling his brain what it had refused to register. Cape dropped the crowbar, the metallic echo bouncing around the deserted building.

The man's throat had been slit from ear to ear. His head sagged forward, his chin buried in the cut, giving the illusion of a clown's smile painted in red across his cheeks. Cape grimaced as he knelt beside the man and examined the wound.

The man's fixed stare showed no hint of surprise, the eyes dull and lifeless. He was Chinese, with longish black hair and a small gold hoop in his left ear. Cape noticed a tattoo on his left forearm, two Chinese characters in blue-black ink. On the floor below his left hand was a Chinese language newspaper, its surface dotted with red spots that looked almost black in the halogen gleam from the flashlight.

Blood from the cut had run down his chest and pooled around his waist, painting the surface of a gun that rested in his lap. Cape couldn't read the markings through the coagulated blood, but it looked like a Beretta 9-millimeter. Cape didn't bother disturbing the scene to examine the gun—it was obvious it hadn't been fired. There didn't seem to be any wounds other than the brutal gash in the man's neck—in fact, he looked utterly relaxed, as if he'd been reading when his attacker struck and couldn't be bothered to struggle or stand up.

A rat scurried across the cement floor, making the hairs on Cape's neck stand on end. He'd been here too long and found too many corpses for one night's work. He'd already decided to leave this one where he found it.

Exiting the way he'd come in, Cape walked quickly but quietly to his car, tossing the crowbar and gloves on the back seat. He was feeling paranoid and had to fight the urge to open his trunk to see if another body was inside, but time was running short and he wanted to get off the streets before sunrise.

It was only ten minutes later that he pulled into his garage and took the stairs up to his apartment, but it felt like an eternity. His body ached and his head was pounding. Without turning on the lights or even taking off his shoes, Cape walked across the loft and lay down on his bed, his mind racing with images from the past twenty-four hours. He had the sense he'd forgotten to do something important, but as he closed his eyes to concentrate, he fell asleep just as the sun came up.

33

"You lied to me."

Sally's tone betrayed her impatience. Dismissed from the meeting with the Dragon Head two hours earlier, she had waited in the shadows of the courtyard for Xan to emerge. An hour ago she watched as Zhang Hong's two sons cut across the courtyard toward the guest houses—she assumed they lived in Hong Kong but were both staying the night.

But still Xan lagged behind, so Sally remained invisible and counted down the minutes. She wanted to confront her teacher far from any rooms, lights, or listening devices.

Xan didn't flinch when she stepped out of the darkness. "You are mistaken," he said in a tired voice. He looked nonchalantly over his shoulder toward the great house, his massive frame backlit by the moon.

"If you recall, you never knew what happened to the film," said Xan, his voice low but firm. "I kept you in the dark."

"As always."

"To keep you safe, little dragon," replied Xan. "But let us be clear with one another. The only person I lied to was shan chu."

Sally stared at him but said nothing.

"An act punishable by death," Xan added.

Sally's eyes remained hard but her expression softened slightly. "Why?"

Xan sighed. "Tell me, now that you've met the Dragon Head, what do you think?"

Sally shrugged. "He seems..." she hesitated. "He seems different than I expected."

Xan smiled without warmth. "Perhaps he seems more human?"

Sally nodded.

"More so each year," muttered Xan. "Some men harden their hearts as they grow older, but shan chu is softening like an overripe pear. In his youth, he was fearless. Ruthless, even." Xan clenched his fists, the knuckles cracking loudly in the empty space. "But now he dotes on his sons, getting himself ready for the next life. What did you think of his sons, by the way?"

"The eldest is formidable," replied Sally, remembering the black eyes and the stillness of the man. "He walks without fear, and there is no life in his eyes. No hesitation." She paused, thinking of the younger brother, the man she'd seen in Tokyo. His weak posture and impatient gestures. A small man acting big. "Wen is a coward," she said simply.

"He is a traitor," hissed Xan. "He sleeps with the yakuza."

Sally visualized that day in the park, Wen and Kano on the bridge, talking like old acquaintances. As her thoughts turned to Kano, the tidal wave of emotions from that night in Tokyo washed over her, and she felt the muscles in her jaw tighten. She looked at Xan, her eyes shining with moonlight.

She said, "Tell his father."

Xan shook his head, a cynical laugh under his breath. "Years ago, yes, that's exactly what I would do. But now? Shan chu would be heart-broken, but I fear he lacks the will to do what is necessary."

"Does his brother know?"

Xan frowned. "I doubt it. I'm told the two don't get along—Wen resents his older brother's power in the society. And while I can't say I have much fondness for Hui, I don't believe he would betray our clan."

"Would you follow him?" asked Sally. "If Hui became shan chu?"

Xan blinked, surprised at the question. "One day I may have to," he said, his tone resigned. "That is the life I chose."

Sally wanted to say something but only nodded.

"But I won't tell Hui, either," said Xan. "He might tell his father, and then I've not only lied to shan chu, I'll have shamed him before his firstborn."

Sally studied Xan's face in the moonlight, the ragged scar twisting like a night crawler as he frowned, his eyes turning back toward the great house. Sally realized Xan could have returned to his quarters unseen, even by her. He knew she would be waiting, and he wanted to tell her something—something he wasn't quite ready to say.

Sally waited until his gaze had returned to her before she spoke. "Then you really don't have any choice about Wen."

Xan nodded slowly, his face flat as a rock.

"You have to kill him," said Sally, her tone matter-of-fact.

Xan looked away again. "Shan chu would look to me," he said, his voice like the rustling of the leaves. "If not for the son's death, then for his protection." He shook his head. "No, I realized Wen must be killed while I am with his father, so any suspicion would turn toward our enemies. The hand of a yakuza must be seen, a single blow with a sword."

This time Sally nodded. "Then I will kill him. Tonight."

Xan met Sally's gaze as he shook his head again. "No, little dragon, too risky. He might have recognized you from Tokyo."

"He didn't," replied Sally. "You saw him tonight."

"He might be a very good actor," said Xan. "I couldn't take the chance."

A chill ran up Sally's spine as she asked her next question.

"Master Xan, why are you speaking in the past tense?"

Xan looked at her a long moment without responding, shattered moonlight shifting in his dark eyes.

"I couldn't send you, little dragon," he said, his voice suddenly ragged. "So I sent Jun."

Sally stared at Xan as the ground fell from under her feet and his voice echoed through the night air, suddenly sounding like he was very far away.

"With any luck," he was saying, "she will already be in bed when you get home."

Xan saw the expression on Sally's face and started to say something else, but he never got the chance. They froze at the sound tearing across the courtyard.

It was a scream, followed by an explosion, and as they turned together toward the guest house, the night erupted into flames.

34

THE GIRL IN THE tight jeans smiled as she ushered Cape into Michael Long's office at GASP headquarters.

She had long black hair and eyes that might have been hazel, but Cape couldn't be sure since he was struggling to maintain eye contact. Her jeans—low on her hips, the lace-up crotch loose at the top—and the gold hoop in her belly button were all too distracting. He breathed a sigh of relief as she exited the room, aware that he had lusted in his heart but proud that he'd kept his pupils free of sin.

The office was bigger than Cape's apartment. He sat facing a mammoth desk, behind which were bookcases lined with trophies, plaques, and assorted books. On the left wall, next to an oak door, were poster-sized photographs of models, male and female, wearing GASP jeans in seductive poses. The wall behind Cape was made entirely of glass and overlooked the Embarcadero and the San Francisco Bay. You could see the span of the Oakland Bay Bridge as it left San Francisco from where Cape was sitting, but the dominant view from the desk was a giant sculpture across the street. From this angle, it blocked almost entirely the view of the water.

Cape remembered the sculpture going up last year. He heard the head of the GAP had donated it to the city and funded the park on which it stood, built alongside the Embarcadero directly across from GAP headquarters. And right next door was GASP, occupying the top two floors of the neighboring building and sharing the same view.

The sculpture was a gigantic bow and arrow, the span of the bow one hundred thirty feet, the feathers on the end of the arrow at least ten feet in length. When he had first heard about it, Cape anticipated a massive bronze sculpture, the arrow pointing out to sea, the bow drawn and ready. Instead, the bow was sunk into the ground, the arrow pointing downward. Cape imagined the city council deciding a grounded bow was somehow less aggressive, not wanting to offend voters in this largely pacifist city.

To add to the effect, the bow was painted gold with red highlights, giving the first impression that a Godzilla-sized cupid had dropped his bow while running past on his chubby cherubic feet.

"I hate that fucking thing," came a voice from behind the desk. Cape turned in his chair to see Michael Long entering the room from the side door.

As Cape stood to shake hands, he caught a glimpse of the jeans Long was wearing and was so shocked he couldn't control his reaction.

He *gasped*.

The jeans Michael Long was wearing were so tight that Cape felt himself chafing just looking at them. The leg seams strained on their journey toward the lace-up crotch, which was held together by leather laces that looked like they might snap at any minute. And though Cape wasn't in the habit of staring at other men's packages, he found it hard to tear his eyes away. Something wasn't quite right, or at least not exactly anatomically correct.

Long chuckled as Cape wrenched his eyes back to the man's face. "Most people react that way at first," he said proudly as he stepped forward. "But you get used to it."

The effect of the jeans was exaggerated, Cape realized, because Long was not exactly someone you'd call in shape. The paunch of his stomach protruded over the waist of the jeans, unimpeded by a wide leather belt.

Cape had stopped wearing Levi's 501s several years back because they were too damned tight in the thighs. It was a tough decision, since it meant admitting he'd hit middle age, since those jeans were cut for men in their twenties. Michael Long looked like he wanted to recapture both his lost youth and the body lost along with it, but that was obviously a long, long time ago. He was balding, with close-cropped black hair ringing his head and a wide handlebar mustache flecked with gray. He smiled as he stepped closer, stopping just three feet in front of Cape.

"Here," he said, reaching toward his crotch. "Check this out." Cape stood, speechless, as Long quickly undid his belt and untied the laces. Spreading the front panels of the fly apart, he reached into his pants.

Cape unconsciously took a step backward and shot a glance toward the door, but by the time he turned back, Long had already completed the motion and held something cupped in the palm of his hand.

Cape blinked in disbelief, but before he could react, Long jerked his hand upward, sending something flying into the air.

Cape caught it by reflex. Turning it over in his hand, he saw that it was a polished wooden rod, roughly the size and shape of a small cucumber.

Or a big cock.

"Lace-up jeans are one thing," said Long, his face beaming with pride. "Diesel's got 'em, so does Levi's. And chicks love 'em—they say sexy without saying it too loudly, you know what I'm sayin'? But for guys, well . . . " He let his voice trail off before continuing. "A lot of guys lack the confidence to wear jeans like this, 'cause they might not have the inventory in the sausage department. That's why I invented the *crotch pocket*. A hidden pocket to add some heft to your package."

Cape stared at Long, not sure if he wanted to laugh or run from the room. "That's really something," he said politely, reaching forward to hand Long his wooden dowel.

"Ain't it, though?" nodded Long, replacing the dowel and walking back around his desk. "Some people thought I was nuts, but men want to look sexy, too, don't you think?"

"Absolutely," said Cape amiably as he sat down, forcing a smile but suppressing a laugh.

"Some even said I was obsessed with the male anatomy," said Long, a disgusted look on his face. "Like I was gay or something. Do I look like a pole smoker to you?"

"Sorry?" said Cape, baffled by the expression.

"A pillow biter?" demanded Long testily.

Cape shook his head, more in bewilderment than agreement.

"An ass bandit?" said Long defensively.

Cape held up his hands, the international symbol for calm. Lecturing Long on his lack of sensitivity, political incorrectness, or his conflicted feelings about his own sexuality wasn't going to help the case one iota, so Cape took the high road and lied through his teeth.

"A visionary," he said. "I'd say you're a visionary."

Long, suddenly appeased, sank back into his chair. "Fuckin-A," he said.

"No wonder your jeans were so popular," added Cape.

"What do you mean, *were*?" snapped Long, coming forward in his chair again.

Uh-oh, thought Cape. *Wrong tense.*

Cape sighed, letting his eyes wander past the madman while he tried to collect his thoughts. He scanned the shelves behind Long, looking at the trophies again. What he had assumed were fashion industry awards were actually bowling trophies, set back on the shelf so the details of the figures were lost in shadow. The plaques all seemed to come from rotary clubs from towns across the Midwest.

Cape shook his head in amazement. He'd met some corporate blowhards over the years, but this guy made used-car salesmen look respectable. He looked back at Long, studying his florid expression for a while before making a decision.

The friendly reporter act was a waste of time. This guy was certifiable, and, if he had anything to do with what Cape had seen in his warehouse, he was also a major-league scumbag.

"I said *were*," said Cape deliberately, "because you had some success initially with your women's line, before the real players like Diesel and Levi's got into the category. But your men's line was a joke from day one, only sold as novelty gifts for bachelor parties."

Long's face reddened as he came out of his chair and around the desk, as if Cape had just insulted his manhood. And, in a way, that's exactly what Cape was doing.

Cape remained seated, egging him on. "Your stock price is in the toilet," he said, "and you're carrying inventory that's almost a year old, because none of your distributors will take it off your hands."

"*How did you*—" Long almost choked on his rage. He thrust his right arm forward, his hand pointing as if he were going to poke Cape in the chest and demand that he leave, or threaten to sue him, or maybe challenge him to a duel.

Cape gave him something better. Before Long could react, Cape sprang from the chair and grabbed Long around the throat with his left hand while his right hand grabbed the laces around Long's crotch. Cape pushed forward with his left arm and pulled back— hard—with his right. Long's eyes bulged, making him look like a character in a Tex Avery cartoon.

"*Wh—who are you?*" It was Long's turn to gasp as Cape tightened his grip on the laces. "Puh—puh—police?"

"No," said Cape, pulling him closer. "Someone much more dangerous—cops have codes of conduct." Another pull on the jeans— Long's expression went from shock to horror. "Tell me everything you know about smuggling, asshole, or your *crotch pocket* is going to be empty for the rest of your life."

Long squealed, his eyes darting to the door. Cape knew they could get interrupted at any moment, but he didn't take his eyes off Long. He could smell the man's sweat mingling with his aftershave, and it wasn't pleasant. Time to move the conversation along.

"Your company's imploding, and you needed cash," said Cape, breathing through his mouth. "So you agreed to let them use your warehouse … how's that for starters?"

He released his grip on Long, who fell as if he'd been deflated. His face was white, his brow lined with sweat as he looked plaintively up at Cape.

"They'll kill me," he said simply.

Cape stood expressionless, waiting.

"I'm not kidding," whined Long, sitting back on his haunches.

Cape leaned down and cupped Long's face in his right hand, forcing eye contact. "Remember the part where I was going to tear your 'nads off? You want to try that again?"

Long flinched involuntarily and shook his head.

"Who's 'they'?" asked Cape.

Long shook his head again. "I don't know—" He caught himself, seeing the skeptical look on Cape's face. "No shit—I was desperate. I didn't know what they were into—I just wanted the cash. Told them they could do whatever they wanted with the warehouse, as long as they paid me."

"*Who* paid you?"

"I don't know—just a guy," replied Long, still on his knees. "A Chinese guy—came to my office one day and said he wanted to make me a rich man."

"You're telling me you don't know who you're doing business with," said Cape.

"They paid cash," replied Long, as if that explained everything.

"What was this guy's name?"

Long shook his head. "You're not listening. I got paid to look the other way—I didn't give a fuck what the guy's name was, as long as his money was green."

Cape spared a glance at the door. "Describe him."

"What the fuck?" muttered Long. "I said he was Chinese."

Cape looked back at him, eyes flat. "And they all look alike, is that it?"

Long shrugged.

"Stand up," said Cape quietly.

Long put his hands up, a pudgy supplicant asking for mercy.

"OK, OK," he said. "He was big—looked like he hurt people for a living, you know what I'm saying?"

"Details," prompted Cape. "I want details."

Long nodded. "He had long hair—wore it in a ponytail. Dressed sharp, only the suits always looked a little stupid on him."

Cape cocked an eyebrow. "How come?"

"He had big fuckin' hands," replied Long, extending his own fingers for emphasis. "Incredible Hulk hands. They stuck out the end of his sleeves like catcher's mitts."

Cape took a step back, images of his trunk flashing across his eyes, Freddie Wang's bodyguard lurking in the shadows. He reached into his jacket pocket.

Long saw the motion and raised his hands up again. "You're not gonna shoot me, are you?"

Cape smiled as he took the photograph out of his pocket. "Not today," he said, letting a little disappointment creep into his voice. "This the guy?" He let the picture fall into Long's outstretched hands.

Long dropped the picture on the rug when he saw the condition of the man propped against the wall, the dead man's eyes staring at Long accusingly.

"Jesus … you killed him?"

Cape didn't answer the question, knowing his only leverage was an implied threat he'd never carry out. "So that's him—that's what you're saying?"

Long glanced nervously from the photograph back to Cape. "Yeah … absolutely."

Cape nodded, bending down to retrieve the photo. Without looking at Long again, he stepped around the desk and picked up the phone, dialing 911. He waited for several minutes before someone came on the line.

"I'd like to report a murder," he said simply. Cape gave the address of the warehouse, said "yes" to a few questions, and then nodded when they asked for his name.

"My name's Michael Long," said Cape pleasantly. "No, I'm calling from my office."

Long was on his feet, staring with his mouth open as Cape hung up the phone.

"What was that all about?" he demanded. There was panic in his voice and a hint of madness in his eyes.

"I forgot to tell you," said Cape, moving to the door. "You're fucked. I found a dead body in your warehouse last night."

Long followed him across the room, as if the bearer of bad news also had the power to make it go away.

"But what am I supposed to do?" he asked desperately.

Cape looked back over his shoulder. "I'd change my pants if I were you, Michael," he said. "I wouldn't want to be wearing those when I got arrested."

Walking out through the reception area, Cape smiled at the pretty girl in the tight jeans but didn't linger, wanting to put as much distance between himself and GASP as possible before the cops arrived. The street beckoned, and Cape knew he was running out of time.

He exited the lobby and stepped onto the sidewalk, looking across the Embarcadero toward the bay. The morning fog had burned off, but the bow and arrow sculpture across the street cast a long shadow, throwing Cape and the building into darkness. His car was parked halfway down the block to his left, where sunlight still held dominion over the city.

He had taken a single step toward the light when he felt a gun press hard against his spine.

35

SALLY AND XAN LEAPT *into hell together.*

By the time they cleared the steps, flames were erupting out of the second floor windows of the guesthouse, and the great room on the first floor was already filled with smoke. The room consisted of hardwood floors wrapped around a large, open brazier, glowing hot coals providing heat for the house in a style reflecting the anachronistic architecture of the school. Above the brazier was a square hole cut in the ceiling, revealing a similar room on the second floor, designed to sit at the center of the guest rooms. Normally large tapestries hung on the walls of the first floor, elaborate embroidery depicting famous battles. But tonight the walls were alive, flames licking the exposed beams and wrapping around the open ceiling to devour the second floor.

But Sally saw none of that, because her eyes were focused straight ahead. The smoke was so thick she could only see in patches, brief glimpses of floor or flames only a few feet away, the open staircase to her right. She saw Xan dart up the stairs, but she could no longer hear him over the roar of the flames.

Yet even with all the confusion, the scene in front of her was all too clear.

Facedown in front of the brazier was the headless corpse of a man, his arms outstretched and twisted—as if he had tried to catch himself, but realized too late he couldn't see the floor because he was already dead. Squinting through the smoke, Sally saw an egg-shaped ball sitting in the hot coals, its surface bubbling in the heat, the egg collapsing inward as she watched. Coals knocked free of the brazier had burned little craters in the floor, sending sparks and flames to dance on chairs, climb up the sides of tapestries, and fill the house with death.

Sally's eyes took all this in without emotion, her mind telling her the obvious, that the man had been decapitated as he lunged, his head sailing backward as he fell forward. But her heart ignored the scene entirely, telling her to keep looking. To find the source of the scream that had brought her running.

She almost tripped, the swirling smoke making it easier to see a few feet away than directly in front of her. As her foot brushed something, she crouched down, extending her hands. What she felt was terribly, horribly familiar.

Jun was kneeling as if in prayer, her body curled in on itself, her head bowed. Next to her was a katana, a Japanese-style long sword, its curved blade bright with blood. As Sally's hand touched her back, Jun collapsed sideways, a small groan escaping her lips. Sally's hand came away sticky, but she didn't pause to look; she already knew what color it would be.

By the time Sally knelt, Jun had rolled onto her back. Twin rivulets of blood ran from either side of her mouth and down her cheeks, and her eyes stared up at the ceiling. Her chest didn't move. Sally saw that Jun's shirt was soaked through and realized the wound on her back had started in her chest. Looking back toward the headless corpse, she saw a gun a few feet away, a small caliber semi-automatic that could easily be concealed under a man's suit jacket.

He had fired as she swept the katana across her body toward his neck, and her momentum carried her forward to finish the strike. He was dead but she got hit anyway. If he had used a sword, she wouldn't even be scratched.

Guns were the only weapon not used at the school, considered the tool of cowards, not warriors. But guns could kill just as quickly as a sword, and it took no great skill to pull a trigger. The reality of the situation hit Sally like a sledgehammer, and she felt her own breath leave her body, the flames above her roaring in anger as they tried to suck the oxygen from the room and the life from her lungs.

She collapsed next to Jun, their faces touching. Gasping, Sally grabbed Jun's face in her hands and turned her head so she could look into her eyes.

Jun blinked.

Sally propped herself up, cradling Jun's head in her lap. Jun's eyes lurched drunkenly in their sockets before focusing again on Sally.

"What happened?" Sally asked, her voice hoarse from the smoke, barely audible above the flames.

Tears sprang from Jun's eyes and ran down her cheeks. Sally's vision blurred and she blinked furiously, not wanting to miss an instant of what Jun was saying. As she watched, Jun's lips moved, but Sally couldn't hear a single word.

"What happened?" she repeated, desperate, her mouth pressed to Jun's ear. "What can you tell me?"

Jun's eyes rolled upward and closed.

Sally stopped breathing. She shook Jun and pressed her face against her cheek, tasting the salt of blood and tears. After a long, endless second, Sally felt fresh tears running down her cheek and pulled back to see Jun looking right at her. With a surging panic, Sally put her ear to Jun's lips.

Every word was seconds long, a helpless agony of anticipation and dread.

"I . . . ," she started, then stopped again. ". . . love you." Her mouth formed the words again in slow motion, as if she were carving each syllable into eternity.

Jun's voice was barely a rustle of fabric, with no breath to carry the words. Years later, Sally would sometimes wonder if she'd heard them at all, or if Jun's last gift had been her final thoughts, sent to Sally in a dream.

As Sally lifted her head to answer she saw Jun start to smile just as the life drained out of her eyes. Sally's mouth was open but there was nothing left to say. She closed her eyes and held Jun, feeling the heat devour her as the entire house started crying out in rage.

A massive hand grabbed Sally by the collar, yanking her upward. She heard Xan shouting her name, but her arms were still wrapped around Jun and she locked them, unwilling to let go. She felt Xan release her and watched as he bent down and grabbed Jun's sword.

With one fluid motion, Xan tossed the katana into the brazier, the blood sluicing across the blade and hissing as it hit the coals. And despite her shock and despair, Sally realized Xan was covering his tracks, removing any sign that the sword belonged to Jun. Erasing any connection back to him.

Sally managed to stand, Jun's head lolling backward, her eyes dull, the fleeting smile lost somewhere in the smoke and ashes. Xan stepped behind Sally and picked them both up, staggering through the wreck-age of the house.

The night air hit Sally like a wave as Xan laid her down in the open courtyard, the sky bright with flame and stars. A sudden roar as beams gave way and the second floor collapsed. Sally rolled onto her back, her hand still holding Jun's, and started shaking uncontrollably. She was colder than she'd ever been, even in winter, and she knew she would never stop shivering.

Sally lay on the ground and felt the cold night air course down her throat, fill her lungs, and squeeze her heart. Clutching Jun's hand tightly in hers, she closed her eyes and smiled, thinking that she must be dying.

Her old friend Death was coming, and this time, at long last, he was coming for her.

36

"GET IN THE CAR."

Before Cape could answer, a tan Buick pulled in front of the GASP building and idled at the curb. Cape could see a lone driver, his features obscured by the shadows cutting across the street.

"*Now.*"

Cape felt the barrel of the gun pressing against his back, urging him onward. He didn't turn around, but he shifted his weight and braced his feet against the sidewalk, letting the man behind him know this wasn't going to be easy.

The man's feet shuffled as he stopped short, surprised that Cape wasn't skipping across the curb. The voice came again but sounded uncertain, not as profane as Cape would have expected.

"I'm not bluffing here."

"That cinched it," said Cape, turning around slowly. "Anyone who says they're not bluffing usually is."

A young man of about thirty stood before Cape holding a Glock at waist height, his index finger straight along the barrel and not curled around the trigger. The way they taught you at the bureau, not the way hired muscle held their guns. The man's blond hair was combed neatly and parted on the side, his blue eyes masked by the his wire-rim glasses. His fair skin was turning red as he struggled to maintain his composure.

Cape smiled, holding his hands out from his sides. "How long you been with the FBI?" he asked pleasantly.

The man's jaw started to drop but he caught it, his eyes narrowing. "I told you to get in the car," he said testily.

"I heard you," replied Cape. "What do you want?"

"I could detain you," said the man, gesturing vaguely with the gun.

Cape looked from the Glock to the young man and gave him the once-over before shaking his head.

"I don't think so," he said matter-of-factly.

The young man's jaw tensed but he holstered the gun, his eyes darting toward the waiting car. It was one thing to jam a gun into a man's back for a quick snatch-and-grab; it was another to stand in the middle of the sidewalk in broad daylight having a conversation.

"I could arrest you," he said.

"For what?"

The man squared his feet with an expression of frustration and anger, looking as if he might take a swing at Cape at any moment.

Cape held up his hand. "While you figure out your next move, I'm going to breakfast," he said, pointing down the street. "See that restaurant with the green awning on the next block? It's called Delancey Street, in case you're not from around here. I'm going to walk there right now and get a table. You and your friend can join me if you want. Then, if you want to arrest me after I eat, that's up to you."

Cape turned without waiting for a response. When he was almost ten feet away, he heard the man behind him curse, not quite under his breath.

Five minutes later Cape was looking over a menu when the man with the glasses walked into Delancey Street behind his partner.

The man in the lead was older. He was black, his hair shaved close and peppered gray at the temples. He was taller than Cape, maybe six-two, with broad shoulders under a tan blazer. Cape put him at one-ninety. His eyes were dark brown and his smile relaxed. He held out a hand as he slid into the booth across from Cape, a knowing look passing between them.

Cape shook his hand. "Cape Weathers," he said. "But you already knew that, didn't you?"

"John Williams," came the reply. "And this here's—"

The younger man jumped in. "Special Agent Dickerson," he said as he lowered himself into the booth. He didn't offer to shake hands.

Cape glanced briefly at Dickerson but brought his eyes back to Williams.

"How come you guys are always *Special* Agents?" he asked. "Aren't there any *regular* agents at the FBI?"

Williams shrugged. "Guess the bureau figures it might impress law-abiding taxpayers."

"I'm definitely impressed," replied Cape, glancing over at Dickerson.

Williams started to laugh but gracefully turned it into a cough. Turning to Dickerson, he reached into his pocket and handed over a handful of coins.

"I forgot to put money in the meter," he said amiably, but something in his tone said he didn't expect an argument. "Wouldn't look right, two government agents getting a parking ticket on the taxpayer's dime."

The muscles in Dickerson's jaw flexed, but he took the money and stalked out of the restaurant. Williams watched him leave, then turned back to Cape.

"Getting you in the car was Jimmy's idea," he said simply. "Jimmy—Special Agent Dickerson—just graduated law school. Hasn't spent much time on the street yet."

"So the bureau teamed him up with you."

"Yeah," said Williams, leaning back against the booth and sighing. "Something like that—so I'm letting him learn from his mistakes, one day at a time."

"Must make for some long days," said Cape.

Williams nodded. "He's a smart kid, wants to do the right thing— we'll see. The bureau goes for those young, gung-ho types, and Jimmy's better than most. Long as no one gets hurt, I got the time."

A waiter came up to the table and stood expectantly, pad and pen in hand. He had a worn, heavily creased face, as if he'd spent many long years someplace much less pleasant than this restaurant. His thickly muscled arms sported tattoos on both forearms.

"I'll have two eggs, scrambled, with bacon and wheat toast," said Cape. "And iced tea."

Williams looked up at the waiter and nodded. "Same, but with rye toast. And coffee." He glanced at the menu. "And some French toast for my friend—and coffee."

The waiter nodded and collected the menus, then left for the kitchen.

Williams turned his gaze on Cape. "Iced tea?"

Cape shrugged. "I could use the caffeine, but I don't drink coffee."

"Why not?"

"I like the idea of coffee," said Cape, "more than I like the coffee itself. When I was younger I'd try it every once in a while, see if it tasted any different than the last time. Finally gave up."

"You shoulda tried it at an inflection point," said Williams.

"What?"

"Inflection point," repeated Williams. "That's how addiction starts. You experience something at a time of personal change. You ask people when they started smoking, smoking pot, drinking coffee—you name it—the answer's always when they changed schools, started dating, went to college—some shit like that. Me, I started drinking coffee when I was ten."

"You had an inflection point?" asked Cape.

Williams nodded. "My Dad died," he said simply. "That man sure loved his coffee. Day after he died, Mom put his cup down in front of me, right on the kitchen table. Didn't say nothin', just filled the cup. Guess it was her way of sayin' I was the man of the house."

Cape nodded but stayed quiet. Williams looked at him for a long minute before saying, "You know why I told you that story?"

Cape shook his head.

"Me neither," replied Williams, shrugging.

"How long you been with the feds?" asked Cape.

"A long time, but not long enough to forget I was a beat cop first," replied Williams. "I got recruited by the bureau when I was in my twenties."

"That must have been flattering."

Williams shrugged. "It was during one of their color drives."

Cape arched an eyebrow. "Promoting and encouraging diversity?"

Williams smiled. "Something like that. For me, it meant a better paycheck, maybe a better class of criminal."

"Is there such a thing?"

Williams shook his head. "Nah, a scumbag's a scumbag, white collar or not." He held Cape's gaze for a minute before blinking, letting him know he was serious about his job. They were talking, but they weren't friends.

Cape nodded.

"Anything else you want to know?" asked Williams. "'Cause, you see, I'm supposed to be the one asking the questions."

"I just figured you already know all that's interesting about me."

"No offense," said Williams, "but you ain't all that interesting. Used to be a reporter—supposedly a good one, whatever that means these days—did some time overseas, right? Then came back and worked the local crime beat."

Cape nodded.

"Got involved in an investigation into a missing girl—sister of one of your friends—found her before the cops did. Figured maybe you could do that for a living. Work standard cases—credit checks, skip tracing, insurance fraud, the usual. Still do some reporting, freelance, when you have to pay the rent. But mostly you find people, am I right?"

"When I can."

"That's it, in a nutshell," said Williams. "Other than you got a funny name."

"We can't all be named John."

Williams smiled. "Read it was short for *Capon*—that true?"

"Yup," said Cape. "A castrated rooster. But I never really went by my given name."

"Can't say I blame you."

Cape shrugged. "Mom sold capons every day—she worked as a butcher."

"Who didn't like men very much?"

"Not at the time," said Cape. "She was in labor thirty-six hours."

Williams, who had been shot twice in the line of duty, grimaced and squirmed in his seat. "Ugh. I couldn't imagine."

"I doubt she was in the right frame of mind to be naming anybody," said Cape.

"You ever think of changing it?"

"Why bother?" asked Cape. "By the time you're old enough, you've already taken all the shit. Plus, the short version's not so bad."

"Makes me think of Superman."

"I wish," said Cape. "So tell me, Agent Williams—if I'm not that interesting, why are you buying me breakfast?"

Williams chuckled. "That was smooth," he said. "OK, I'll get the tab if you answer some questions."

"Go ahead and ask," replied Cape amiably. "But I can't make any promises."

"You've been talking to Freddie Wang," said Williams matter-of-factly.

Cape didn't say anything at first, his face deadpan. An image of the corpse in his trunk flashed into his mind.

"Since that was a statement and not a question," said Cape slowly, "I'm not really sure what you're asking."

Before Williams could answer, Special Agent Dickerson and the waiter arrived simultaneously. The scowl on Dickerson's face suggested he didn't approve of dining with suspected felons, but Williams gestured toward the chair next to Cape.

"Got you French toast," he said amiably.

Dickerson's scowl faltered as he sat down. It was hard to stay mad in the face of French toast.

Williams nodded toward Cape but looked at Dickerson. "Mister Weathers here was just telling me what he and Freddie Wang had to discuss."

"Freddie's a bookie," said Cape tentatively.

"Among other things," replied Williams, clearly not taking the bait. "You saying you're placing bets with Freddie?"

"What?" said Cape. "You don't think I'm a gambler?"

"Oh, I'd say you're a gambler, all right," replied Williams, "otherwise we wouldn't be havin' breakfast together. But I doubt you're placing any bets with Freddie." He smiled before adding, "But you didn't expect me to believe that, did you?"

Dickerson shifted in his chair, clearly uncomfortable with the friendly tone of the conversation, but said nothing. His mouth was full of French toast.

Cape spread his hands. "I was talking to him about the refugee ship," he said simply. "But you already figured that, too, right?"

Dickerson coughed, turning in his chair to face Cape. He swallowed rapidly and tried to clear his throat, but Williams held his hand up, palm out.

"Eat your breakfast, Jimmy," he said, his eyes never leaving Cape's. "Go on."

Cape shrugged again. "I want to know what happened on that ship."

"You got a client?"

"Sure," said Cape, holding Williams's gaze. Liars always blink, and they always look away.

"Who?" demanded Dickerson, having recovered from his near-death experience with the French toast.

Williams cut him off again. "Doesn't matter, Jimmy. Besides, I doubt even Mister Weathers is *that* cooperative."

Cape smiled.

"So here's the deal," said Williams, leaning forward to sip at his coffee. "This is a federal case, with lots of important people expecting guys like us," he jutted his chin forward, indicating Dickerson, "to find the bad guys, quick. In case you're not up on current events, the State Department has an interest in keeping things nice and friendly with the Chinese."

"I read the paper," replied Cape, "and, despite my view of most politicians, I even pay my taxes. So why don't we move past the foreplay and you tell me what you have in mind."

Williams leaned back in his chair and nodded. "What did Freddie have to say for himself?"

"You don't have his place bugged?" asked Cape.

Williams didn't respond.

"He didn't say anything directly," replied Cape, " but he suggested I follow up on the cargo."

"And you did?"

"That's why I was next door," said Cape, "visiting Michael Long of GASP jeans. It was his shipment, his cargo."

Williams nodded. "Another pair of agents is going to see him later today."

"I doubt it," replied Cape. "The cops are headed this way to pick him up."

Williams sat forward in disbelief. "What did he tell you?"

"It wasn't exactly a confession," replied Cape, "but it was enough."

Dickerson banged his fist on the table, the suddenness of it like a gunshot in the small restaurant. In the silence that followed, all three men heard the sound of sirens coming toward them.

Williams started laughing.

"Son of a bitch," he said as he fished some money out of his wallet. "You coulda mentioned that when we sat down."

"Then you wouldn't have bought me breakfast," said Cape.

"True," said Williams. "Just one more question, cowboy."

"Shoot."

"You done with this?" Williams asked. Cape knew he wasn't talking about breakfast.

"Just getting started," replied Cape. "I don't know where it's going, but I'm definitely not done yet."

Williams nodded. "Then neither are we," he said. "We'll be talking to the cops and see what comes next—see if this Michael Long has anything to say."

"You get him motivated," replied Cape, "and he'll talk."

"You did strike me as the motivational type," said Williams.

"That's me," said Cape, "a regular Anthony Robbins."

"That's why I bought you breakfast," said Williams. "See, Jimmy and I have to follow the rules—and the rules for the feds are even worse than for the cops. So by the time we get an assignment, the necessary clearance, and the warrants, the clues have faded and the suspect has fled the vicinity."

"Must be frustrating."

"It pretty much sucks," agreed Williams, who seemed untroubled as he said it. "But a man like you, he can do whatever he wants. By the time I get a warrant and coordinate with the local authorities, you've come and gone."

"And had breakfast," added Cape.

"Exactly."

"That's one of the few advantages to being me."

"I don't give a shit about your case," said Williams. "And I don't expect you to give a shit about mine. But having looked at your background, I think you're straight."

"Thanks."

"So I want you to call me."

"What if I told you I was more inclined to call the cops?"

"They ever buy you breakfast?"

"Once or twice."

"Go ahead and call them," said Williams. "Like I said, I don't give a shit. Just don't leave me out in the cold."

"What's my motivation?" asked Cape.

"Well, *Mister Anthony Robbins*," replied Williams, "how about this: you could have a friend with the feds, or you could be an asshole."

"Do I have to choose now?" asked Cape.

Williams smiled and shook his head.

"And what if you find something?" asked Cape. "You saying you'll return the favor?"

Williams held up his hands. "Can't promise that," he said. "National security, all that shit. But I'll say this—you call me, and I promise you won't be the only one doing the talking."

Cape nodded and stood to leave. He held out his hand. Williams extended his own and shook.

"Thanks for breakfast," said Cape.

"It's the taxpayer's money," replied Williams. "So in a way, you bought me breakfast."

"Swell." Cape nodded at Dickerson, who sat sullenly chewing the last of his French toast. Cape wondered what the two mismatched partners would say to each other after he left.

Two police cruisers sat outside the GASP building, their lights rotating silently, painting the street in lurid reds and blues. A small crowd of tourists had gathered on the sidewalk to see what was happening. Cape imagined Michael Long would be escorted out of the building any moment. He turned up his collar and stuffed his hands in his pockets, walking in the opposite direction, taking the long way across the street to retrieve his car.

He wondered if Long would say anything about the photograph Cape had shown him. Long might be too scared and confused about the body in his warehouse. With any luck it would be hours before the cops worked their way back from the warehouse to Long and ultimately to Cape, assuming his part came to light during the questioning.

Cape hoped it would take at least that long. The feds hadn't asked about the warehouse, because they didn't know about it yet, but Williams hadn't said anything about the dead body Cape left in Chinatown, either. That meant they hadn't made the connection to Freddie.

Or it meant they didn't know about that body, either.

Cape felt something in his pocket and suddenly remembered what was so important, the lost thread from last night. He pulled the rough card into the light and looked at the heavy lines of the blood red triangle painted on its back. Turning it over, he read the address on the front of the card and frowned.

It was time to go back to Chinatown.

37

XAN WAS STILL COVERED in soot, the long sleeves of his shirt singed and torn in places. Dawn was breaking by the time he left Sally at the infirmary, Jun's body on a cot next to her. Xan strode purposefully to his office, pushing past the throng of students and instructors gathering in the courtyard.

A folder in his blistered hand, Xan made his way to the great room upstairs, knowing he had just been there but feeling it had been a lifetime ago. As he cleared the second floor landing, Xan saw the door had been left open, the rice paper across the threshold already torn.

Hui was standing in front of the desk facing the door, as if he were expecting Xan.

"I came to see your father," said Xan impatiently.

Hui's handsome face and black eyes were expressionless as he spoke. "My father is dead."

Xan stopped in mid-stride and opened his mouth, but before he could speak, Hui stepped to the side of the desk, and suddenly Xan *forgot what he was about to say. Zhang Hong sat in his chair, face down on the desk, his arms and hands splayed at strange angles. Two hundred darts pinned him there.*

Xan forced himself to look away and met Hui's gaze, his own face a mask.

"Did you kill him?" asked Xan, his tone making it sound like a threat.

Hui frowned, looking disappointed. "And wait for you to arrive?" He shook his head. "My father was a great man, once." Hui paused and looked over his shoulder. "But lately a sentimental old fool. He lost his youngest son tonight because he led his sons down the darkened path. When our mother died, he brought us into the Triad. Into this way of life. To my father, that made him responsible for Wen's death, and it was more than he could bear."

Xan studied Hui from across the room. Hui barely blinked and never looked away, save for when he turned toward his father. His voice never faltered. Watching him, Xan was reminded of Zhang Hong as a young man and thought of the old man's words from only a few hours ago.

The darts kill instantly. There is a cloud of death, ten feet in diameter, hovering directly over this desk.

"Did you kill him?" Hui's voice drifted across the room, breaking into Xan's reverie. The two men still stood a good twenty feet apart, each taking the measure of the other.

The scar on Xan's face twitched as his jaw muscles clenched. "I served your father before you—"

Hui waved his right hand dismissively. "I wasn't speaking of my father," he said calmly.

234

Again Xan stood motionless, seeing Hui in a new light. "Your brother Wen was killed," he said deliberately, "with a yakuza sword." Without stepping any closer, Xan tossed his folder at Hui's feet. As it spun in the air, the photographs inside spilled across the floor. "I lied to your father," Xan continued, an edge coming back into his tone. "To protect him, because I knew he could not bear the news. Your brother was pan twu—a traitor to this house and the memory of your father."

Hui bent down to look at the photos and was slow to respond, turning each one over as if some further explanation might be found behind each picture.

"The girl took these?" he asked.

Xan nodded.

"And the other girl?" said Hui, standing now. "She was killed in the fire?"

Xan shook his head. "She was shot."

Hui raised his eyebrows. "By whom?"

"No one in the society would have such chyeh nuo," Xan said deliberately. "Cowardice does not become us, even a traitor." He met Hui's gaze, daring a challenge, counting on the stigma of carrying a gun in his father's house and doubting Wen had told anyone. "The yakuza carry guns as well as swords."

Hui pursed his lips. "Why kill my brother with a sword, then?"

"A ritual killing," replied Xan, feeling himself stepping onto firmer ground as his lie took shape from truth. "Reserved for traitors. Your brother must have been passing information both ways."

"But why kill the girl with a gun?"

Xan smiled bitterly. "Because it was the only way to kill her."

Hui nodded as if satisfied, then asked, "But why was she there?"

It was Xan's turn to look disappointed. "To protect your brother, of course," he said calmly. "I had seen the photographs, and I know the yakuza cannot be trusted."

"Master Xan, you seem to have thought of everything." Hui's eyes were so dark it was impossible to read his expression.

Xan's gaze cut to the human pin cushion that had been the Dragon Head and he shook his head, his expression grim. "Not everything."

The two men stood silent for several seconds. Finally Hui bowed his head slightly, his eyes still on Xan.

Hui said, "I will need help burying my father." He had chosen his words carefully. Xan knew he meant much more than putting the body in the ground. "Can I count on you to help?"

Xan looked from father to son and back to the father, lying dead, before he let his eyes wander around the room. Xan realized his world was as small as those four walls and had been that way for a very long time. When he spoke, he was talking to himself as much as Hui.

"I will continue to serve the society," he said simply. "As I always have."

Hui nodded. "Then let us bury our dead," he said, "and not speak of this again. My brother died in the fire, along with the girl. And my father's heart failed him."

Xan looked down for a moment before looking back at Hui and nodding. He started toward the desk.

Hui took a step forward before he caught himself, a frown appearing on his handsome face.

"But we're forgetting something," he said. "The other girl…"

Xan stopped. "Who?"

"The girl who was here tonight," said Hui. "The one who took the pictures—the one you and my father called little dragon."

"What of her?" demanded Xan, conscious of the tone creeping into his voice.

"She knows," said Hui, matter-of-factly.

Xan didn't move. "She will tell no one."

Hui nodded. "I know she won't," he said, his tone light. "But after we're done here, you'll bring her to me, won't you? Just so we can talk." Hui didn't wait for a reply as he stepped around the other side of the desk, his eyes turning even darker as he looked over the ruined body of his father.

Xan said nothing. He was suddenly conscious of the burns on his arms and hands, the blood where his shirt was sticking to his body. He could still smell the fire in his clogged nostrils and taste the soot in the back of his throat, and he realized that he had done more than pull Sally and Jun out of the fire. He had brought a little bit of hell with him, too.

And that meant the devil must be very close.

38

CAPE PULLED INTO THE parking lot adjacent to Marina Green, checking his watch as he turned off the ignition. The morning fog had burned off, but the afternoon sun was already low on the horizon, shards of light ricocheting off the bay. Grabbing his sunglasses off the passenger seat, Cape locked his car and headed across the grass.

The field at the Marina was a San Francisco landmark, the biggest patch of open grass outside Golden Gate Park. At any time of day you'd find runners headed toward the Golden Gate Bridge, visible from any point along the wide sidewalk fronting the field. The crowded jetties marked where the grass stopped and the ocean began, the docks home to scores of fishing boats, sail boats, cabin cruisers, and even the occasional yacht.

Mitch Yeung sat on a low retaining wall that separated the field from the sidewalk, maybe twenty yards from a cluster of teenagers flying kites. About fifty yards farther down the field, another group that looked older—maybe college students—were playing touch football, and beyond that a volleyball game was underway. Mitch held a hot dog in his right hand, which he waved like a baton as Cape approached.

"Have a seat," he said amiably, jabbing the hotdog toward the kites. "You'll get a kick out of this."

Cape studied the group. The boys ranged in age from maybe fourteen to twenty and were all Chinese. Two of the older kids stood side by side facing the open field, clutching large plastic handles to which multiple kite strings were tethered. Behind them, the rest of the boys had split into two groups, each shifting right and left as the boys controlling the kites circled each other in a bizarre dance. Both groups were yelling excitedly in Cantonese and throwing money on the ground as their champions' kites soared.

The boy on the left was controlling three separate kites, each in the shape of a different animal. A green dragon, phoenix, and eagle plummeted and swooped only a few feet above the heads of people running across the field, the strings of his kites criss-crossing those of the boy next to him. The boy on the right held sway over only two kites, a red dragon and a butterfly.

"Look at the kite strings," said Mitch, his mouth full as he swallowed the last of the hot dog. "See those flashes of light?"

Cape looked skyward and saw the reflection, darts of light shooting out randomly from the strings. "What are they?"

"Razor blades," replied Mitch, smiling.

"You're kidding," said Cape. He narrowed his eyes, but the kite strings were a blur. The boy on the right did a quick stutter-step, grabbed the plastic handle with both hands, and twisted his wrists violently counterclockwise. Both dragon and butterfly lurched to the left, the breeze off the bay making an angry slapping sound against the fabric of the kites. A sudden twang signaled his move had worked, and Cape watched as the phoenix fell into a flat spin and plummeted to the ground.

The boys on the left started shouting vehemently as their opponents scooped money from the ground and yelled back, exultant for the moment. Each contestant slowly passed the plastic handle to another boy from their team, careful to keep the two remaining kites aloft. Once the hand-off was completed, the shouting resumed as the new combatants squared their feet and planned their next attack.

"Pretty cool, huh?" asked Mitch, hand raised to block the sun.

"I come down here a lot," said Cape, "but I've never seen this before."

Mitch nodded. "They come here maybe once a month," he said. "These are two local gangs, settling minor differences. In the old days it would be a knife fight, sometimes swords—even over a slight insult. Don't get me wrong—they still kill each other from time to time, but for minor stuff they let the fighting kites decide."

"Maybe there's hope for today's youth, after all."

"Well, it's fun to watch, anyway," said Mitch, leaning forward. "You wanted to meet?"

Cape nodded. "How's it going on Treasure Island?"

Mitch shook his head. "Nothing new," he said in disgust. "The people who can talk, won't. And the people who are still too sick probably couldn't tell us anything, either. I'll probably go back to my real job after tomorrow."

"What do you think?"

Mitch hesitated before answering. "I think those people were going to be slaves when they landed, and they knew it."

"But they came anyway."

Mitch shrugged. "My parents once told me that slavery can look a lot like freedom when you're desperate. Maybe being an American slave is better than being a Chinese peasant."

Cape knew this was personal, so he waited, watching the kites twist and turn. The green dragon had sent the butterfly spinning toward the bay, but the red dragon was still flying high. Mitch tore his gaze from the kites and looked at Cape for a full minute before saying anything.

"You want to know what I think?" he said quietly. "I think someone decided to kill the bastards that ran that ship. And speaking as a cop, I hope we never catch the guy who did it."

It was the answer Cape had been hoping for. Reaching into his jacket, he removed the card with the red triangle.

"This mean anything to you?" he asked, handing the card to Mitch.

When Mitch saw the red triangle etched into the back of the card he flinched, dropping the card on the wall as if it were on fire. Glancing at Cape with an expression that was half consternation and half embarrassment, he gingerly picked up the card and turned it over in his hands.

"Where did you get this?"

Cape told him of the orange-haired youth that had almost knocked him over.

Mitch shook his head as he stared at the card. "Incredible."

"You want to let me know what's so incredible?" asked Cape, snatching the card back from Mitch.

Mitch blinked. "You've been summoned."

"By whom?" asked Cape. "On the card it says *One-eyed Dong*. Is that a person or a Chinese euphemism?"

Mitch managed a short laugh. "Is this where you start in with the dick jokes?"

"You've heard them before?"

"When you're Chinese, you hear them all," replied Mitch. "I had friends named Wang, Dong, Long, Ding, Hung, you name it."

"And I thought I had it rough."

"Not by a long shot," replied Mitch. His tone turned serious again as he added, "but this isn't a joke, Cape."

"What is it, then?"

"See this?" said Mitch, his index finger following the lines of the triangle. "It's a Triad symbol."

"What do the characters stand for?" asked Cape, pointing to the Chinese letters below the triangle.

"Man, heaven, and earth," replied Mitch. "That's what the three sides stand for. Triads sometimes call themselves the Heaven and Earth Society."

"OK," said Cape. "And One-eyed Dong?"

Mitch looked at Cape and frowned. "Never heard of him."

"Is that bad?" asked Cape. "You look worried."

"Triads are *secret societies*," replied Mitch. "That's why they were founded and that's how they operate, so the closer you get to the real power—"

Cape cut him off. "The less you know?"

"Exactly," said Mitch. "Guys like Freddie Wang—they're punks—high-profile gangsters that the feds can watch without breaking a sweat. But the guys in the shadows pulling the strings, they're invisible. Somebody's uncle, a local businessman, someone you'd never suspect."

"You're not making this any easier."

"And you found this as you were leaving Harold Yan's place?"

"Yeah."

"Makes you wonder."

"Yeah," Cape said again.

"Why are you telling me this?" asked Mitch.

"Because I have no one else to tell," replied Cape. "And you seem like one of the good guys."

Mitch glanced at the tattoo on his arm, the faded ink a constant reminder of the brother he'd left behind. "I don't know about that," he said simply, "but I'm not one of the bad guys, either."

Cape nodded but didn't say anything, watching the kites as he considered what Mitch had said. The green dragon had clipped the red one, tearing through one of its wings. The boy holding the string cursed rapidly in Cantonese but somehow managed to keep the red dragon aloft, the flapping of the torn fabric sounding like a drum. It made Cape think of battle, unseen armies lurking just out of sight.

Cape turned the card over in his hands. "And this is an invitation?"

"More like a strong suggestion you show up."

"When?"

"It doesn't say," replied Mitch. "Which means you're probably already late."

39

THE OLD NURSE TOLD Xan she would sit with Sally until she regained consciousness, then notify him right away. She held the girl's hand and sang to her softly, stroking her hair.

Sally's eyes moved feverishly behind their lids as, for the first time in months, she dreamt of her parents. She could remember their faces when she awoke but nothing else. No sense of whether the dream was happy or sad. Just their faces and eyes—full of love, devoid of judgment, telling her without words she still had much to do.

Sally opened her eyes and started at the face leaning over her. She recognized Ping as a nurse who had been at the school since Sally first arrived. Last year, Ping had watched over Sally for two days while she recovered from a concussion.

The old woman smiled and leaned back, patting Sally's hand.

"Welcome back, little dragon."

Sally blinked herself awake and tried to sit up, groaning as she pushed against the pillows.

"Ping, where is … ?" she began, then looked past the old woman's shoulder at the cot next to hers.

Jun lay there, her eyes closed, arms straight by her sides. Her skin already looked marbled, as if she had slowly turned to stone while Sally slept.

"I'm so sorry … ," said Ping, her voice trailing off as she watched Sally's face. "Master Xan insisted we put her here, next to you, until he returned."

Sally appeared not to have heard. She swung her legs over the side of the cot and stood shakily. Ping started to object but saw Sally's expression and moved aside. "You'll probably want some time alone," she said, stepping toward a curtain that separated this part of the infirmary. "Master Xan will want to know you're awake."

This time, at the mention of Xan's name, Sally turned, her brow furrowing. For a moment Ping feared the girl might have sustained another concussion and was disoriented, but then Sally's face cleared and she smiled briefly at the old nurse.

She said, "Some time alone would be nice."

Once Ping had left, Sally sat next to Jun and ran her hand slowly across her face, feeling Death's cold embrace in every fingertip. After a long moment she bent down and kissed Jun lightly on the lips, then put her mouth next to her ear and whispered.

"It should have been me."

Sally blinked, but no tears came. The part of her that shed tears had atrophied to the point that she no longer expected them. She knew Jun was long gone from this body, and no amount of sorrow or crying was going to bring warmth back to her flesh. Sally turned toward the curtain and breathed deeply, trying to clear her head. Xan would be here soon.

Though her dream remained elusive, the image of her parents had flashed into her mind again at the mention of Xan's name. And though she didn't yet know what she was supposed to do, she suddenly realized where she had to go.

Sally reached for the pile of clothes sitting on her nightstand. Slipping out of the compound in broad daylight would be difficult, but not impossible. After all, it was what she was trained to do.

She was over the wall before Xan reached the infirmary.

"She's gone?"

Xan's scar writhed back and forth as his expression changed from impatience to disbelief. But when it finally settled down, Ping could have sworn Xan looked more relieved than angry.

"She's gone," he repeated quietly. Ping remained mute and nodded.

Xan looked around the infirmary, now empty save for Jun's body. He took in a deep breath and nodded to himself before pulling the curtain closed. Then he turned to face Ping.

"Tell no one."

40

CAPE WAS DRIVING DOWN Battery when his cell phone rang. He pulled over next to a hydrant, aware that his driving was questionable even when he wasn't talking on the phone.

He knew the reason for the call as soon as Beau's voice came booming out of the tiny handset.

"Thought maybe you lost your phone," he said, the phone vibrating. "Third time I called."

"Sorry," said Cape. "Meetings."

"You got a digital camera?"

Seemed like a good idea at the time. "Sure," said Cape, his tone guarded.

"Take any pictures lately?"

"Sure."

"*Mail* any pictures lately?"

"You mean the Golden Gate Bridge at sunset, the Ferry Building, that sort of thing?"

"How about dead Chinese guys?"

"Oh, that picture," said Cape. "How'd you know it was me?"

"The envelope had your return address on it."

"I didn't want you to worry about a sociopath on the loose."

"I always said you were thoughtful," replied Beau. "Matter of fact, that's what I'll say at your defense hearing. Your honor, he was stupid, irresponsible, had no regard for the law, but he was one *thoughtful* motherfucker."

"I had second thoughts after sending it."

"How 'bout second thoughts when you were *taking* it?" The phone almost jumped from Cape's hand. "You ever hear *don't leave the scene of a crime*?"

"Fuck you," said Cape. "You ever hear of the anonymous tip?"

Cape could hear Beau sigh on the other end, a long whistling through the speaker.

"Where is he?" demanded Beau.

Cape blinked. "Who?"

"I'm not playin' here," said Beau. "This is my job we're talking about. I get a picture of a dead man in the mail, I'm supposed to find the dead man *and*—this is the important part—find the dude who killed the dead man in the first place."

"You don't have the body," Cape said stupidly.

"What am I saying here?"

"You saw the sign in the photo?" asked Cape. "The Chinese Merchants Benevolent Association, the plaque in the background?"

"Now you're insulting me?"

Cape frowned. Of course Beau had seen the plaque—that's why Cape framed the photo that way. Stir things up, get local cops involved again. For all the feds or the police knew, this murder was unrelated to the immigrant ship, so homicide would have to take the lead. And Cape's real motivation—get the cops talking to Harold Yan, someone with influence in Chinatown who could pull a few strings. Get someone with power to take an interest in solving this case.

"You still there?" Beau's tone was insistent.

"You talked to Yan?" Cape asked, feeling the answer forming in the pit of his stomach.

"Busy man," said Beau. "But polite as can be."

"He never saw the body?"

"Didn't recognize the guy, neither," said Beau. "'Course, he thinks we have the body and were just lookin' for an ID—I'm not advertising a missing body just yet."

"You press him?"

"You crazy?" asked Beau. "No, wait—let me rephrase that. It didn't seem *prudent* to suggest to Harold Yan, the mayoral candidate, that he might be full of shit."

"Fuck me," muttered Cape.

"What?" said Beau.

"Nothing," said Cape, a little too quickly.

"OK, let's try again," said Beau deliberately. "Where did the body come from?"

"I found it."

"Where?"

"In my trunk."

"Just like that," said Beau. "Next to the spare tire."

"Next to the jack, actually. He was on top of the spare."

"Damn, that changes everything," said Beau. "Where were you?"

"Talking to Freddie Wang."

"A-ha."

"A-ha?"

"You bet your ass, a-ha," replied Beau. "Now we're gettin' somewhere."

"We are?"

"You've seen him before?"

"Yeah. At Freddie's, maybe ten, fifteen minutes before I left."

"Perfect," said Beau. "Gives me someone to talk to—that's what good police work is, you know. Talkin' to people, till somebody says something stupid."

"Aren't you going to ask me if I killed him?" said Cape, sounding a little wounded.

"Why? Did you?"

"No."

"Then why should I ask?"

Cape didn't have an answer to that.

Beau said, "You're gonna have to come in and make a statement."

"Figured as much."

"Tonight."

"OK," said Cape. "Later, though, if it's all the same to you."

"Was stupid to move the body," said Beau.

"I was trying to get your attention."

"Well, 'less you want to lose your license, you might want to leave that part out."

"Got it."

"Guess I don't need to ask why you were talkin' to Freddie?"

"Uh-uh," said Cape.

"How's that going?"

"I think someone's trying to kill me," said Cape.

"Good," replied Beau. "Saves me the trouble."

Then he hung up.

41

The small house was nestled in the hills behind Causeway Bay, not far from where the boats, junks, and sampans jostled for position beneath the elevated expressway. Generations of families had lived on some of the boats, too poor to pay rent anywhere in Hong Kong but with nowhere else to work.

Li Mei worked in her garden, thinking of her youth on one of those boats. Her parents dead these many years, her brother drowned when he was ten. She was the first in her family to have solid ground beneath her feet at the end of the day. Though still close to the water, she was a world away.

She groaned slightly as she stood, putting her right hand behind her hip for balance. Nothing reminds you of your age like your knees. She took off her gloves and dropped them next to the back door, turning the knob and stepping into relative darkness. She blinked as her eyes adjusted from the morning sun to the cool shade of her kitchen.

"Hello, Li Mei."

Li Mei gasped and almost fell over, her hands jumping out from her sides. As the sun spots left her eyes, a figure materialized at the small kitchen table, Li Mei's startled mind matching the voice to the shape before her.

"Sally!"

Sally stood slowly and embraced the old woman, who still looked like the oldest person Sally had ever seen. It had been almost two years since Sally had visited. She'd told herself she was too busy, but realized now she'd been avoiding Li Mei for another reason. It was one thing to look in the mirror, but another to face someone who knows you and see yourself in the process. Li Mei broke their embrace and sat down, her silence invitation enough for Sally.

She told Li Mei everything, starting with her trip to Tokyo and leading to the events of the night before. Li Mei's ancient face cracked at times, new creases lining her brow, but she said nothing. Something in Sally's eyes told the old woman that this was just a preamble.

When she had finished, Sally stared at Li Mei for a full minute before speaking again, her eyes calm. "Li Mei, how did you know about the school?" she asked quietly. "About the Triads."

Li Mei opened her mouth and hesitated, just for an instant, but it was answer enough. Sally leaned forward and took the old woman's right hand in hers and said, "You stepped through the red gate, didn't you?"

Li Mei's eyes betrayed her.

"You went to the school as a girl," Sally continued, "and became a consort. A concubine. A spy."

The old woman nodded, her eyes going out of focus with the memory. "Yes, child. For a very long time, that was my life."

Sally squeezed her hand, then nodded. "That's how you knew Xan."

"Yes," Li Mei replied. "I wanted to give you...a choice." Then added, "And the power to make one."

Sally ignored the comment. "You said a very long time...how long?"

"What does it matter?"

"Because I'm leaving," said Sally

Li Mei blanched. "They won't let you."

Sally smiled sadly, then let her eyes wander around the walls of the kitchen. "This is such a nice house, Li Mei."

"I'm comfortable," said Li Mei, following Sally's gaze.

"And you bought it yourself?" asked Sally idly.

Li Mei balked, then yelped as Sally dug her thumb into the soft spot between the old woman's thumb and forefinger. She tried to pull away but Sally's grip was firm, and as Li Mei squirmed in her chair, the pressure on her hand slowly increased. Sally looked across the table at her former nursemaid, marveling at how detached she could be about the old woman's pain. She knew it should bother her but at the same instant knew that it never would.

Sally leaned in close, her voice almost a whisper. "You used me to buy your freedom from the Triad," she said evenly. Sally realized the answers were there her whole life but she'd been too blind to see them. "Which means you were still part of the black society when you were working for my parents. Maybe too old to be someone's concubine, but a spy just the same."

Li Mei couldn't meet Sally's gaze, and tears started to run down her cheeks. She stammered as she began talking. "Your...your father was a very important man in the U.S. Military. He was head of Army Intelligence, stationed in Japan. That's where he met your mother."

Sally eased the pressure on Li Mei's hand but held fast to her wrist.

"The Triads ran many smuggling operations," said Li Mei. "Some heroin, mostly guns—even people."

"People?"

"Illegals from China, smuggled onto Japanese freighters in Hong Kong," said Li Mei matter-of-factly, as if telling a friend about the price of pears. "Very profitable."

"What's that got to do with my father?"

"The gun trade was a major concern for the Japanese government— there are no guns in Japan by law. And it was also a concern for the U.S. military, because guns were disappearing from Army bases. So your father was asked to assist in their investigations."

Sally's jaw clenched but she remained motionless. "And you were sent to watch over my father."

Li Mei nodded.

Sally released her hand. "Tell me about him."

Li Mei looked up, her cheeks damp, surprised by the question. Over the years Sally spoke of her parents only rarely. "What do you mean?"

"What was he like?" asked Sally. "My father."

Li Mei took a deep breath, trying to relax. "Your father was a great man."

A great man. Sally's brow furrowed, as if the phrase were an oxymoron.

"He treated everyone with respect," continued Li Mei. "He was honest. He loved your mother, and he adored you." She smiled at the memory. "At that time America was held in high regard by many people—and your father, with his blond hair and blue eyes—I think, to me, your father always seemed very American. Of course, I've never been there."

Neither have I, thought Sally. "How do you know he was honest?"

Li Mei's eyes darted away but came back. There was no lying left in her. "Because they tried to buy him off, get him to stop his investigation. But the first time a gift was left at the house—money in an envelope, left in the mailbox—your father walked into the middle of the street and tore it to pieces. He knew they would be watching the house."

"And my mother."

Li Mei smiled sadly. "Smart, beautiful. And she was never afraid—of anything. Just like you. Your parents were..." Li Mei's voice trailed off, unsure of what to say.

Sally worked the muscles in her jaw again. She could put this off another hour or just say the words. When they came, she almost spat them across the table.

"My parents were murdered."

Li Mei's face broke apart, the tears running down gullies of age too deep to measure. "I... I never knew anything would happen to them, Sally," she sobbed. "Someone in the society made a deal with the yakuza—they worked out an arrangement for the guns. The next thing I knew, your parents had been driven off the road by a truck. I... never really knew it wasn't an accident."

Sally nodded, feeling the puzzle pieces lost in memory take shape. None of it surprised her, but it came with a sickening, awful finality that confirmed she was completely and utterly alone. Since the age of five, she had been a pawn in someone else's chess game, and there was nothing she could do to knock the pieces off the table and start over. All she could do was leave the table.

Sally stood up, looking down at the woman she'd loved as a child but feeling nothing but disdain. Even pity was beyond her reach now.

"I'm leaving."

Li Mei looked up, snot running down her nose, her eyes red. "But ... they won't let you."

Sally laughed, a short barking sound that surprised even her. "You forget where I went to school," she said simply. Then she turned and walked out the door, leaving the old woman alone with her guilt, her house, and the view of the boats where she used to live.

42

THE ADDRESS ON THE card wasn't on a map, and Cape knew better than to ask around Chinatown for directions. He'd followed the street numbers to a dead end and assumed at first it reemerged a few blocks later, like so many streets in San Francisco that disappeared into hills or landmarks and showed up a mile away.

But that would take him out of Chinatown, which didn't make sense, so fifteen minutes later he found himself back at the end of an alley, looking at empty boxes, broken vegetable crates, and shadows, wondering when the genie was going to appear and tell him the secret word.

The alley was half a block deep, with a grocery and tobacco shop flanking either side of the entrance, but the stores and the cross street seemed a world away. This far back, all Cape could hear was the wind and maybe the scuttling sound of a rat eating its way through the trash.

It was a rat. Pulling a pocket Maglite, Cape shone the light along the brick walls on either side, careful to keep the beam tight and his body between the light and the street. As it passed over a wooden crate, two red eyes glared back, followed by a rustling glimpse of a long tail. Based on the spacing of the eyes and the length of the hairless tail, Cape figured the rat must outweigh him by about forty pounds. He focused the light on the ground as he stepped forward gingerly.

This was starting to look like a dead end. Cape considered turning around when he saw it: a manhole cover, the grated kind, set into the corner of the alley. Shining the light through the top, he saw a ladder running down the side, disappearing into the darkness.

Panning the light over the nearest wall, Cape saw a blood red triangle etched into one of the bricks. Squatting down, he put his thumb in the center of the triangle and pushed.

He jumped as the manhole cover swung open with a muffled *clang.*

You've got to be kidding.

Turning off the flashlight, Cape lowered himself down the ladder, feeling for the rungs with his sneakers as he gripped the cold metal bars. His instinct was to make as little noise as possible, though he suspected an alarm had sounded somewhere once he triggered the trap door.

Fifteen feet down the hole, the darkness softened to a gray haze. Twenty feet down he could see the floor, light spilling into the tunnel. Thirty feet and he touched bottom, almost blinded by the sudden glare coming from an opening on his left. Blinking, Cape looked into another world.

Colored lanterns hung from the stone ceiling, brick walls were adorned with tapestries in muted reds and golds, and the cloying smell of incense permeated the air. Sofas, chairs, and cushions of different periods and styles crowded the small space, along with the occasional sculpture or desk, making it impossible to take in the entire room at once. Thick carpets had been piled on the stone floor, sometimes layered, giving Cape the feeling that the floor undulated beneath his feet. Toward the back of the chamber the light dimmed, but Cape could see another tunnel leading off to the right, no doubt connected to other chambers and more holes cut beneath the city. A low grinding sound emanated from the center of the room, like a ball bearing rolling across a sheet of glass.

Taking a deep breath, Cape stepped forward.

Two sets of hands grabbed him from each side, pulling him forward gently. He let himself be frisked, surprised at the soft touch. These guards were a cut above Freddie Wang's goons. As his eyes adjusted, he saw two men dressed in suits, Chinese in their mid-thirties, moving in an efficient, practiced manner as they checked him for weapons. Both released him at the same time, returning to their positions by the entrance. The one on the right nodded at Cape politely before pointing over his shoulder, indicating he should keep going.

Stepping around a folding screen, Cape stopped short as he came upon a man sitting behind a large desk. Next to him on a small tray was a silver tea service, steam coming from the pot. The man's face was in shadow, his arms spread as he rolled a white marble back and forth across the desk. The grinding sound rose and fell as the marble spun from hand to hand.

"You're late, old chap."

The man raised his head and Cape's eyes went wide, causing the man to chuckle softly. Smiling, he tilted his head back, letting the light spill across his face as his right hand came down and trapped the marble in his palm.

Gray-black hair sprouted from a high forehead, pulled back in a ponytail behind ears that looked two sizes too big. Deep lines ran from his forehead down his cheeks, underscoring his smile. His right brow arched over a dark brown eye as he returned Cape's stare. His left eye, however, was missing.

A ragged black hole flanked by scar tissue marked the missing orb, and Cape found his eyes drawn morbidly to that side of the man's face.

"Sorry," said the man pleasantly. "Just need to clean it." Bringing his right hand up, he popped the marble into his mouth and rolled it around like a gumball before spitting it back into his hand. Pulling his ravaged eyelid up with his left hand, he popped the marble into the hole with his right, jabbing himself with his index finger until it settled. Cape now found himself looking at a man with two brown eyes, the left only slightly askew.

"Gets distracting, doesn't it?"

Cape nodded, temporarily mute.

"So you're Cape, then?"

Cape nodded, pulling his gaze toward the one working eye.

"And you must be the white rabbit."

The man behind the desk laughed. "I knew I'd like you," he said amiably. "One-eyed Dong, at your service."

"Guess I don't have to ask how you got your name," said Cape.

"Fondue accident," replied Dong. "Least that's what I told me mum. But your name—can't say I've ever met anyone named Cape before."

"It's short for capricious."

Dong laughed again.

"So you obviously know all about me," said Cape, pulling out one of the desk chairs. "How 'bout I ask some questions?"

Dong bowed his head. "By all means."

"Where are you from?" asked Cape. "Your English … ?"

"It's the Queen's English, not mine."

"That's what I was wondering."

"Wonderful schools in Hong Kong," said Dong. "Used to be a British colony, you know."

Cape nodded, thinking of the red triangle. "The Heaven and Earth Society?"

Dong smiled, his right eye glittering. "The Black Society, Heaven and Earth, White Lotus. There are so many names."

"But all Triads."

"Just so." Dong nodded.

"Where do you fit in?"

"I don't," replied Dong, his tone suddenly flat. "Not anymore."

Cape waited.

"I was *heung chu*," said Dong, pride in his voice. "Incense Master for one of the most powerful Triads in Hong Kong. And I was going to be elevated to *fu shan chu*—deputy to the Dragon Head."

"What happened?"

"I was betrayed," replied Dong. "Along with the entire clan. The Dragon Head I served was murdered, his position usurped." Dong took a deep breath as if trying to control his temper. "I could either flee or be murdered in my sleep—I chose to live underground."

"Literally," said Cape, looking around.

"Indeed." Dong followed Cape's gaze, his good eye drifting out of focus as he contemplated his surroundings. "After the 1906 earthquake they built tunnels connecting many of the basements in Chinatown so residents could escape even if their building collapsed." He turned his gaze back to Cape. "I've only been in San Francisco a short while but studied the city before I came. One of the disadvantages of my current existence is the need to keep moving."

"I like what you've done with the place," said Cape. "But why did you invite me here?"

"And here I was beginning to think you were so bright." Dong shook his head sadly. "My dear boy, I just wanted to see if I could trust you," he said. "But I didn't *invite* you anywhere."

Cape shifted in his chair and fingered the card in his pocket. "Then who did?"

Before Dong could answer Cape saw movement in the back of the chamber. As he stood, he saw the boy with the orange hair come out of the side tunnel, the one who had given Cape the card. A sullen expression was on his face, eyes narrowed, crooked teeth making his mouth seem too small for his face, his narrow shoulders lost inside a loose jacket covered with pockets and zippers. Cape squinted in the dim light as he approached.

The boy stood behind Dong and smiled, incisors and cuspids jutting out at crazy angles. Then he stepped to the side, took a deep breath, and spit his teeth onto the floor at Cape's feet. Before Cape could react, the boy reached up and tore off his nose, flinging it across the room.

The wig came off last, dark hair falling around the shoulders, obscuring the face as it shook back and forth. When the head came up, green eyes met Cape's stare, framing a perfect nose dotted with freckles.

Sally smiled broadly as his jaw hit the floor.

"Miss me?"

43

XAN RETURNED TO HIS quarters and sat heavily in his chair, not bothering to turn on the lights. He'd had harder days, perhaps, but none
longer. He wanted to drink but lacked the energy to make one, inertia
winning out, at least for the moment.

You are getting old.

The thought occurred to him just as he felt the edge of the knife
against his Adam's apple.

"Welcome back, little dragon," he sighed, sounding more resigned
than afraid.

Sally removed the knife and stepped from the shadows to stand a
few feet in front of the chair, just beyond striking distance. She nodded once in greeting.

"I thought you left," said Xan.

"I came back."

"To kill me?"

Sally shrugged. "We'll see."

Xan almost smiled. "You think you could?"

Sally did smile. "Without a doubt, Master Xan."

Xan gestured toward the low couch against the wall behind Sally. "Please."

Sally took a step backward and sat without looking over her shoulder. "Did you know my parents were murdered?"

Xan studied her. "You went to see Li Mei." His tone even, not accusing, more curious than anything.

"Was that a yes?"

"No," replied Xan, "I suspected it—we all did. Was it coincidence a yakuza was driving the truck that killed them?" Xan shrugged. "But does it matter now, little dragon? You killed the man that murdered your parents."

"No." Sally shook her head. "Jun did."

Xan nodded. "I only knew for certain when I saw the pictures you took. Wen had covered his tracks well."

"But you didn't tell me."

"Why?" Xan sat up in his chair, his tone suddenly angry. "So you could run to your death?" Xan looked away, the dim light casting shadows across his ruined face. "Did you never wonder how I got this?" he asked, tracing the jagged scar with his index finger.

Sally said nothing.

"I had a wife," said Xan, looking again toward Sally. "And a daughter. They were murdered in front of me." Xan smiled bitterly. "So I went in search of revenge—by myself."

Xan leaned forward, moonlight igniting the scar as he spoke.

"I wasn't trained then, and there were five of them," he continued. "But I managed to kill three with my bare hands before I was hit from behind and knocked unconscious. When I came to, I realized they had tied me to a large piece of driftwood. There are sharks in the

265

harbor, you know, especially in the winter months. One of the men leaned over me, wanting to make sure I was conscious—I can still see his smile—that's when I saw the knife."

Xan touched his face again, remembering. "I was in the water for three days before a junk pulled me onboard in a fishing net."

Sally leaned forward. "But you survived."

Xan nodded. "And came here," he said. "To study."

"And serve."

Xan didn't answer.

"And the two men?"

"One was killed in a gunfight in a bar a few years later," replied Xan.

"And the other?"

"It took me five years," said Xan. "But I found him." He paused, and for a moment Sally thought he was finished, but then he added, "I cut off his arms and legs and threw him in the harbor. After what I'd lived through, I didn't trust the sharks."

"But it didn't bring back your wife?" asked Sally, annoyed at her own impatience. "Or your daughter. Is that the lesson, Master Xan?"

"No," said Xan softly, shaking his head. "I wanted you to understand that you and I are not so different, little dragon. And that I have already lost one daughter."

Their eyes met, and Sally nodded her understanding. Xan held her gaze for a long time before turning away. Sally was the first to break the silence.

"If I were to ask shan chu about my parents' death, could he tell me anything?" she asked, changing the subject back to the reason she was there.

Xan shook his head. "No," he said tiredly. "He was ignorant of his son's treachery. And I'm afraid you are too late to visit with the old man of the mountain."

Sally thought at first Xan meant the hour was too late until she registered the look on his face.

"He's dead?" she asked, incredulous. She had only been gone one day.

Xan told her of the events since dawn, his voice heavier by the minute.

"Do you think Hui killed his own father?"

Xan shrugged, sounding almost apathetic. "Supposedly only shan chu had the combination to the safe, so why dial the wrong one unless you desired a quick death? But then again, Hui exudes the warmth of a cobra."

"Will he be made the new Dragon Head?" asked Sally.

"Not necessarily." Xan frowned. "There will have to be an election."

"Can he win, given the circumstances?"

"The real circumstances are known only to me," replied Xan. "And as you said, Hui is formidable—I would not underestimate him."

"So what are you going to do?"

Xan shifted his weight, the legs of the chair creaking under him, Sally imagining it as the sound of his joints. Looking at her teacher, she felt for the first time the decades between them. Before he could speak, Sally answered her own question.

"What you've always done," she said simply.

A smile flashed across Xan's face briefly. "There is no other place for me in this world, little dragon. I have become what I am, and there is nothing that can change that. I have walked too far down this path."

"Can you trust Hui?"

Xan shrugged. "As long as he can trust me."

Sally nodded, then held his eyes for a long second.

"I'm leaving."

"I know," replied Xan, adding, "I'm sorry about Jun."

Sally blinked but didn't respond.

"Where will you go?" asked Xan.

Sally shook her head. "You might hear from me," she said. "But don't try to follow me."

"I won't," replied Xan. "You have my word."

"But others might?"

"Not while I'm here," said Xan.

"What will you tell them?"

"The truth." Xan smiled. "If they follow you, they will not return."

Sally nodded once, then stood and bowed, keeping her eyes locked on his.

"Goodbye, Master Xan."

Xan stood and returned the bow, his face a mixture of warmth and sorrow.

"Goodbye, little dragon."

44

Xan hated being lost, especially in a city as small as San Francisco.

Chinatown had sold its soul, lifting its skirt for anyone with a dollar in his pocket. Plastic dragons, pagoda keychains, *mild* Szechuan cooking. What started as an ethnic neighborhood had become a cesspool of tourism.

But he was making progress, and there were some who still remembered where they came from. Some believed his story—a worried uncle looking for his niece—others saw him more clearly. They might not know Xan, but they had known men like him.

Fear was an excellent motivator.

45

CAPE REALIZED HE WAS grinning like an idiot.

Staring at Sally, he said, "You're not dead," realizing how stupid that sounded. Then he said it again.

Sally smiled. "You said that already."

"Just wanted to make sure."

The two friends looked at each other, neither one moving. In all the years they'd known each other, they had never embraced, but their bond was palpable in the confines of the small chamber. Cape knew he wouldn't be standing there if not for Sally, who had saved his life more than once, often putting her own at risk. When Sally looked at Cape, she saw the second man she had completely trusted, the first a half-remembered father from a childhood stolen long ago.

"What's so funny?" asked Cape, seeing her expression.

"You remind me of my father."

"I must have aged while you were gone."

"Maybe that's it," replied Sally, adding, "thanks for coming."

One-eyed Dong interrupted. "I already told him he was late."

Cape shrugged. "I've been busy."

"I know," said Sally in a conspiratorial whisper, sitting on the edge of the desk.

Cape looked from Sally to Dong and back again.

He asked, "Someone mind telling me what's going on?"

Dong turned to Sally and said something under his breath. Sally shook her head and responded with a torrent of Cantonese, gesturing toward Cape as she talked. He always marveled at how seamlessly she moved from one language to another. Unlike Dong, Sally spoke American-English with no discernible accent, able to curse like a sailor or play Scrabble with the best of them. Cape suspected the same was true for her other languages.

Sally gave Dong one more dose of Cantonese before turning back to Cape. "Where do you want to start?"

Cape caught himself before a hundred questions jumped out at once. He'd been so focused on finding Sally and making something—*anything*—happen, he hadn't stopped to think.

"Might be easier if you asked questions," suggested Sally. "I don't know what you already know."

Cape nodded, trying to organize his thoughts. *Might as well start at the beginning.*

"Were you onboard that ship?"

"No."

Cape let out a breath he didn't know he was holding.

"But someone…" He tried to find the right words. "Someone *like* you was there."

"Her name is Lin," said Sally, sounding very tired. "She went to the same school, was trained the same way. Her older sister was

271

my—" Sally's eyes clouded over for an instant. "She was ... my roommate."

Cape wanted to ask something else but left it alone. "She was injured, wasn't she?" He described the blood outside Sally's place.

"Badly." Sally's expression was grave.

"You brought her here?"

Sally nodded. "Dong sent word to me—a card with a red triangle. He somehow knew Lin was coming."

"I may be exiled," said Dong, "but I still have friends."

"My place wasn't safe," added Sally. "I patched Lin up, then she passed out. She's been unconscious until last night."

"*Why* is she here?"

"She stole something," replied Sally, "and smuggled it out of Hong Kong."

"What?"

Sally turned to Dong, who was stirring sugar into his tea. With a theatrical sigh, he shook his head and ducked under the desk, only to reappear a moment later. He held something roughly the size of an orange wrapped in burlap, which he placed on the desk with a resounding *thunk*.

He unwrapped it slowly, revealing the blood-red stone, the finely carved scales, the curves that made it look, at first, like a human heart. Cape addressed his next question to Dong:

"What is it?"

Dong smiled, arching the eyebrow over his good eye. "Isn't that obvious?" he asked playfully. "'It's the stuff dreams are made of.'"

Cape studied the stone heart that looked like a dragon when the light caught it in a certain way. *The stuff that dreams are made of.* He looked at One-eyed Dong. "Is that your best Humphrey Bo-gart impersonation?"

"I was doing Shakespeare," said Dong defensively. "*The Tempest.*"

Sally interrupted by lifting the dragon off the table and handing it to Cape. He hefted it in his right hand, surprised at its weight. It felt warm, and as he turned it in the light, the dragon's eyes seemed to glow.

"So what is it?" he repeated, looking at Sally.

"It's a talisman," she said. "A charm."

Dong cut in. "If it's in your possession, your victory is assured."

Sally lowered her voice. "*He who holds the heart holds the future.*"

Cape frowned. "You sound like a fortune cookie."

Sally shrugged. "I'm not saying I believe it, either." She glanced at Dong. "I'm just telling you why it's important."

"To whom?"

"The Triads," answered Sally before Dong could say anything. "When you think *Triad*, you probably think organized crime, and you're right. But these societies, or clans, or whatever they call themselves—they go back hundreds of years."

Dong added, "The original secret societies in China were established to overthrow an unjust emperor. They were patriotic, highly disciplined—"

Sally cut him off. "And very superstitious."

Dong made a pouty face and poured more tea.

Sally continued. "Rituals, ceremonies, names."

"Names." Cape looked at Dong. "Like Incense Master?"

"Exactly." Sally nodded. "These things have real power in the world of the Triads. And since the Triads have power in the real world…"

Cape finished the thought. "The power behind these things is real, whether you believe in them or not."

"Yes."

"So it's valuable," said Cape.

"That's not why she stole it," said Sally.

Dong said, "She was supposed to deliver it to someone."

"Who?" asked Cape. "You?"

"Heavens, no," said Dong. "Someone you know, here in San Francisco."

Cape knew the answer before Dong said the name.

"Harold Yan."

46

Xan looked at the man's eyes and saw nothing but terror.

Truth always came from fear. He followed the line of the man's arm as he pointed through the shop window, toward the alley across the street.

Xan released the man and nodded.

He was getting close.

47

"Harold Yan," said Cape.

Sally and One-eyed Dong nodded in unison.

"The mayoral candidate."

"The same."

"And Lin—the girl on the ship—she said Yan told her to steal this dragon's heart?"

"No." Sally frowned. "She just said she had to find him. Remember, she was delirious—she was bleeding and had a fever. She didn't even tell me she had the stone—I found it on her when I dressed her wounds."

Cape frowned. "If she was looking for Yan, why come to you?"

Sally shrugged. "She knew I was in San Francisco, and she was hurt. She couldn't risk passing out while talking to Yan's receptionist or falling down in the street. Someone could find the dragon's heart and steal it."

"But why does Harold Yan want the heart? It doesn't make sense."

"Of course it does," said Dong.

Cape looked at him. "Why?"

"Isn't that obvious?" asked Dong. "He's about to enter a contest—an election. The heart would assure his victory."

Cape looked at the elaborately carved piece of jade sitting on the desk in front of him.

"But you just told me the dragon's heart was part of Triad history."

"Right," said Sally.

"Which means Yan is part of a Triad."

"Or under their influence," said Dong.

"C'mon."

"My dear boy," said Dong, his tone just this side of condescending. "You'd be surprised how many politicians are criminals."

"I've been saying that for years," said Cape. "Every time I pay my taxes. But a Triad?"

Dong huffed. "Do you have any doubt the Mafia has infiltrated American politics over the years?"

Cape chewed on that for a minute. Last year a local Congressman got caught taking bribes in exchange for his vote on funding for the new Bay Bridge project. The investigation found the construction company paying him off had mob connections.

"OK," he said to Dong. "Say Yan has connections to a Triad, or, as you said, the Triad has some leverage over Yan."

"If Yan gets elected, it gives the Triad a foothold in San Francisco."

"And?"

"That would be very, very bad."

"Very, *very* bad?"

Dong leaned forward. "There are tongs, street gangs, and a handful of criminals in this city that already have loose connections to the Triads."

"Like Freddie Wang," said Cape.

Dong frowned. "An unsavory example, but a good one."

Dong loved being the center of attention, but Cape wanted to cut the lesson short. "You're saying there's no central organization here, no power base like Hong Kong."

"Or Shanghai," said Dong. "Or even New York."

"So?"

Sally cut in. "Remember those people on the ship?'

Cape thought of the faces he'd seen on Treasure Island, the brutal stories Mitch had told him. "Yeah?"

"Multiply that times a thousand."

"She's right," said Dong. "Right now smuggling people is a side venture for the Triads—they make more from heroin and guns, with less risk. But occasionally they'll exploit a situation, pull together a temporary organization to turn a profit."

"Hire a snakehead," said Cape, remembering the lesson from Mitch.

Dong raised his eyebrows. "Precisely."

"But if they had a permanent base here in San Francisco..." began Cape.

Sally finished his thought. "Things could get a lot worse."

"It's a disgusting business," muttered Dong.

Cape looked at him again, wondering when the English sophisticate became the Incense Master. Maybe Dong preferred the heroin trade, considered it more gentlemanly. The man was charming on the surface, but Cape had no doubt Dong could molt like a snake at a moment's notice. He turned his attention back to the ship and something that had been bothering him since the beginning.

"Why did Lin kill the crew?"

"They deserved to die," replied Sally without hesitation. She breathed through her nose, then in a calmer voice said, "Lin was trained to shadow and kill men. Men who are killers—not women and children. Even in death, there is a code."

Cape studied his friend, wondering where you drew the line after you'd crossed it so many times.

"The crew were *sze kau*," said Sally. "Triad thugs. At school, we called them 49s."

Cape remembered Beau's description of the ship, the number drawn in blood.

"Everyone in a Triad has a name and a number," explained Dong. "Based on tradition. The Dragon Head is 489, or sometimes 21, which is 4+8+9. Mine was 438. The foot soldiers are 49s."

"Numerology is a big deal in China," added Sally, shrugging. "It gets complicated."

Cape looked at Sally, thinking *complicated* didn't even begin to describe her upbringing. He rubbed his temples and tried to concentrate.

"But why would Yan take the risk now?" he asked.

"The heart," replied Dong. "The election."

"I don't know," said Sally, forever the skeptic.

"Why don't we ask Lin?" suggested Cape.

Sally and Dong exchanged a look.

"What?"

"We've got a little problem," said Sally. "Lin has disappeared."

48

Xan taught his students the value of patience, though he had none himself.

It had been a long day, and the night was turning cold. But as he looked across the street toward the alley, Xan smiled for the first time in days.

Patience had its rewards, after all.

49

SALLY TOLD CAPE THAT when she came back last night, Dong was asleep, his two guards were unconscious, and Lin was gone.

Sally had mistakenly assumed Lin was too weak to move. And since their view from the bunker was limited, Sally had gone out to patrol the neighborhood.

Cape asked why Lin had run.

"If Lin recognized Dong—and it's not hard, with that eye rolling around—she'd know he was forced out of the Triad. She could have fallen into a trap, or a plot to steal the dragon's heart for himself."

"Wouldn't she have trusted you?" Cape had asked. "You said you were close to her sister."

Sally's eyes hardened. "That was a long time ago," she said, adding, "And I'm not there anymore." She looked at Cape but her eyes were still somewhere else. "Lin is who I would have become, had I stayed. Trust isn't part of her vocabulary."

"You think she went to Yan without the dragon?"

Sally shrugged. "She wasn't strong enough to risk stealing it, even if she knew where Dong kept it hidden. I might have come back at any minute. This way, at least she could tell Yan where it was. That's better than being trapped, or dead underground."

"I thought I was paranoid."

Sally shook her head. "You're not even close," she said. "Lin was *trained* to be suspicious."

Time was running out now that Lin was missing. They needed to get an angle on Yan quickly, otherwise they'd be going in blind. And since Yan was a respected public figure and they were an exiled criminal, a trained assassin, and a private investigator with questionable judgment, the best they could hope for would be to get arrested.

So Cape climbed the ladder and crawled out of the hole. His phone couldn't get a signal in Dong's underground lair, and reception wasn't much better between the buildings. He walked the length of the alley, checked the signal on his phone, and dialed Linda's number.

It rang almost ten times before there was an answer.

Linda didn't like to get too close to phones, so when it rang, she dashed across the room, pushed the button for the speakerphone, then retreated to a safe distance and shouted, which always made her sound angry.

"*It's the middle of the night!*" she yelled, making Cape think maybe she really was angry. He visualized her hair lurching forward as she reprimanded his disembodied voice.

"Sorry," said Cape. "But Sally and I—"

"*Sally's OK?*" shouted Linda.

"Oh, yeah," said Cape. "I forgot—"

"*Then why are you calling?*" demanded Linda, sounding pissed again.

"Remember when I asked you to look into Harold Yan?"

"*Didn't you get my message?*"

Cape held out his phone and checked the screen, which read: *2 new messages.* Beau had mentioned he'd called several times, but he wouldn't have left more than one message.

"I got it," said Cape, putting the phone to his ear. "I just haven't listened to it." He imagined Linda's hair crouching down, ready to strike.

"*Why not?*"

"I've been in a tunnel," said Cape. "Under a manhole cover."

That put Linda at a momentary loss.

"So what did you find out?" asked Cape.

"Almost nothing," said Linda, her voice dropping to a normal pitch. Cape could tell she was standing closer to the phone, fears of electromagnetic menace temporarily gone. "Lots and lots of press clippings, going back ten years, but it's all pretty standard stuff for a public figure. The more public he became, the easier the trail is to follow."

"OK," said Cape, discouraged. "Is that what you said in your message?"

"No," said Linda. "The Sloth and I tried to go back, to before Yan left China."

"And?"

"And nothing," said Linda. "Before immigration, the guy disappears."

"Isn't that because you're trying to access records in China? That must be next to impossible."

"Not for the Sloth," said Linda. "He even has a program that can translate the characters into English as you scroll down a page."

"So?"

"So either Yan had a really, really boring life in China," said Linda. "Which I doubt. Or ... he's a criminal."

"Who changed his name when he came to the States," said Cape. "Because he wanted to get into politics."

"Where the real power is."

"The real power is in politics?"

"I heard that on an episode of *West Wing*."

"Then it must be true. OK, so he gets a new identity."

"Exactly," said Linda. "Not that hard, really, if you know the right people."

"But if I can prove Yan has a criminal past ..."

"You've got some leverage," said Linda. "You could really screw up the election."

Cape started to get excited until he realized he didn't have a single piece of evidence.

"I don't have jack shit besides this conversation, do I?"

"I'm afraid not," said Linda, her voice even softer. "Unless ..."

"Yeah?"

"Sloth said you'd need his fingerprints."

"Fingerprints," said Cape to himself. "And then?"

"Then you'd need a friend at Interpol, the CIA, NSA, or the FBI."

The last three letters of the alphabet soup got Cape's attention. Linda was still talking but he'd taken the phone from his ear. Carefully he reached into his right-hand coat pocket and touched the sides of a round disk with his thumb and forefinger. As he pulled his hand from his pocket he saw the red and white letters against a blue background: *Yan for Mayor*.

Absently he raised the phone to his ear and said "thanks," hanging up before she could answer. Gingerly dropping the button back into his pocket, he called John Williams at the FBI and left a message.

Ten minutes passed.

When his phone rang, Cape nearly jumped out of his shoes.

"You're up late," said Williams.

"Can you run a set of prints for me?" asked Cape. "Through Interpol, or maybe the Hong Kong authorities? The records might go back ten or even twenty years."

Williams coughed for almost a full minute before getting it under control. "You must have the wrong number—you want me to pick up your dry cleaning, too?"

"You said you wanted a lead on the ship."

"We already got the jeans guy in custody," said Williams. "You remember, the asshole you should've given to us, but instead gave to the police?"

"Big deal," said Cape.

"We got him on conspiracy, murder, and tax fraud, for starters."

"You think he's the mastermind behind this?"

Williams was silent on the other end.

"Neither do I," said Cape.

Williams grunted. "What've you got, cowboy?"

"A thumbprint, maybe," said Cape. "On a button."

"Not much," muttered Williams. "What do you want?"

"A name."

"That's it?" said Williams skeptically. "And what do I get?"

"A name," said Cape. "And maybe some answers."

"Maybe?"

"That's all I can offer," said Cape.

Several long seconds passed. "OK."

"How soon can you have it?"

"This is the FBI, junior," said Williams. "Not the 1-hour photo."

"Can't you say it's a matter of national security?"

"Is it?"

"Isn't everything these days?"

"You got a point," said Williams. "When can you bring it in?"

"I can't," replied Cape. "Can you pick it up?"

"Jee-zus, you are high maintenance." Cape heard Williams cupping the phone, muffled voices in the background. "Where are you?"

Cape gave him directions to the nearest corner.

"OK, look for a blue Honda."

"The FBI drives a Honda?"

"We might be on a budget, but we're not stupid," said Williams. "If you don't drive an import in California, everyone thinks you're a cop."

"Sneaky."

"That's the idea."

"One more thing."

"What?"

"My prints are on this thing, too."

"No problem, you'd be in the files 'cause of your license." Williams held the phone away from his mouth again and shouted to someone in another room, then came back on. "Never mind—my man in the car will have a kit—stick your hand through the window, he'll take your prints. It'll save us time."

"Thanks."

"If this pans out, we're even."

"You'll call me either way?"

"Sure," said Williams. "Give me your number."

Fifteen minutes later the car pulled quietly up to the curb next to a hydrant and cut its lights. Cape reached through the window and dropped the button into a plastic bag the driver held open, then extended the fingers of his right hand and felt them rolled across an ink pad one at a time. The whole exchange took less than two minutes.

Cape walked back up the block and turned down the alley. He had gone less than ten feet when he sensed someone behind him. Pivoting on his left foot, he raised his left elbow high and spun around, just as he felt an electric jolt across his shoulders. His body twisted backward as the muscles in his neck started to spasm, black spots appearing at the edge of his vision. He felt the breath leave his lungs as his momentum completed his turn, bringing him face to face with a man with a jagged scar cutting across his right eye and down his cheek.

Xan smiled, the scar dancing in celebration, as Cape felt the ground fall out from under him and saw the lights at the end of the street go out one by one.

50

THE DRIVER'S LICENSE SPUN like a leaf as it fell, tapping sounds chasing after it as the plastic edge ricocheted off the rungs of the ladder.

The guard nearest the tunnel turned as the card hit the stone floor. Bending down, he saw there was a note wrapped around it, Chinese characters drawn in short bold strokes. He quickly stepped across the room and dropped the license onto the desk, then bowed and returned to his position at the bottom of the ladder.

The first thing Sally saw as Dong unwrapped the note was Cape's picture on the license.

"*Ta ma de*," muttered Sally. Oh shit.

"That doesn't even look like him," said Dong, taking the license. "How does the Department of Motor Vehicles do that? You know, in Hong Kong—"

"*Dong.*" Sally's voice was full of warning. "What does the note say?"

Dong read aloud. "'Bring the heart.'"

"That's it?"

"It gives a location—Buddha's Universal Church."

"Just a few blocks from here, on Washington."

"At this hour the church will be deserted," said Dong miserably. "Yan has set a trap, and your friend is the bait." He blew out his cheeks as he handed the note out to Sally.

Sally's eyes grew wide as she looked at the slip of paper.

"Yan didn't write this note."

"How do you know?" Dong reached for the note but stopped when he saw the grim expression on Sally's face. When she looked up, her eyes were hard and her voice flat.

"I recognize the handwriting."

51

Harold Yan looked worried.

"Drink this," he said as he handed a mug to Lin. "It tastes bitter, but it will help the healing process."

"*Mh goi.*" Lin winced as she extended her arms but nodded her thanks.

"That shoulder looks bad," muttered Yan. "You didn't go to a hospital?"

"No," said Lin.

"Smart girl," said Yan approvingly. "The hospital has to report gunshot wounds to the police."

Lin nodded as she blew into her mug, the steam making her eyes water. "The bullet passed right through."

"You're very brave."

Lin forced a smile before sipping tentatively. He was right, the drink tasted awful. She hated this, sitting in Yan's house, the front room that doubled as a home office, trying to explain herself without telling him what really happened. She didn't even know Yan, beyond what she'd been told. A true friend, someone we can trust. She tried to think of someone she could really trust and came up empty, save for a dead sister she only remembered from pictures.

Yan looked nice enough, professional, well-mannered. Comparing him to men she'd known, he seemed more like the Dragon Head or a businessman than the thugs and killers she usually hunted. Not anything like the *sze kau* pigs on the ship. He already asked her about that, something in his voice warning her to stretch the truth. She said someone tried to steal the heart—that shut him up, got Yan saying wait one minute, then going to the next room for tea. Lin suspected he didn't care about the women and children in the hold any more than the crew, so there was no point trying to explain. Lin knew how to follow orders—she'd made the trip, didn't she?—but *how* she completed an assignment was up to her.

"I have a few more questions, if you don't mind," said Yan pleasantly. "I'll keep it short tonight—I know you're still weak."

Lin nodded, clenching her jaw. She *was* weak, a feeling new to her. She'd never been injured this badly in all her years of service, but now she could barely stand without seeing spots. Yan had her sitting in a high-backed chair with wooden arms, something she could hold onto as she drank her tea. Her shoulder burned, the bandages still wet with blood. It had taken her almost two hours to find this house, on the border of Chinatown and North Beach, an old two-story Victorian in the middle of a short, twisted road that was more alley than street. She never could have found it that first night, half dead and soaking wet. If Sally hadn't been home, Lin knew she'd be dead.

But then she woke up underground, betrayed. One-eyed Dong had been exiled, a price on his head. Sally hadn't left the society, after all—she must be part of the conspiracy to steal the heart. Lin cursed her lack of strength, unable to risk anything except running away. But at least she was alive and free, able to tell Yan where it was.

Now they just had to get it.

Yan stepped around his desk and sat on its edge, only a few feet in front of her.

"Do you know why you're here?" he asked idly. "What did the Dragon Head tell you?"

"*Lung tau* gave me the heart," Lin began.

"But you knew he would tell people you stole it?"

Lin nodded. "He explained there are traitors within our society, planning to steal the heart and kill him."

"But he couldn't hide it."

"No," said Lin, shaking her head emphatically. "If he moved the heart himself it would be an act of fear, a sign of weakness. His enemies would gain support."

"So he stole the heart from himself," said Yan. "Brilliant."

"He said to tell you everything," said Lin. "But no one else knows, not even Master Xan."

"Your . . . ," Yan paused, searching for the word. "Instructor."

Lin nodded again. "The Dragon Head told Xan there was a situation in China that needed attention, and he requested that Xan send me—to Fuzhou."

"Where you caught the freighter."

"Yes," said Lin. "He gave me the heart, wrapped in cloth so I could hide it in my clothes, then explained how to board the ship." She sipped more tea, which tasted less bitter the more she drank.

She could feel herself starting to relax, her shoulder less painful. Her eyes felt heavy, hands tingling, legs almost going numb. She blinked as Yan watched her, his eyes full of concern.

Yan stood and looked down at her cup. "It's helping, isn't it?" He smiled though his eyes had gone flat, expressionless. Stepping behind Lin's chair, he put his left hand gently on her shoulder. "Yes, you are very brave," he said admiringly.

Lin started to respond but gasped as Yan dug his fingers into her shoulder.

"But very stupid." Yan's voice was pure disdain as he twisted his thumb savagely against her bandages. Liquid fire ran down her arm and Lin dropped the tea in her lap, but she couldn't feel it against her skin. Her legs were completely numb. Yan seized the back of the chair with both hands and pulled, slamming Lin onto her back, stars exploding behind her eyes. She started to hyperventilate as the numbness in her legs crept across her stomach toward her heart.

"You had the most powerful weapon in Triad history," seethed Yan, stepping in front of the chair. "And you lost it."

Lin watched, helpless, as Yan raised his right foot and brought it down slowly onto her shoulder. The numbing poison had made it to her chest, squeezing the air out of her lungs, but it left the nerve endings in her shoulder raw and exposed. The heel of his shoe pressed down, Lin's head twisting back and forth on the rug as she tried to scream, managing only a strangled cough as tears ran down her cheeks.

"But you're still of some use, and with your help, perhaps I can get the heart back." Yan's eyes shone with a fanatic's zeal. Lin stared, wheezing and thrashing, as Yan reached behind his back and tugged at his belt. The room was getting dark, and Lin realized she was blacking out.

That's when she saw the knife.

52

BUDDHA'S UNIVERSAL CHURCH IS still the largest Buddhist church in North America, even though it was built in 1961. Although Buddhism has become the fastest growing religion in the United States, the size of its churches have remained relatively modest. But the founders of this church in the heart of Chinatown lacked the funds to build from scratch, so they converted an abandoned nightclub and renovated the dilapidated building themselves over a ten-year period. Today the interior is filled with colorful murals and mosaics, and the rooftop garden has one of the best views in the city.

Cape had never seen the view at night, and under different circumstances would have enjoyed it. But sitting with his hands tied behind his back gave him little opportunity to see more than ten feet in front of him. A crescent moon stared down at the roof, a malevolent eye covered by a cataract of thickening fog. Since the church was the tallest structure on the block, very little ambient light found its way to the garden from the streetlights and neighboring buildings.

Beyond that, the garden was nothing but shifting shadows against the night sky.

Xan emerged from the darkness at the edge of the roof and strode through the garden. He was wearing a loose-fitting, long-sleeved black shirt and black cotton pants, with sandals on his feet. As the sparse light found him, his grizzled scalp and broad face flickered in and out of focus, making him appear headless.

"The street is deserted," he said in English. His voice was deep and full of gravel, with a slight accent that seemed to come and go depending on how fast he talked. "They should have come by now."

Cape said nothing at first, not sure if Xan was thinking aloud, but then said, "Maybe they don't like costume parties."

Xan smiled and leaned over Cape, getting in close. Cape could see the raised scar tissue coursing its way across Xan's cheek, making one eye seem larger than the other.

"Cut yourself shaving?"

Xan gently squeezed Cape's left shoulder.

Cape jerked backward, his body spasming as if struck by lightning, knocking his head back as a scream caught in his throat. He coughed violently, wheezing as air rushed from his lungs, bile rose, and his eyes started to water. His head struck the tiles again, hard, as vertigo hit like a sledgehammer.

An eternity that lasted only a few seconds passed and Cape opened his eyes, relieved to see the roof wasn't spinning. Twisting his body, he managed to sit up and saw Xan standing ten feet away, idly passing something from hand to hand.

It was Cape's wallet.

"The cards in your wallet say your name is Cape...?" He made it sound like a question. "Except, of course, this card." Xan held up a brown card with a red triangle. "This card doesn't seem like the others, does it?"

Cape took a deep breath, knowing Xan was only a step away from squeezing his other shoulder. "One of these things is not like the others?" he asked. "Who are you, a Muppet gone bad?"

Xan's jaw clenched but he didn't move. "Where did you get this card?"

Cape looked at Xan and said nothing. He couldn't move his left arm at all but tried to roll his shoulders to keep some blood circulating to his hands. He wondered if he could roll to the edge of the roof and ... *what*? A five-story drop onto hard pavement was starting to sound pretty good.

"Do you have any other cards like this?" asked Xan patiently.

"Go fish."

Xan took a step forward but his manner remained calm, unthreatening. "I have no interest in hurting you."

Cape almost laughed but it came out as a cough. "Gee, that's reassuring. I'd hate to know what it feels like when you are interested in hurting someone."

"One-eyed Dong," said Xan. "You've met him?"

Cape nodded. "Charming guy, treats his guests much better than you," he said, seeing no reason to lie. Xan wasn't about to believe Cape found the card on the street.

"And what business does a *gwai loh* have with One-eyed Dong?" Xan held up another card. "This says you are a 'licensed investigator' in the state of California."

"I'm considering another line of work," replied Cape. "And how about you—a massage therapist?"

Xan raised his head slightly, and said with a hint of pride, "I am a teacher."

Cape squinted, blinking his eyes dry. "Reading, writing, or arithmetic?"

"Life and death." Xan's eyes were two pieces of obsidian.

"Let me guess," said Cape. "A girls' school." It was out of his mouth before he could stop it. *Fuck it—maybe it'll get him talking— more time to think, less time to writhe in agony.* He sat up straighter, shaking his head to clear it.

Xan's eyes grew wider as he studied his captive. After a long moment he started to walk in a slow circle around Cape.

"Did you know that more than half the assassins in the world are women?"

"I dated a girl who tore my heart out."

Xan ignored the remark and kept circling, making Cape think of a shark.

"It's true," said Xan. "What better way to get close to a man, especially a dangerous one? Women make men stupid, careless. Even a dangerous man is vulnerable when he's with a woman."

Cape thought of Sally, wondering how far back the two went. *Keep him talking.* "That can't be easy, turning women into killers."

"They are *weapons*," said Xan. "But you miss the point—it's impossible to teach women anything. They are stones, worn hard and smooth by waves of disappointment and years of sorrow, as predictable and stubborn as the tides."

"Was that a haiku?"

Xan's eyes flashed a warning but he never broke stride. "But *girls*—girls are made of clay. Especially girls who lost their childhood to broken homes or tragedy. Start young, fuel their anger, and you can mold them, teach them, make them anything you want."

Cape again thought of Sally—the Sally he knew. "One problem with your theory."

"What?"

"Girls tend to grow up into women."

Xan scowled. "By then they've chosen a path," he said. "You can't change who you are just because you're old enough to drink. No one, not even a woman, can change their past."

"Maybe not," said Cape. "But they can make their own decisions."

Xan waved his right hand dismissively. "Free will is an illusion, *gwai loh.*"

"Our fate is set?"

Xan nodded.

"Then why do you keep looking over the edge of the roof?"

Xan stopped circling and looked impassively at Cape.

Oh, swell. You pissed him off.

"He's got a point, Xan." The voice was muffled slightly, making it hard to pinpoint the location, but it seemed to come from directly behind Xan.

Xan whirled and thrust his right arm forward, his hand open and turned sideways.

Cape watched as a chain twenty feet long shot from Xan's sleeve, its barbed tip flying through the air toward the bamboo stand at the edge of the roof. By its speed alone, it would impale anyone in its path. The sound of wood splintering was followed by a sudden clang of metal against metal, and Xan lurched forward, suddenly off-balance as the chain was torn from his arm.

Xan grunted and peered into the darkness as he rolled sideways, changing his position before a counterattack could begin.

He was too slow.

Three *shuriken* whistled through the air, the first two spinning over Cape's head, their sound the only way to track them. The third throwing star also made a sound as Xan bellowed with rage. Turning his head, Cape saw why.

The six-pointed star, three inches in diameter, was embedded deeply in Xan's right knee. He staggered and brought his left arm up in a swinging motion as he struggled for balance. Metal darts glinted in the half-light from the moon as they flew from his hand. Xan strained his ears for sounds of impact, but as he shifted his weight onto his left leg, a shape darker than the shadows materialized behind him.

The wooden sword swung low and wide, knocking Xan's legs out from under him. Even as he fell, Xan managed to pull a knife, a *tanto*, from his belt, but the sword caught his wrist on the backswing with a loud crack. The knife slid across the roof, coming to a stop between Cape's legs, the point of the blade barely penetrating the crotch of his jeans and nicking his thigh.

Cape's breath hissed through his teeth in a mixture of primal fear and relief. With an effort, he tore his eyes from his crotch and saw the cloaked figure had dropped the sword to bring both hands down in a chopping motion, so fast that Cape never saw the impact, but Xan's head jolted sideways. The hands came up again, repeating the strike, Xan slumping face-first onto the tiles.

From where Cape was sitting, spread-eagled at knife point, he couldn't tell if Xan was still breathing. He didn't need Sally to remove the black cloth from her face to know who had come to his rescue and almost castrated him in the process.

Sally shook out her hair and looked from Cape to the knife and back again.

"Oops." Sally winced apologetically. "A couple more inches and that would have really hurt."

"A couple more inches … you referring to the knife, or was that meant to be ambiguous?"

Sally smiled and shrugged her shoulders.

Cape exhaled loudly. "Thanks." He nodded with his chin toward Xan. "I take it you know him."

Sally looked down at Xan and nodded slowly.

"He was my …" She started to say *teacher* but stopped. When she turned to Cape, she had a bemused expression on her face.

"Let's just say I grew up in his shadow."

"Don't you think you were a little rough on him?"

Sally looked at Cape, a slight smile on her face but her eyes as cold as emeralds.

"Do you have any doubt he would have killed you?"

"Nah, he was just warming up to me."

Sally shook her head. "You're delusional."

Cape let it go, holding his arms up and back as Sally cut the ropes binding his wrists. Both arms tingled from lack of circulation.

"Ready to go?" he asked.

Sally shook her head. "Not yet."

She walked over to Xan and turned him over. Blood soaked his pants around the right knee. Sally pulled the throwing star free and

Xan grunted but remained unconscious. She wrapped the cloth that had been covering her face around the knee and pulled it tight, then turned to Cape and held out her hand.

"Hand me those ropes."

"You sure?"

"Definitely," replied Sally. "He's coming with us."

53

ONE-EYED DONG NEVER CLAIMED to be a brave man, and though he'd count himself smarter than most, he considered his real strength to be self-awareness. He knew he could never adapt to the new Dragon Head, so he left. Well, he *fled*, but that's only because he couldn't trust the bastard not to kill him. Dong was as mercenary as anyone else, even if he did have better table manners, and the Dragon Head couldn't risk him jumping to a rival clan.

Zhang Hong, the previous Dragon Head, had lasted a long time, as respected and trusted as a career criminal could be—bold, visionary, and undeniably ruthless, but still fair in his own way. He honored his ancestors and kept to the code. But his son, Zhang Hui, was a bloody shark. Dong had no doubt Hui had killed his father to become Dragon Head. He suspected Hui would knock off his own mum if there was profit in it.

His only hope was to keep moving long enough for Hui's greed to be his undoing. But sitting in a tunnel beneath a strange city, Dong wondered if even he had the patience to wait that long, or if his desperate circumstances would force him to act. He was running out of cities, and his chances were getting worse the closer he came to being cornered. He rolled his glass eyeball back and forth, letting the noise lull him into a trance where time and distant enemies held no sway.

Footsteps broke his reverie. Shen, the taller of his two guards, was approaching the desk. Shen and the other guard, Lok, were brothers whom Dong had rescued from abject poverty by recruiting them into the Triad. Fearless young men with flexible moral constitutions were always in demand, so Dong made arrangements to have money sent to the boys' family every month. They were fiercely loyal and had risked everything by coming along on his self-imposed exile.

Lok's name meant *happy*, and he certainly was, even in this cluttered, damp basement that had become their base of operations. Shen's name meant *deep-thinking*, but tragically he was as dumb as a dish of soap.

Dong popped his eye back in and waited patiently for Shen to speak. After a minute of looking hopefully at the eager young man, Dong exhaled loudly and made the first move.

"Yes?"

"A package was delivered."

"Where?" asked Dong. He hadn't heard the trap door, and Lok had moved to guard the rear tunnel.

"At the opening of the south tunnel. Lok went out to buy more food at the grocery that stays open all night, just a few blocks away. I disabled the trap door and covered for him. He found the box ten feet inside the tunnel, where it opens near Stockton Street."

"And?"

"I have the package."

Here we go, thought Dong. "And?"

"I opened it."

"*And?*"

"I thought you'd want to know what was inside."

"What?"

"I said, I thought you'd want to know what was inside the package."

Dong blew out his cheeks. "*What* was inside?"

"A note," replied Shen. "And … something else."

Dong decided he wasn't a patient man, after all.

"Just give it to me," he said tersely.

"I don't have it."

"Where is it?"

"Lok has it."

"Of course." Dong pressed his palms against the desk and stood up, turning toward the back of the chamber. Shen followed two steps behind.

Lok stood maybe twenty feet down the tunnel, behind a metal grate with a door set into it. On his belt was a flashlight, and over one shoulder was a sword. Over his other shoulder was a Heckler & Koch MP5 submachine gun.

"Lok!" Dong's voice echoed down the tunnel.

Lok turned, smiling. He was always smiling, as long as Dong could remember. At first Dong assumed it was gratitude for being plucked from the Hong Kong slums, but now he suspected Lok suffered from the same cranial confinement as his brother.

"The box?"

Lok nodded and extended his right hand, palm up. It was a small cardboard box, the kind where the top slides over the bottom, the size that might hold business cards. Dong took it from Lok, who was still beaming, and held tight to the lid with his left hand, pulling the bottom down slowly with his right. The lid came off with a small popping sound.

Dong stared inside the box for a full minute before putting the lid back. His hands were shaking.

"We're leaving," he said, looking from Lok to Shen.

The two brothers looked at him and then at each other. "When?" They asked in unison.

"Immediately," replied Dong. "Bring only what's necessary. I will bring the heart."

"What about the woman?" asked Shen.

"What about the *gwai loh*?" asked Lok.

"*I'm fine, thanks.*"

The three men jumped as the voice echoed down the tunnel, Dong almost dropping the box. Lok clicked on a flashlight to reveal Sally and Cape moving toward them, Cape holding Xan's legs, Sally with her arms around his torso.

Dong waved awkwardly. "We were just—"

"Turning around," said Sally, disgust in her voice. "Open the door." She looked pointedly at Dong as Lok complied. She and Cape pushed past them and stutter-stepped to the nearest couch, where they deposited the still-unconscious Xan.

Dong's face registered shock at seeing Xan, but Sally didn't give him a chance to say anything. "A suspicious person might think you were about to steal the heart."

Dong's good eye narrowed as he stepped forward and handed her the box. "You insult me too easily," he said quietly. "In another life, you would have worked for me."

"I left that life behind for a reason," said Sally. "In your world, people can only be trusted one moment at a time." She broke eye contact with Dong and opened the box. Her jaw set as Cape stepped beside her.

A finger lay at the bottom of the box, severed just below the third knuckle. It was a woman's finger, judging by the tapering and the nail, and Cape was pretty sure it was the pinky from the left hand. He had no doubt where it had come from.

Beneath the finger was a note written in Chinese, blood spotting the paper. Sally pulled the paper out of the box and read it aloud in English. "*Bring the heart or I will send you hers,*" she said in a monotone, then turned to Cape. "What time is it?"

Cape held up his watch. "Almost three in the morning."

"We don't have much time." Sally put the paper back in the box and closed the lid.

"Where?" asked Cape.

"Ross Alley," replied Sally. "The bakery."

Cape nodded. "It's Monday morning, isn't it?" he said. "They're closed Mondays."

Sally looked at Dong. "Naturally he doesn't want to meet at his office, or his home."

Dong's face was grim. "Lin's already dead, *little dragon,*" he said, his voice barely audible. "You of all people must know this."

"That why you were leaving?" asked Cape.

Dong waved his hand impatiently. "He knows about the south tunnel," he said. "We're sitting ducks."

Sally shook her head. "He won't come here—he doesn't know what's down here. If he was coming to us, he'd be here by now."

"I can't take that chance."

Sally looked at Dong and smiled briefly, then stepped intimately close and whispered, "Yes, you can." When Sally stepped away, Cape caught a glimpse of her eyes and was very glad he wasn't standing in Dong's shoes.

Sally turned her back on Dong and walked over to the couch.

Cape took his cell phone from his pocket and checked the screen. It had rung twice on the way over, but dropping Xan to answer the phone, though tempting, didn't seem like an idea.

2 missed calls. 1 voice message. No signal.

It would have to wait.

He moved toward the couch as Sally leaned over Xan. Taking a new length of rope, she bound Xan's wrists, ran the rope around his ankles, then brought the rope over the back of the couch and across his throat. He'd choke with every swing of an arm or kick of his legs.

"This guy that dangerous?" asked Cape.

"He trained me."

"You sure one rope's enough?" asked Cape. "Maybe we should drop an anvil on his head, or a safe."

Sally ignored him. Cupping Xan's neck in her right hand, she tensed her fingers and squeezed where the neck met the skull, then set her left hand under his chin and twisted violently, stopping the motion after just a few inches.

Cape grimaced. "I had a chiropractor do that once."

Sally nodded but kept her eyes on Xan. "It's the same basic movement. If I keep going, it would break his neck." She released

Xan's head and took a step back from the couch, then started counting just under her breath.

"Five … four … three …"

54

LIN OPENED HER EYES.

Her pupils were dilated, her vision blurry. Her shoulder was cold, almost numb, but she could feel something warm and wet running across her elbow and assumed she was still bleeding. She blinked and tried to take deep breaths to clear her head, but her lungs felt like they had collapsed, an invisible elephant sitting on her chest.

Her arms were tied behind her back and she couldn't feel her hands. Rocking forward, she shifted her weight, and on the third try managed to sit upright and get her legs under her. Almost immediately her left hand started to pulse, then throb, until she almost fainted from the pounding and the dull, ragged pain.

That's when she remembered the knife.

She didn't have to see her hand to know her finger was gone. She tried to control her breathing, the way she'd been taught, but she could only manage shallow breaths. Her head was still cloudy, and she struggled to keep her eyes open.

She was sitting in a small room, almost a closet, maybe four by four with a ceiling roughly eight feet high. Buckets and mops had been pushed into one corner, and shelves covered the wall to her left, stacked with toilet paper, paper towels, tampons, and cleaning supplies. The wall behind her was empty, painted white. To her right was a door with a deadbolt lock. Directly in front of her, set against the far wall, a video camera rested on a rolling table. The red light above the lens was illuminated.

Beneath the camera was a monitor, a new TV with picture-in-picture, a little square in the corner of the screen showing one scene and the big screen showing another. On the big screen was a room dominated by some kind of conveyor belt running down the center, with a large central structure jutting upward like a smokestack toward the ceiling. At the end of the conveyor was a beige mountain almost ten feet high—she couldn't be sure, but it looked like a pile of fortune cookies.

It took Lin a moment to make sense of the image in the small screen until she moved, because she didn't recognize herself. Haggard and bloody, she bore no resemblance to the girl who boarded that ship in Fuzhou such a short time ago.

Lin closed her eyes. When she opened them again, she saw the bomb.

She saw it on the monitor first, sitting on the floor next to her, in plain sight but off to the side. A gray square with texture like clay, wires wrapped around it leading to a digital clock. Lin squinted at the small screen and then twisted her head around. The clock was counting backward in minutes.

She said the number as it changed, as if saying it aloud would give her control over its inexorable decline.

"Fifty-three…"

55

"... TWO ... ONE."

Xan opened his eyes.

He turned his head slowly and studied the ropes binding his hands, then looked at Cape with a bemused expression. Then he noticed Sally and almost smiled. When he saw Dong standing a few feet away, he scowled.

He turned back to Sally. "So it's true," he said in Cantonese.

"What?" she replied in English, wanting Cape to follow the conversation.

"You're part of the conspiracy, little dragon?"

"What conspiracy?"

Xan shook his head sadly and changed to English. "You're denying you have the heart?"

"No, we've got it."

"You admit it!"

"Aren't you going to ask where we got it?"

"You stole it, obviously."

313

"Why is that obvious?"

"It was stolen," said Xan. "And you have it."

Sally shook her head sadly. "You haven't changed."

"What does that mean?"

"Things were never complicated for you."

Cape noticed a change in Xan's eyes, as if he were about to say something and caught himself. Cape didn't know Xan, but he knew Sally. He wondered if she had been the only complicated thing in Xan's world.

Xan asked, "Then where did you get it?"

"Lin brought it here."

"Lin is in Fuzhou."

Sally raised her eyebrows but said nothing, challenging him with her eyes.

"I sent her there myself," said Xan indignantly.

"On whose orders?"

"What does it matter?"

"Lin boarded a freighter in Fuzhou," said Sally. "She took the heart, smuggled herself onboard, and came here."

Xan stared at her, then looked over at Dong, who nodded.

Cape stood back, watching Xan's reactions, surprised at how little emotion he betrayed for a man tied to a couch. The wound in his leg had to hurt, but he did not flinch, totally focused on the mission that brought him here. It reminded Cape of Sally. She hadn't said *hello, nice to see you after all these years, you're an asshole, why didn't you write?* Nothing mattered but the present situation and her ability to control it.

Sally studied Xan for a minute, then said, "You didn't know."

She produced a knife and bent down to cut the ropes.

Dong, watching, raised his hands. "Are you sure … ?"

Sally waved him off as Xan slowly shook off the ropes. He remained seated in a non-threatening pose and tilted his head from side to side, sharp cracking sounds coming from his neck.

"You caught me off guard," he said.

"You're an old man," said Sally. "And I'm in my prime."

Xan gave her a look.

Sally asked, "Why are you here?"

"To kill you."

Cape unconsciously took a step forward at the same time Dong took a step back. Sally didn't move, saying "Didn't you once tell me students should become better than their teachers?"

"Was that a challenge, *little dragon*?" asked Xan.

"Which one of us was tied to the couch?"

Cape interrupted. "She's got a point."

Xan looked at Cape with a puzzled expression. "Who *are* you?"

"A friend."

Xan looked at Sally. "A friend of yours?"

Sally nodded and smiled as if laughing at some private joke.

"This *man*," said Xan. "Is a friend of *yours*?"

Sally nodded again.

Xan glanced at Cape. "What does he do?"

Sally stopped smiling. "He tells the truth."

Xan met Sally's gaze and the room went quiet. After a minute, Cape cleared his throat.

"Looks like you two have some catching up to do—mutual friends, orders to kill each other, that sort of thing—think I'll go check my phone." Stepping around the couch, Cape met Dong on his way to the rear entrance and whispered, "You trust this guy?"

"No."

Cape considered the source. "Do you trust anyone?"

Dong seemed to think for a moment. "Not really," he said. "Probably why I'm still alive."

"Let me ask that another way—can I trust this guy?

"He's a beastly chap," said Dong. "But I'd say he's telling the truth."

"How can you be sure?"

Dong looked over toward the couch. "Because he's talking to *her*."

Cape watched Sally, talking to Xan but still standing in front of the couch, just out of arm's reach. He turned back to Dong. "I'm going outside," he said. "Don't lock the door."

"What about Yan?"

Cape shook his head. "Sally's right. He won't come here. I only met him once, but he's the kind of guy who wants to be in charge. He chose the playing field—he wants us to come to him."

Dong spoke deliberately. "The girl is dead."

"Maybe," said Cape. "But we won't know sitting here, will we?"

Dong glanced at Sally. "You're as mad as she is, aren't you?"

Cape shrugged. "Guess that's why we get along."

"Bollocks." Dong sighed heavily.

Cape left Dong muttering under his breath and stepped through the metal grating. The tunnel was almost seven feet in diameter, so he could walk easily, but the floor was damp and the first thirty feet pitch black. He should have borrowed one of the guard's flashlights. Finally he saw a small patch of light and picked up his pace.

The opening in the Stockton Street tunnel was a sewer grate. Since the only things passing through the tunnel during the day were cars, and this part of San Francisco was dead at night, the possibility of anyone spotting the entrance was slim. But Cape saw no reason to risk going outside if he could get a signal right here. Holding the phone up to the grate, he checked the screen—three small bars flickered above the antenna symbol.

The message was from Agent Williams. Cape listened to the message twice, then scribbled some notes. He considered calling back, since Williams had threatened to kill him if he didn't, but Cape rejected the idea. There were too many variables and not enough time. He liked Williams, but the FBI would have to handle this by the book, just like the cops. By the time they knocked on the door with a warrant, Yan could have killed the girl and taken off. Cape thought of Sally's words. *We don't have much time.*

He turned away from the light and headed back down the tunnel.

56

FORTY-FOUR

Lin jumped at the sound of the deadbolt.

Harold Yan leaned through the open door, his serpentine smile making Lin tense involuntarily, her instincts telling her to strike, vertigo hitting as her muscles flexed against her bonds. She shut her eyes as bile burned the back of her throat.

Yan looked smug. "The poison is still working," he said. "You don't think I'd leave someone of your—station—free to move around, do you?"

Lin opened her eyes and managed a deep breath, getting enough wind inside her to spit across the small room. A wad of saliva smacked against Yan's pants just below the crotch. Lin felt faint from the effort but managed a smile of her own.

"*Yat-zeu.*" Go to hell.

"*Baat poh.*" Yan's eyes turned cold. "I'll meet you there, bitch." He forced a smile, adding, "But don't die just yet—I'm expecting company and you're the main attraction, so don't forget to smile

318

for the camera." He pulled the door closed and slid the deadbolt into place.

Lin stared at the locked door for a moment, then turned to the monitor and concentrated on her image in the corner of the screen.

"Thirty-nine..."

57

"It's too risky."

Cape heard Dong before he could see him over the jumbled furniture. As he neared the center of the chamber, he saw Sally sitting across from Xan, with Dong standing next to her, the guard named Shen a few feet away.

Sally turned toward Dong. "You have a better idea?"

"He'll be expecting you," replied Dong, nodding toward Xan and adding, "Or someone like you."

Xan nodded. "Surprise is lost, the field of battle is under his control. *The Art of War*—"

"—is irrelevant," snapped Sally. "Because we have no time."

"He won't be expecting me," said Cape.

All heads turned.

"Think about it," he said. "Yan met me only once, and I asked for his help. He may not trust me, but I doubt he thinks I've got the heart."

"*We've* got the heart," said Dong. "Not to put too fine a point on it."

"I have plenty of paperweights already," said Cape. "But Yan thinks I'm just a *gwai loh*—and I must be, because everyone keeps calling me that."

"It's colloquial Chinese for someone who is white—an outsider," said Sally. "It means devil."

"White devil, actually," added Dong. "Nothing personal, of course."

"Of course," said Cape. "But Yan is expecting someone who's Chinese, not me. Someone connected to the heart is supposed to walk through the front door."

"What do we do?" asked Dong.

"Come through the back door." Sally turned to face Dong. "You'll be relieved to know I want you to stay here."

"With the heart?'

"Not a chance," said Sally.

Dong looked crestfallen. "And the guards?"

Xan shook his head. "*Sei chun.*"

Sally glanced at Cape. "He said 'stupid.'"

Cape looked at Shen, who seemed oblivious to the remark. He had a pistol holstered on his hip, which Cape pointed to as he addressed Dong. "Mind if I borrow that?"

Dong barked something in Cantonese and Shen came over and handed Cape the gun, an H&K 9-millimeter semi-automatic, black metal and composite with a contoured grip. Cape got the same sensation he always had holding a gun, an almost primal fear mixed with an undeniable sense of power. It sickened him to admit how good the weight of the gun felt in his hand. He glanced up to find Sally looking at the gun, a somber look on her face.

Cape caught her eye. "We can't all leap tall buildings."

"You should try sometime."

Sally walked toward the south tunnel and came back with a sword slung across her back. She was still wearing the black clothes she'd had on the night before.

Xan stood. "How far away is this bakery?"

"Five blocks," said Sally. "But if we take the tunnels, we can cut it to three."

"Don't forget what was in the box," said Dong. "This man is dangerous."

Cape looked at Sally, then at Xan. "So are we. Besides, I might be able to distract him."

"How?"

"I know something about him." Cape patted the pocket where he'd put his notes.

"What?" asked Xan.

Sally said, "We don't have time."

Cape slid the gun into his belt and pulled out his shirttails. "I'll tell you on the way."

58

DAWN WAS BREAKING AS Cape walked down Ross Alley. The sun was still asleep, but it had yawned and stretched enough to crowd the darkness, turning the sky a deep blue.

Ross Alley was about as short as its name implied, a minor twist in the Chinatown maze barely a block long. The Golden Gate Fortune Cookie Factory was tucked between two small storefronts, the metal and glass doors incongruous next to the old wooden sign at the entrance. *20,000 fortune cookies made daily. Visitors welcome. Admission free.*

Cape stopped a few feet from the door and looked around, but the street was empty. Xan and Sally had circled around the back of the alley. Xan's job was to find Lin. Sally didn't say where she would be, but Cape took comfort in that. He was used to her being invisible. His job was to distract Yan for as long as possible.

You'll think of something. With his right hand, he casually brushed the back of his shirt and checked the position of the gun, which he'd moved to the small of his back. Satisfied it wasn't going to fall out of his pants the moment he stepped across the threshold, Cape took a deep breath and tried the door.

It was unlocked.

The front room was crowded with boxes, rolls of plastic mounted on metal spools, a long counter, and a cash register. Cape moved his head slowly, scanning the room, but no one jumped out and pointed a gun or yelled in Chinese to get lost. But looking up, he noticed the small video camera mounted above the door at the far side of the room, its red light blinking.

Cape raised his right hand to his lips and blew a kiss.

Three steps later he was through the door and inside the factory. A low humming sound came from fans overhead, recessed into the ceiling. It was an L-shaped room, and Cape found himself in the short section, surrounded by stacked wooden barrels and blind to the rest of the factory floor. Several barrels near the door were open, revealing thousands of fortune cookies jumbled together, waiting to be wrapped in the next room. Unable to resist, Cape took one from the nearest barrel and cracked it open.

You will live long and prosper.

Cape popped the cookie in his mouth and took another.

The future is uncertain.

And another.

Trouble awaits you just around the corner.

Cape threw the last cookie onto the floor. "Should have quit while I was ahead." Crunching quietly, he stepped past the barrels into the open, holding his hands out from his sides.

Two large conveyors sat side by side, throwbacks to another age, when bakeries were not massive factories outside the city but small assembly lines in tiny storefronts like this one, the machines feeding the dough to workers who shaped the cookies. Next to the conveyors sat two metal chairs, where each day two old Chinese women would sit, pressing paper fortunes onto the flat dough, then using a metal rod to fold the dough by hand before it cooled. At the end of the machine was a pile of fortune cookies almost eight feet high. Cape walked halfway down the conveyor before he could see the rest of the room.

The first thing he saw was Harold Yan.

He was standing next to the mountain of cookies looking at Cape. He wore a white button-down shirt with no tie, a blue blazer, tan slacks, and loafers. A local politician making the rounds in his community. Cape noticed a small water stain on his pants, just below the crotch. *Maybe he's nervous, too.*

Behind Yan was a rolling cart holding two video monitors, the one on the left obscured by Yan, the other showing the view from the security camera in the front room. To Yan's right and standing maybe fifteen feet behind him was another man, someone Cape had never seen before. He had short black hair and a thin mustache drooping on either side of his mouth, scar tissue around his eyes. His trapezius muscles had taken the place of his neck, and his shoulders were stretching the fabric of his black jacket. Cape didn't bother asking what he did for a living. He locked eyes for a minute, figuring prison logic applied in this case, then turned his attention back to Yan.

"Thanks for inviting me."

Yan was nonplussed, even though he'd seen Cape on the security camera.

He said, "What are you doing here, detective?"

Cape shrugged. "Jackie Chan wasn't available."

Yan forced a smile but his left eye twitched. "This doesn't concern you."

"I got your finger in the mail," said Cape. "And it pointed in this direction."

Yan's eye twitched again. "What are you talking about?"

"I thought you wanted the dragon's heart," said Cape nonchalantly, turning toward the entrance. "I must have the wrong address."

"Stop."

The tone was half command, half plea, Yan still not sure how to play this. But his pants were down and there was no turning back. "You have the heart?"

Cape nodded.

"*You*, a—"

"—white devil?"

Yan stared at him. Cape reached into his left-hand pocket very slowly, conscious of the thug in the corner. He raised his cell phone. "I call and it's here in five minutes."

Yan studied Cape for a minute, then seemed to make a decision. He didn't know how, but Cape had something he wanted, and that was enough.

"You say you have the heart, but of course you don't have it with you," said Yan, gesturing toward the man with no neck. "You don't mind if Shaiming checks, do you?"

"Yes." Cape put the phone back in his pocket. Shaiming didn't move, waiting for a sign from Yan.

Yan spread his hands. "And if you don't call ... say you've been injured ... or worse?"

"Then you don't get the heart," said Cape. "Just the cops."

Yan clenched his jaw and nodded. Since the heart was a Triad treasure, Cape figured Yan never expected anyone involved to call the police. This was a meeting for criminals only.

"It seems we have a stalemate," said Yan, stepping to the side and revealing the monitor directly behind him.

Cape squinted as he tried to make sense of the image. The woman on screen looked younger than Sally, but so disheveled it was hard to tell. She was sitting against a white wall, slumped to one side, her left hand wrapped in bloody gauze. Cape took a shallow breath and tasted bile.

He fought the urge to rush Yan. *Keep him talking.*

"I thought she was working for you," said Cape.

"So did she." Yan half turned to admire his handiwork, then looked at Cape with a gleam in his eye. "Can you see the clock?"

Cape had been transfixed by the image of Lin and his own inability to act, but now he saw it, a small rectangle in the corner of the screen. He recognized the gray square under it immediately. It was identical to the bomb he'd found under his car.

Yan had taken a step backward and now held something in his right hand.

"I also have a cell phone," he said. "But it works a little differently from yours." He held up the phone. "There's two numbers that only I know." He moved his thumb back and forth over the keypad. "One disarms the bomb, and the other triggers the detonator. I just input the second number, so if I push send now, well ... you know the rest, detective."

"What about the clock?"

Yan grinned. "That's my insurance. You have—" He glanced over his shoulder. "Eighteen minutes to produce the heart, or the girl dies in a very messy explosion. But get me the heart and I'll make the call. You can have the girl."

"I don't want her." Cape kept his voice as flat as he could. He sensed Yan taking control of the situation and needed to keep him off guard. "I don't even know her."

Yan wasn't buying it. "Then why are you here, detective?"

"To get rich."

Yan hesitated, finding it hard to argue with greed. "You want money, but not the girl?"

"Are hearing problems common in your family?"

Yan's eyes narrowed. "So you don't care if I push this button?"

"Go ahead," said Cape. "But after the big *boom*, don't you think the cops will come? Or the fire department? Kinda hard to negotiate with those sirens blaring."

Yan lowered the phone but held it tightly in his right hand. The image on the monitor shifted and Cape's heart jumped, lines running across the screen for an instant before the picture returned to normal. Lin still sat there, eyes half closed, the clock now reading seventeen. Cape assumed Yan didn't have time to set up some elaborate system, but the cell phone made him nervous. Lin might not even be in this building.

Yan's back was to the monitor. "What do you want?"

"Lots and lots of money," said Cape. "I thought I'd keep it simple."

"How much?"

"What's it worth to you?" asked Cape. "You're obviously willing to kill for it, so it must be valuable. To me it's just a lump of green stone."

"You're an ignorant fool, detective."

"Is that why you tried to kill me?"

Yan smiled, the cat completely out of the bag now. "How did you know it was me and not Freddie Wang?"

"I didn't, until just now."

Yan studied him but remained silent.

Cape said, "I found a dead body and bomb behind my car, but Freddie could have killed me inside his restaurant."

"Then why did you leave the body outside my office?" asked Yan.

"I don't know," said Cape, shrugging. "It seemed like a good idea at the time."

"That's it?"

"To be honest, I thought it might stir things up, make you take an interest."

"You never suspected me?"

Cape shook his head. "Not until the body disappeared," he said. "But when you told me to check out the cargo on the ship, that made me wonder."

"I read the police arrested Michael Long," said Yan.

"A failed jeans designer masterminded a human smuggling operation?" Cape frowned.

"The authorities seem satisfied."

"I showed Long a picture of your dead thug," said Cape. "It scared the hell out of him. The cops don't know that."

Yan blinked several times. "You're not as stupid as you look, detective."

"It's the broken nose," said Cape. "Throws them off every time."

"So what do you want?"

"I already told you," said Cape, stealing another glance at the monitor. *Ten minutes.*

"A million dollars," offered Yan.

Cape coughed.

"Not enough?"

"I was thinking at least five," said Cape.

Yan started to raise the cell phone. "Let's say I believe you don't care about the girl," he said slowly. "That's still a lot of money—what makes you think I have it?"

"I figure I'll need to disappear," said Cape. "Especially if you push that button. You know, change my name, get a new identity... the whole Joan Rivers treatment. Maybe even get my nose fixed."

Yan was watching him very closely now.

"What did it cost when you did it?"

Yan's jaw dropped.

"Want me to guess your real name?" asked Cape. "I already know it's not Rumplestiltskin."

"Who *are* you?"

"That's not the question," said Cape. "Who are you?"

Yan's voice was defiant. "I'm *Harold Yan*, the next mayor of San Francisco."

"Liar," said Cape.

"*President* of the Chinese Merchants Benevolent Association."

"Criminal."

"Respected member of the City Council."

"Murderer."

"Mayor of Chinatown."

"Moron."

Yan took a step forward but stopped, his eyes burning holes in Cape. He started to say something but Cape cut him off.

"You were the worthless son of a Triad leader," he said. "You betrayed your father, then faked your own death to come here."

Yan's shoulders slumped as he listened, but his eyes remained hard. His nostrils flared when Cape spoke again.

"Your name is Wen," said Cape. "Zhang Wen."

59

"ZHANG WEN."

Sally had bellowed with rage when she first heard the name.

When Cape said it during their run through the tunnels, Xan had to restrain Sally from running ahead. After a furious exchange in Cantonese, Xan released her. But judging by the expression on his face and the vein pulsing on his forehead, it took all Xan's self-control not to sprint down the tunnels himself. Cape didn't ask what had been said, but when Sally told him how she knew Wen, he said, "We don't have to stick with the plan."

"It's a good plan," she replied. "We need you to buy us time."

But now there was no time left. A million questions roared through her brain, but all she could do was count down the minutes. Sally watched Cape talking to Wen, the men only ten feet apart but fifteen feet below her.

She hung upside down like a spider, legs curled around a black nylon rope. She wanted to go lower but knew she'd risk being spotted by the goon in the corner, whose eyes were still riveted on Cape.

She heard Cape say the name again, daring Wen to respond. As he talked, Cape nonchalantly brushed his right hand across his hip, as if wiping sweat from his palm. Sally had seen Cape do that before. He was getting ready to draw his gun.

Taking a deep breath through her nose, Sally relaxed her grip on the rope.

The man who was no longer Harold Yan smiled involuntarily at the sound of his real name.

Ten minutes ago this *gwai loh* had walked into his plans, somehow in possession of the heart, catching him red-handed with a girl and a bomb. He knew right away he would have to kill the detective; he just wanted to get the heart first. But when their conversation took an unexpected turn and Wen heard his name spoken aloud for the first time in ten years, instead of being afraid, he felt *relieved*.

No more lying and obfuscation. Just life and death—two old friends Wen had known since he was a boy. He'd never been stronger than his brother but was always more clever, which is why he came out ahead even when others were arrested or killed. Like that *yakuza* swine Kano, so many years ago. Today was no different. After this was over, he could put the mask on again and become Harold Yan, charming politician. But for this moment he could be himself, Zhang Wen. Ruthless, powerful, and smarter than everyone else.

As he looked at Cape across the factory floor, he ran his left hand across his face. "They told me the plastic surgery would be painless," he said. "They lied. I couldn't smile for almost two years. My jaw ached. My scalp itched constantly."

"Head lice?" asked Cape.

Wen ignored him. Nothing the *gwai loh* could say was going to ruin this chance to stop acting for a few minutes—to be free to say whatever he wanted—because no one in this room would live to talk about it. The girl would be dead in less than ten minutes, one way or another, then he'd play hardball with this buffoon detective. See how cocky he was after a few minutes with his bodyguard Shaiming. And even if he didn't get the heart today, Wen knew he would eventually. Kill enough people and you'll find someone willing to make a deal.

The detective was talking again.

"Why the ship?" he asked. "Why smuggle those people from China—why take the risk before the election?"

Wen shook his head, marveling at how someone so stupid could know so much about him. "Do you have any idea what political campaigns cost?" he said. "That ship brought in more cash from those families than a hundred fundraisers."

"What about that speech in your office? How this affected—"

Wen cut him off. "All citizens of San Francisco? You think the socialites in Pacific Heights spent more than two minutes at cocktail hour talking about that ship?"

"I was thinking more of the folks here in Chinatown."

Wen laughed, a sharp sound even to his own ears. "Not all Chinese are equal, detective. There are people with power, and there's everyone else—that's true in China and it's true here. Those families were a means to an end. They just happened to be Chinese."

"So it was just for the money."

"And the heart," said Wen. "Don't forget why you're here."

"You actually believe the heart would help you win the election?"

"You wouldn't understand," replied Wen. "If you hold the heart, you cannot be defeated in any contest."

"If you say so."

"Where is it, detective?" asked Wen. "You're running out of time."

"How do I know you're not going to double-cross me, like you did Michael Long?"

Wen smiled at the memory. Long was desperate to save his company, said yes to everything Wen had suggested. He even offered the use of his warehouse. "This is a different situation."

"Yeah, maybe. But I saw the guy in the warehouse, with his throat cut—I assume that was your handiwork."

Wen glanced over at Shaiming with a look of pride, then said something in Cantonese.

———————

Cape didn't like the expression on Yan's face—or Wen's face—and was having a hard time deciding what to call this asshole from one moment to the next.

Wen had gone from looking surprised to worried when Cape first walked into the warehouse, but now the guy looked almost euphoric, like every question Cape asked was a trip down memory lane.

He was pretty sure Wen, Yan—the man in front of him—was nuts.

It's all out in the open now, thought Cape. *He's going to kill the girl, then me.* Cape realized Wen thought he had an accomplice, someone to call on his cell phone that would bring the heart. But Wen's expression said he figured it would still be for sale later, after Cape was dead. There wasn't any leverage if you didn't want the heart for yourself—you either valued the heart or you didn't, in which case it was only worth something once it was sold. One way or another, Wen would get what he wanted, with no witnesses.

Cape saw the Shaiming nod at Wen and unbutton his coat, revealing a snub-nosed revolver sticking out of his pants. Cape stole a glance at the monitor and wiped his hand across his hip.

———————

Lin had managed to drag herself against the door, perpendicular to the monitor and video camera. She could barely keep her head up, but she managed to raise her right foot and kick, once.

The video camera crashed to the floor just as the door over her head splintered below the deadbolt.

———————

Xan kicked a second time, separating the door from the frame. A third kick knocked the door off the top hinges, leaving it hanging and twisting against the broken lock. Wrapping both hands around the door, he heaved backward.

———————

The screen behind Wen turned to static as Cape drew his gun and pointed it somewhere between Wen and Shaiming, who was already holding the grip of his revolver.

Wen raised his phone and brought his thumb down on the keypad.

Shaiming took a step forward and pointed his gun at Cape.

Sally let go of the rope.

Cape took aim and pulled the trigger.

60

SALLY PLUMMETED HEADFIRST TOWARD the factory floor.

She was a black blur in Cape's peripheral vision as the automatic jumped in his hand, the slide cycling backward with the spent cartridge ejected from the chamber. The roar of the shot deafened Cape instantly, leaving only a ringing in his ears. He couldn't hear Shaiming's gun fire but saw the muzzle blast of the revolver, shards of cookies stinging his face as the mountain of fortunes next to him exploded.

Cape adjusted his aim and squeezed off another round.

The second shot slammed into Shaiming's chest, knocking him back on his heels as Cape fired again, hitting him in the gut this time. The revolver flew from Shaiming's hand as the back of his head hit the floor, the gun spinning across the cement and bouncing off the wall.

Sally tucked her chin to her chest and reached behind her head, drawing the *katana* from its scabbard as she turned 180 degrees in mid-air.

Pivoting on his right heel, Cape saw Wen draw a palm-sized automatic and point it at him. He was going to fire before Cape completed his turn.

Sally landed directly in front of Wen, coming up from a crouch with her sword raised, her left foot leading her right.

Wen staggered back a step but kept the gun up, his eyes wild. Cape couldn't see Sally's face, but Wen's expression changed with a flash of recognition, his eyes narrowing as he pointed the gun at Sally's chest.

Slow motion took over. *He's got her*, thought Cape, rocking onto the balls of his feet, his legs feeling glued to the floor. *No one's that fast, not even her.* He felt the heat of the gun across his fingers, the sweat in his eyes, the weight of his own heart as it tried to beat faster, but he couldn't see past Sally to get a clear shot.

The door at the back of the room slammed open and bounced off the wall with a sound like a gunshot, so loud even Cape could hear it. All heads turned as Xan kicked the door again as it swung back at him, Lin cradled in his arms.

It took a fraction of a second for Wen to see Xan was unarmed, but it was enough. He snapped his head back toward Sally and, sensing movement, squeezed the trigger.

Sally swung the *katana* in a vicious arc, stepping into the cut as the blade cut through flesh, her momentum pushing the sword as her weight shifted. Wen's head flew from his shoulders like the cork from a champagne bottle, tumbling in mid-air before landing dead center in the pile of broken fortune cookies.

Wen's torso wobbled for an instant before crumbling, the gun clattering to the floor, a trail of smoke coming from the barrel.

Sally stood over the body, her nostrils flared and her eyes wide, the edge of her sword glistening red. She lowered the sword and turned toward Wen's head. Taking a step closer she spat, her saliva landing right between the eyes, still open and frozen with fear.

Cape took a panicked step toward Sally but she held up her hand and he froze. Reaching beneath her shirt, Sally tugged at something between her breasts. When her right hand reemerged it held the dragon's heart, still wrapped in cloth but with a tear across the fabric where the bullet had been deflected. Sally looked at Cape and shrugged.

Cape felt dizzy and realized he'd stopped breathing. As the ringing in his ears subsided, he turned to look at Xan, who was standing over Shaiming, turning the man's head to one side with his foot.

"You have good timing," said Cape.

Xan nodded, jutting his chin toward Shaiming. "You shot him?"

"I had to," replied Cape, feeling the weight of it settle in his stomach.

"Never apologize for killing someone," said Xan gruffly, sounding like a math teacher Cape had in tenth grade. "Especially if they deserved it."

Cape gestured toward Lin. "How is she?"

Both men turned as Sally crossed the factory, her attention focused on Lin. Xan squatted and sat on the floor, cradling Lin in his lap like a child. A small trickle of blood ran from the corner of her mouth.

He said, "She's leaving us, little dragon."

Sally ignored him, touching Lin's face with her right hand.

"The bomb?" asked Cape. He hadn't heard an explosion, but after the first gunshot he hadn't heard much of anything.

Xan shook his head. "Disarmed. I pulled the detonator from the plastic explosive."

Sally looked at him. "Poison?"

Xan nodded. "Wen killed her long before we arrived," he said. "She just refused to die before you got here."

Sally felt something stir against her hand. Lin's eyes fluttered open, her lips coming apart with a wet crackling sound. Sally pressed her face against Lin's, holding her head in both hands, their noses touching.

Sally's voice was barely a whisper. Lin's eyes rolled around before focusing on Sally. Her mouth moved in slow motion. Cape couldn't hear what they said, but tears sprang from Sally's eyes and fell onto Lin's face. Cape had never seen Sally cry. After a moment he blinked, his own eyes welling up.

The three stayed there, unmoving, Sally sobbing silently, Xan watching her, Cape trying to absorb everything that just happened. It was a long time before Sally sat up and ran her hand across Lin's eyes. Taking a deep breath, she stood and looked around the room, as if she'd forgotten where she was.

Cape touched her shoulder. "We have to leave," he said softly.

Sally looked at him and nodded. She had stopped crying, but her eyes told him she was somewhere else.

"Do we leave them?" asked Xan, waving a hand toward Shaiming and Wen's bodies. "Or take them to the tunnels?"

Cape caught Sally's eye and spoke very deliberately. "If they don't find Lin, they'll think you were on that ship."

Sally held his gaze but didn't respond. It took Xan a moment but he got it, turning to Sally and saying, "He's right, little dragon." Then to Cape he said, "You have a plan?"

Cape's eyes never left Sally's as he answered.
"Yeah," he said. "I think I do."

61

It was almost 7:30 in the morning by the time Cape walked into the Hall of Justice on Bryant Street. After passing through the metal detectors, he rode the elevator to the fourth floor, where Homicide Detail was located. Many of the desks were unoccupied, and the small office at the back was empty.

Vincent Mango sat behind his desk, black hair slicked back, dressed immaculately in a dark gray suit, yellow tie, and loafers. He looked more like next month's *GQ* cover than a homicide detective.

Cape gave him a wave, crossed the room, and took a seat in front of the desk. He checked his watch, then nodded at Vincent.

"Where is everybody?"

Vincent looked around the room as if he hadn't noticed. "It's that time of day. Most of the bad shit happened already, in the middle of the night, so we got people on the street. And the bad stuff that's gonna happen today, well, it hasn't happened yet. Still too early in the morning."

"Where's Beau?" Cape jutted his chin toward the desk behind Vincent.

"Went home about two hours ago," replied Vincent. "You know how he hates this time of day."

Cape nodded. "I'm here to make a statement."

"I heard," said Vincent, turning toward his computer. "Beau told me. Said you were supposed to come in last night."

"I fell asleep."

Vincent turned and gave Cape the look, just for an instant, that said *keep the bullshit to yourself.*

Cape asked, "You want to hear it or not?"

Vincent pulled a pair of reading glasses from his jacket pocket and turned back to his computer, fingers on the keyboard.

"You're not going to write it down?" asked Cape, motioning toward a yellow pad on the desk. "Beau always writes it down first."

"You ever seen my handwriting?" asked Vincent. "Even I can't read it. Besides, what do you care?"

Cape shrugged. "Curiosity."

"Killed the fuckin' cat," said Vincent. "You sent us a picture of a dead guy—or a guy who looks dead—only we can't find him. How's that for a start?"

"OK." Cape talked for several minutes, getting the occasional look from Vincent but otherwise without interruption. When he had finished, Vincent swiveled in his chair and took off his reading glasses.

"That's it?" he asked. "You found a body and didn't call?"

"My phone wasn't working."

"You ever hear of a pay phone?" demanded Vincent. "Or 911?"

"You know how hard it is to find a pay phone in this city?"

Vincent thought about that for a minute. "Yeah, it's impossible. They pulled 'em all out once everybody started carryin' cell phones."

"Exactly," said Cape. "How about getting a cab?"

"A taxi?" said Vincent. "Even worse—you know, the other night the wife and I were—" He caught himself and scowled at Cape. "You enjoyin' yourself?"

"Sorry, Vinnie," said Cape. "It's fun to see you get worked up about these things."

"I got Beau busting my balls all day, thanks," said Vincent. "Him, I gotta work with. You, I could arrest if I wanted."

Cape held up his hands. "Point taken, Detective Mango."

"So get to it."

"What?"

"The point, dickhead, *the point*. Where's the fuckin' body?"

"I don't know," said Cape, shrugging. "I told you already—I found it by Harold Yan's office—you talk to him again?"

Vinnie shook his head. "He's not around, least not yesterday. We call or stop by and his secretary says he's out shaking hands, tryin' to get elected. He'll be back soon."

"You check the office?"

"No way. Yan is connected. Guy's running for mayor, for chrissakes." Vincent dropped his voice a few notches. "*Excuse me, judge, but we have this picture that might be a dead body—but we're not sure—and it might have been in front of Harold Yan's office—but we're not sure—and we were wondering if you could give us a warrant to search his offices, even though he'd call the press, accuse the current mayor of harassment and get us all fired.*" Vincent shook his head. "How's that sound?"

"You need probable cause, huh?"

"You must watch those police shows on TV," said Vincent. "What I need is a dead body."

"Sorry, all I've got is a picture."

Vincent started to respond when the phone on his desk rang, loudly. It rang like a real telephone, before you had to plug phones into an outlet and they started chirping like birds. The bell on Vincent's phone was loud enough to wake a dead man.

Cape watched as Vincent cradled the phone in his ear and dragged a yellow pad across his desk. After a string of *uh-huh, when, yeah, right away*, he finished the call by saying, "And tell them not to touch anything."

As he hung up the phone, Cape asked, "What was that?"

Vincent looked at Cape for a moment before answering.

He said, "*That* was probable cause."

62

AT THE PRECISE MOMENT Cape started talking to Vincent Mango, an explosion destroyed Harold Yan's office on Grant Street.

The second floor windows facing the street were blown out, sending a light snow of glass onto parked cars. The ceilings on the first floor cracked, plaster hitting the hardwood floors in clumps, but the real damage was contained to the second floor. Xan had used just the right amount of plastique. Neighboring buildings were untouched. A fire started in the reception area outside Yan's office, which seemed to be the source of the explosion.

The fire department arrived within ten minutes from the station less than four blocks away, knocking down the door and rushing up the stairs. At first they feared a gas leak that could spread to other buildings until they realized Yan's offices used electric power and heat. That was when they considered arson. But when they found the body of a dead Asian male with gunshot wounds to the chest in Yan's office, they didn't know what to think.

Ten minutes later Vincent's phone rang.

As he grabbed his coat, Vincent told Cape they weren't finished, would talk later, and Cape just nodded. He walked to his car and waited a few minutes before pulling away from the curb. By the time he approached Grant Street the block had been cordoned off, the cop cars and truck from the medical examiner stacking up next to the fire engine. Cape kept driving.

He desperately wanted to sleep but forced himself to drive down the Embarcadero to park in front of Town's End restaurant, known for serving one of the best breakfasts in the city. Cape knew the owners and wanted to be seen in public for a few more hours. He also didn't want to go home just yet. If someone wanted to find him today, he didn't want to make it that easy.

He grabbed a table next to the window and nodded at the cooks behind the counter, managing a half-assed smile. He felt his eyes go to half-mast and thought about ordering coffee but knew he'd hate it when it arrived. He thought of Agent Williams and waved down the waitress to order iced tea and scrambled eggs.

Cape wasn't hungry when the food arrived, and after an hour the tea was eating a hole in his stomach. He'd been holding the paper in front of him but couldn't remember a single sentence. The radio behind the counter finally broadcast a news update that mentioned the explosion at Yan's office, but it didn't give any details. He felt his stomach cramp up and walked to the men's room and splashed cold water on his face, then washed his hands. They looked clean, but he could still see the blood all over them.

He dried his face and looked in the mirror but couldn't find any answers in his own eyes. He turned away and stepped back into the restaurant to find someone sitting at his table.

John Williams looked up from the paper and smiled.

"Your eggs are cold."

Cape shrugged. "Lost my appetite."

"That's too bad," said Williams. "I just ordered."

It almost made Cape smile as he sat down. "Coffee?"

"You bet," said Williams. "And eggs and hash browns."

"Bacon?"

"Goes without saying," said Williams. "Getting your appetite back?"

"We'll see."

"Most important meal of the day."

"It's almost lunchtime."

"Yeah, but these folks serve breakfast all day," said Williams. "Your kinda place."

Cape nodded absently. "How'd you find me?"

Williams jerked a thumb at the window. "Not that many beat-up convertibles in this town, where everybody's gotta own a Lexus or a Mercedes. 'Sides, you parked on the biggest road in the city. Figured I'd check the streets in front of the breakfast places first."

Cape felt himself relax. He reached for his tea, reminding himself why Williams was such a good cop.

"What's up?"

"There was an explosion at Harold Yan's office this morning."

Cape pointed to the radio. "I heard that," he said. "What's the deal?"

"Bomb went off," said Williams, getting right to it. "Plus they found a dead body."

"Yan?"

Williams studied Cape for a moment. "Heard you sent the *police* a picture."

349

He hadn't answered Cape's question, an old cop trick. "So it wasn't Yan?"

Williams shook his head. "Another fella, Asian male in his thirties."

Cape concentrated on keeping eye contact. Liars always drift. "He died in the explosion?"

"He might have, if he hadn't already been shot."

"And you've never seen this guy before?"

"I haven't, but that don't mean much," said Williams. "But it turns out he's got a record." He took a sip of coffee and looked over the rim at Cape, adding, "He's not the guy in your picture, though," making that last part sound almost like a question.

"You sure?"

"I'm never sure," replied Williams. "Plus it was a shitty photo."

"I took it at night," said Cape. "With a digital camera."

"What did the cops have to say about that?"

"They're pissed," said Cape. "Said I should have stuck around."

"They're right," said Williams. "But you had someplace you had to go, huh?"

"Something like that."

"Don't suppose you were awake at seven thirty this morning?"

"Sure," said Cape. "I was over on Bryant Street, talking to the police."

Williams raised his eyebrows and his mouth twitched, but he stopped the smile before it appeared. "That's quite an alibi."

"I'm flattered," said Cape. "But shouldn't you be talking to Harold Yan?"

Williams leaned forward on his elbows. "See, that's the problem. The police had the same idea, and after they found the dead guy, no judge is gonna stop them from going over to Yan's place and letting themselves in."

"So?"

"They found an unidentified female in her late twenties, minus one finger, Harold Yan, and Harold Yan's head."

"Dead?"

"Yeah, all three of 'em," replied Williams. "Yan's definitely dead, so's his head, and the girl's been shot with a small caliber automatic, clutched in Yan's hand."

Cape grimaced and looked down at his plate. He could still feel the kick from Yan's gun in his hand and see the small hole in Lin's chest. Leaving Sally's sword next to Lin was easy, but shooting a girl he once hoped to save wasn't something he could shrug off. Sally told him it didn't matter, Lin was dead and gone, but even she turned away after they spoke of it. It was Cape's plan, and something he had to do alone.

When he looked up, Williams was watching him closely.

He said, "Seems Harold Yan wasn't who he appeared to be."

Cape met Williams's gaze and held it for a minute, then nodded. Williams was giving him an opening.

"No, he wasn't," said Cape. "He set up the smuggling ring."

"You saying Michael Long is innocent?"

"No," said Cape. "I'm saying he's stupid, and he broke the law, helped finance the operation. But Yan arranged for the ship, then when it went bust, he killed the guy in the warehouse and put the finger on Long."

"You can prove this?"

"No," said Cape. "But I can tell you Yan used a middleman, the guy in my picture."

351

"Who was he?"

"He was supposed to be a bodyguard for Freddie Wang, but he was really working for Yan."

"Doing what?"

"Making an impression on Michael Long, getting the money, scaring the shit out of him," said Cape. "That was Yan's idea, to frame Freddie Wang if the cops started looking any deeper. If Long identified the guy, no one would connect him to Yan, so Freddie ends up behind bars."

"This middleman . . . you killed him?"

"No," said Cape without hesitation.

Williams nodded and said, "Probably Freddie. Don't suppose he'd be too happy about one of his guards two-timing him."

Cape felt at least one of the knots in his stomach unwind.

He had accounted for all the killings except for the guy in his trunk, who obviously had been in the process of planting a bomb underneath Cape's car. And Cape had rejected the theory that the man suffered a sudden heart attack but had just enough strength to lock himself in the trunk before he died. His neck had been broken by a professional.

Cape knew Sally had been going out on patrol at night and asked her about it. At first she just looked at him, her green eyes betraying nothing, but after a moment she smiled and said, "Don't mention it."

He never would.

Williams delicately picked up a piece of bacon between two fingers and took a bite. "That button you gave me, Yan gave it to you?"

"Yeah," said Cape. "Figured you'd get to that right away, with his name on it."

"Still talking to Interpol, but they're pretty excited, want to know why I'm asking about some dude who's been dead for ten years."

"What did you tell them?"

"Said he was busy running for mayor," said Williams. "Want to know what else?"

Cape waited.

"Once the cops finally called us, we checked the dead girl's prints."

"And?"

"They were all over the ship."

Cape nodded. "Case closed?"

"Kinda neat," said Williams. "Don't you think?"

"You mean everybody being dead?" asked Cape. "Seems kind of messy to me."

Williams took another bite of bacon. "Remember when I said you weren't all that interesting?"

"How could I forget?"

"Changed my mind," said Williams. "Know what that means?"

"You started a file."

Williams nodded. "Sorta have to, if I want to keep my job, but it's no big deal. In your case, there ain't jack shit to put in there 'cept random bits of information that seem to come to you from above."

"You leading up to a question?" asked Cape. "'Cause I noticed you have this roundabout way, sort of like you're sneaking up on me."

Williams chuckled. "You gonna tell me how you came by this information on Harold Yan?"

Cape seemed to think about it. "Not today," he said. "That alright with you?"

Williams pursed his lips. "Yeah, I guess so," he said slowly. "You obviously ain't one of the bad guys, and truth is, this case'd be nowhere if you hadn't stirred things up."

"You think I stir things up?" asked Cape indignantly.

"Don't push it."

"OK," said Cape, holding up his hands.

Williams glanced at Cape's plate, the eggs runny and frigid. "Sure you don't want something to eat?"

Cape looked over at the waitress, then glanced back at Williams. "You buying?"

Williams shook his head. "Not a chance."

"What the hell," said Cape. "Maybe I'll have some pancakes."

63

LINDA'S HAIR WAS BARELY visible over the top of the newspaper, shifting back and forth as she read aloud.

"*...believed to have died in the explosion, his identity being withheld pending notification of next of kin... the suspected gas leak was confined to Harold Yan's offices...*" Linda lowered the paper, her hair lurching forward as she addressed Cape across the table. "I thought you said he was shot?"

Cape shrugged.

"And that there wasn't any gas."

Another shrug.

Linda scowled and raised the paper, muttering under her breath. "The *Chronicle* never gets their facts straight." Her hair nodded in silent agreement as she resumed reading. "*...police later found Yan in his home with an unidentified female, both apparently the victim of foul play...* blah, blah, blah... *the mayor was quoted as saying 'The city has lost a valued public servant, and I have lost a worthy* *opponent and good friend, unless it turns out he was a criminal, in which case I am shocked and deeply concerned ...'*"

Cape arched an eyebrow. "It didn't say that."

Linda held up a hand, calling for silence as she continued. "*... the mayor's aides later denied any statement had been made, saying a press conference would be called tomorrow.*"

Linda lowered the paper just as their food arrived.

They were having dinner at one of the many restaurants with *Hunan* in the name, two doors down from Freddie Wang's place. It was an understated restaurant with very little tourist traffic—most of the neighboring tables were filled with young Asian couples or families. Linda was surprised when Cape suggested it but didn't object. She had an abiding passion for sizzling bean curd.

"I thought you'd had enough of Chinatown for one week."

Cape broke his chopsticks apart and rubbed the splinters off them. "Just the underside of Chinatown, the part I never knew existed. This part"—he paused as he skewered a fried wonton—"*this part I miss.*"

Linda concentrated on her bean curd for a minute before looking up. "Thanks for telling me what happened."

"Thanks for your help," replied Cape. "Sorry the Sloth didn't come." His friend rarely ate out, eating so much slower than everyone else.

Linda nodded. "He's counting on some leftovers, so try to restrain yourself."

"Yes, ma'am."

Linda smiled, the lines around her eyes multiplying. After a moment, she said, "You left some things out, didn't you?"

It was Cape's turn to smile. "You always were a great reporter."

"The messy parts?"

"Yeah," said Cape, looking more serious now. "Very messy."

Linda studied him. "You OK?"

"Ask me again in a week."

They ate quietly for a while, the background chatter of the restaurant soothing, fits of laughter, snatches of happy voices, all sending a subliminal message that everything was normal again.

Linda broke the silence first, saying, "How's Sally?"

"I can never tell, really," said Cape. "And this was hard on her. She's taking a few days off, going to visit some old acquaintances."

"Really?" said Linda. "Where?"

"Hong Kong."

Zhang Hui sat behind his desk, the only light coming from the small halogen next to the phone. It cast his face half in shadow, the left side pale, the right all but invisible. Both eyes were cavernous, the sockets dark pools, taking all of the light and giving none of it back. He raised his head idly as Xan stepped into the room and stood just beyond the shadows.

Hui asked, "Did you bring it?" His tone was casual, two old colleagues picking up where they left off.

"That's what I said when I called."

"So?"

"Your brother is dead."

"So I heard," Hui said indifferently.

"He was supposed to be dead ten years ago."

"Was he?" asked Hui, leaning into the light.

Xan refused to be baited. "We were both here, *with your father.*"

357

The mention of his father got Hui standing, both hands on the desk.

"Don't forget your place, *Master* Xan."

"I never have."

"Neither one of us is innocent." Hui stood up straighter, his hands pressed in front of him.

"True," said Xan. "I looked the other way when you killed your father, and I—"

"—tried to kill my brother," said Hui.

"That's not what I was going to say."

"But it's true," replied Hui.

"Yes." Xan looked into Hui's eyes, wondering where the pupils were hiding.

"So how are we any different?"

Xan bit his tongue. "Who was killed ten years ago?" he asked. "Who died in the fire?"

"Does it matter?"

"I'm curious."

"This trip to America has made you nostalgic, Xan." Hui paced back and forth. "You've had ten years to ask this question."

"Seeing your brother surprised me."

"How did he die?"

"The first time or the second?"

"The first time was a *sze kau*," said Hui testily. "A foot soldier assigned to guard the guest house. My brother killed him, then took his clothes and fled."

"He killed one of our soldiers," said Xan evenly. "One of *my* men."

Hui scowled. "Men like that were deserting all the time. Did you miss him?"

Xan didn't say anything for a minute. "You helped your brother?"

Hui stopped pacing. "Of course."

"Your father would not have approved," said Xan.

Hui gave a bitter laugh. "You think the old man was killed by poison darts because he *approved*?"

"He told you and Wen the combination to the cabinet."

"We were his sons."

"You're ruthless."

"Thank you."

"And you changed the combination so he would trigger the darts."

"Wen did that, as well," said Hui. "My brother lacked charm, but he was always thinking."

"And you sent the heart to him, so he could win his election?"

"Think of the possibilities, an alliance with the *mayor* of San Francisco."

"It's against our laws."

Hui shrugged. "That's why I told you it was stolen."

"You tortured men to find it—our men," said Xan. "And I helped you."

"It had to be convincing," said Hui with a note of pride. "Would you have gone after it?"

"You lied to me."

"You sound surprised."

"Then why send me to bring it back?"

Hui spoke as if talking to a child. "It was lost, you fool. It didn't arrive on time."

"So you saw an opportunity to settle an old score."

Hui nodded. "I heard Dong was in San Francisco." He smiled, delighted with his own genius. "I knew you would assume he'd stolen it and kill him—if, indeed, he had the heart."

"He did."

Hui's eyebrows shot up, though his eyes were still too dark to see. "You killed Dong?"

"No."

Hui's hands slapped down on the desk. "Why not?"

Xan ignored the question. "Your brother betrayed the society."

Hui waved his right hand dismissively. "Nonsense. He forged *alliances*, made us stronger."

"I'm a soldier," replied Xan. "I don't deal in semantics."

Hui studied Xan as if he had just walked in the room, a complete stranger. "I thought we had an understanding ten years ago that none of this—*none of this*—is personal. You were always stubborn but never naïve, Xan."

Xan didn't answer.

"What has changed?"

Xan shrugged. "Perhaps I have."

"You ... *change*?" Hui gave a short laugh and sat down. "I'll die before that happens."

"Perhaps you're right."

Hui narrowed his eyes, catching something in Xan's tone he didn't like.

"*Where is it*?" he asked impatiently. "Where is the heart of the dragon?"

"Right here." Xan moved to one side.

Hui saw two legs step into the faint pool of light beyond the desk, right then left. Another step and the torso appeared. It was a woman. He couldn't see the face, but a flash of light revealed the curved blade of a sword.

Hui glanced toward Xan but saw nothing but shadows. As he reached for the phone, Sally stepped into the light.

———————

The taxi Linda had called was sitting at the curb.

Cape opened the passenger door and Linda stepped down from the sidewalk, resting her right hand along the top of the door. She turned toward Cape and asked, "You sure you want to walk?" He nodded and she ducked her head inside the cab, telling the driver to wait.

Linda stepped back onto the sidewalk and hugged Cape, her head against his chest, hair tickling his nose and almost making him sneeze. When she let go, he asked, "What was that for?"

Linda smiled as she got into the cab. "I'm glad you're not dead."

"Me, too." Cape gave a quick wave as the taxi pulled away.

———————

Xan reached into the dragon's mouth and pulled its jaws apart.

The lid of the three-legged incense burner opened with a rasp of ancient hinges, the elaborately carved dragon's face lifting to reveal the velvet-lined interior. The bronze legs seemed to twist and change position as Sally studied the carvings, coils and scales intertwining above clawed feet that bit into the wood of the desk. A dozen eyes watched as she slowly unwrapped the cloth around the heart.

The stone felt warm in her hands, as it had the first time she held it. The dragon that looked like a heart studied her, glowing red eyes daring her to steal the heart, keep it for herself. The bloodstone seemed to glow from within as Sally placed it carefully inside the bronze stand.

"Here's your rock," she said unceremoniously.

Xan sighed. "That rock saved your life."

"I took a man's life," replied Sally. "That's what saved mine."

Xan closed the lid, the dragon's mouth leering back at him. He said, "You don't believe in anything, do you?"

Sally smiled sadly. "That's the difference between us."

"What?"

"I believe in myself," she said. "Not this." She gestured toward the incense burner.

"This is tradition," said Xan. "It is—"

"*Sin ka lan*," said Sally. "Bullshit—it's an excuse."

"For what?"

"For not starting your life over again."

Xan's eyes narrowed, his scar twitched.

Sally asked, "How long since your family was murdered?" Xan's face reddened but Sally spoke again. "Killing other men for the Triad hasn't brought them back. They're as dead as my parents."

Xan's voice was as quiet as the grave. "Do not presume you know what's in my heart, little dragon."

Sally nodded in acknowledgment but didn't back off. "Everything inside these walls was a lie, from the time I was a child. Nothing has changed."

"Things could change now," said Xan. "Zhang Hui is in hell, where he belongs. There will be an election."

"You think Dong will come back?"

"Of course."

"He had fled the tunnels when I got there," said Sally. "He is a coward."

"He is a survivor," said Xan. "And he is not an animal, like Hui, or Wen."

"*Lay yow mow low gah*?" asked Sally. *Do you have a brain?*

Xan clenched his teeth. "It could be different. You could come back."

"You could leave, Xan."

It sounded strange, even to her, saying his name without *Master* preceding it. Xan looked at Sally with a tired expression, the lines around his eyes deepening.

"You've grown up, little dragon."

"I had to," said Sally. "A long time ago. Maybe it's time you did, too."

Xan shook his head. "Where would I go? You don't just leave—"

"I did."

Xan frowned.

"You could be a teacher," said Sally.

"I am now."

"Someplace else."

"Where?"

Sally gestured at the incense burner. "Where did that come from?"

Xan looked puzzled. "What?"

"The dragon's heart," said Sally. "Your precious relic. Didn't it come from the five ancestors?"

"Yes, but—"

"Five Shao Lin monks."

Xan nodded.

"Not criminals," said Sally. "Not smugglers, bookmakers, or murderers."

"No, they were—"

Sally held up her hand. "Patriots. Yes, I know the story. They were honorable men, warriors—not thugs pretending to be those things."

"That was a long time ago," said Xan. "Different times."

"There is a Shao Lin monastery near the peak," said Sally. "With roots stretching back hundreds of years."

Xan shifted uncomfortably. "Why would they accept me?" he asked. "It is a closed order."

"They would welcome someone with your training." Sally picked up the incense burner, pushing it into Xan's hands. "Especially if you came bearing gifts."

Xan stared at the dragon's face in his hands, then looked back at Sally. "You've put a lot of thought into this."

"It's a long flight."

Xan nodded. "I'll give it some thought."

"Just do it."

"You sound like one of those American commercials. You've spent too much time there."

"It's home," said Sally. She stepped away from the desk and bowed deeply, keeping her eyes on his.

"Goodbye, Xan."

Xan returned the bow. "Goodbye, little dragon."

Cape started walking. It was still early and the street was busy. Across from the restaurant, two old men sat playing mah jong on a folding card table, the same two he'd seen the other night. Young couples crowded both sides of the street, some Asian, many interracial, their faces lit by the glare of neon from above. Cape looked at the signs, the strange characters and symbols that never became more recognizable no matter how many times he studied them. A few days ago that had bothered him, but now it just made him smile.

A few blocks and a left took him past Sally's loft. The grocery downstairs was open, but the second floor of the building was completely dark. Cape wondered when he would see Sally again but no longer worried *if* he would. He realized that he could no more keep Sally safe than control the weather. But he could be there when she called, as she always had for him.

At the corner, Cape came to a manhole cover and stopped. He looked down into the darkness, thinking about places long forgotten, a side of the city rarely seen, and a part of himself he wished would stay hidden, as dark as the hole beneath his feet. He stepped over the manhole and crossed Broadway, the demarcation line between Chinatown and North Beach, an asphalt border between two different worlds. At the far corner, Cape turned and looked back, a wistful smile on his face. He knew he'd return, he just didn't know when.

That night Cape slept like a dead man and didn't dream at all.

ACKNOWLEDGMENTS

Though it would be impossible to list them all, I would like to thank some of the people who helped make this book a reality.

My agent, Jill Grosjean, for faith and stamina when I almost ran out of both. My amazing wife, Kathryn, for her positive energy, insight, and willingness to read every word, even the ones I misspelled the first time around. My two beautiful and smart daughters, Clare and Helen, for keeping me young at heart. My brother, Bob, and Jody Dempsey for never doubting this would happen. Mike, Suzanne, and Michael Bloom for always being there for my entire family. All the folks at FFS for keeping a dream alive. The Marshalls, for being such great friends and neighbors. Orest Stelmach for paving the way. The Zinns for staying close. Everyone at the Book Passage Mystery Writers Conference, especially Tony Broadbent and Kirk Russell, two great writers and mentors. The extraordinary team at Midnight Ink: Barbara Moore for realizing the potential of these characters; Gavin for a perfect cover; Karl for his patience and critical eye; Kelly, Alison, and the entire sales, marketing, and promotions team. The many people who read early drafts of this novel—without your generosity and support, Cape and Sally would never have existed outside the restaurant where I wrote the first draft.

TVM
November 2006

Beating the Babushka

A Cape Weathers Investigation

Coming October 2007 from MIDNIGHT INK

A movie producer hurtles to his death from the top of the Golden Gate Bridge, an apparent suicide that shocks the film community and puts a two-hundred-million-dollar production in jeopardy. When a female colleague comes forward claiming it was murder, the police are skeptical and preoccupied by a sudden drug war that's erupted between the tong gangs of Chinatown and the mob. They listen to her story and send her packing.

She turns to a private detective named Cape Weathers, who believes her just enough to let her pay his day rate. His conscience is telling him to drop the case when two Russian gangsters show up on his doorstep and tell him to drop it or die. Soon Cape discovers how dangerous the movie business can be when millions of dollars are at stake and putting a price on someone's head is just another line item in the budget.

Cape and his partner Sally—a female assassin raised by the Triads—take on the Russian mob, a major movie studio, and a recalcitrant police department by enlisting the help of rogue cops, computer hackers, and an investigative journalist who just doesn't give a damn. But with a sniper on their trail, the challenge will be staying alive long enough to find out the truth.

BEATING THE BABUSHKA is a novel that explores man's quest for immortality, the price of fame, and the mystery of what happens when Russian *Mafiya* and movie moguls collide.

ABOUT THE AUTHOR

Tim Maleeny is a graduate of Dartmouth College and Columbia University.

His short stories have appeared in *Alfred Hitchcock's Mystery Magazine* and *Death Do Us Part*, an anthology from the Mystery Writers of America. *Stealing the Dragon* is his first novel, the start of an ongoing series featuring detective Cape Weathers and his deadly companion Sally. The second book, *Beating the Babushka*, will be available October 2007. To contact Tim or learn more about his writing, visit www.timmaleeny.com.